VODKA DOESN'T FREEZE

VODKA DOESN'T FREEZE

LEAH GIARRATANO

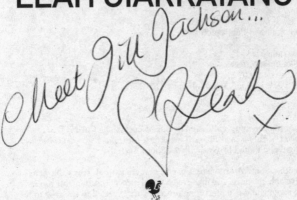

Meet Jill Jackson...

Leah x

BANTAM

SYDNEY AUCKLAND TORONTO NEW YORK LONDON

Vodka Doesn't Freeze, although inspired by real Australian crimes, is a work of fiction. All the characters in this book are fictitious and any resemblance to any actual person, living or dead, is purely coincidental.

A Bantam book
Published by Random House Australia Pty Ltd
Level 3, 100 Pacific Highway, North Sydney, NSW 2060
www.randomhouse.com.au

First published in Australia and New Zealand by Bantam in 2007
This edition published by Bantam in 2008

Addresses for companies within the Random House Group can be found at www.randomhouse.com.au/offices

National Library of Australia
Cataloguing-in-Publication Entry

Giarratano, Leah.
Vodka doesn't freeze.

ISBN: 978 1 86325 588 2 (pbk.)

A823.4

Cover photography and design by Luke Causby/Blue Cork
Typeset in Sabon by Midland Typesetters, Australia
Printed and bound by Griffin Press, South Australia

Random House Australia uses papers that are natural, renewable and recyclable products and made from wood grown in sustainable forests. The logging and manufacturing processes are expected to conform to the environmental regulations of the country of origin.

10 9 8 7 6 5 4 3 2 1

My thanks to my patients and colleagues who taught me that vodka doesn't freeze.

Thanks also to my family and to Ray Black.

This book is dedicated to Joshua George. True grit.

Prologue

THE RAZORBLADE JUST felt cold and clean as always; her blood warm and soothing. Carly Kaplan had expected something more dramatic this time, the last time, but like always, she simply felt calm and still.

The bathwater darkened around her, and she sighed; everything was finally going to be all right. The blood always reassured Carly that she was real, alive. Today would be the last day she needed to check.

As usually happened at this point, Carly's perspective suddenly shifted and she now watched herself from somewhere up near the ceiling. She felt quietly sorry for the girl in the bath; her face wet with soap bubbles, tears and blood. She studied the scars and shadows that marred her once innocent skin. She watched the whites of her own heavy-lidded eyes emerge. She saw her breathing grow ragged, her mouth and nose slipping under the water.

Her essence now part of the steam near the ceiling, Carly saw her mother burst through the door and struggle with the body in the bath. It was kind of sad, but her vision was sepia now, the colours in the scene below her transparent. Her mother's hold on the body slipped once, twice. The scars on Carly's arms and legs seemed faded; maybe the blood bath had finally cleaned her.

Carly's mother lifted her face to the ceiling, her mouth open in a silent scream, her eyes beseeching. Carly gazed down at her, somewhere faintly troubled by her mother's pain, but there was nothing she could do.

It was finally time to leave.

1

JILL LOVED THIS BIT. Her legs burned as she drove them mercilessly on the pedals, halfway up the hill of Arden Street, Coogee. She liked this part best because she knew how much Scotty hated it. If she could get enough of a lead on this hill, she could beat him this time.

She could only hear her own regular gasps now – she was pulling away from Scotty, and the thought of him cursing behind her drove her harder. Her blonde hair was pulled into a ponytail beneath her bike helmet and the heat of the Sydney morning burned the back of her neck. The humidity was almost complete; it felt nearly as though she was swimming. As her body undulated with the movement of the bike, the scales-of-justice tattoo on her deltoid slipped in and out of her T-shirt, which was slicked with sweat to her flat stomach.

Each breath tasted like metal now as Jill pulled air through her raw lungs. Her thighs were screaming. And then, when the pain got too bad, she stopped feeling it, just as she always had.

Thoughts about work replaced the street scene. Despite their cutthroat competitiveness when were they working out together, on the job Jill knew Scott Hutchinson had her back. She couldn't have wished for a better partner, especially at a time when half the unit wanted her out. It was like being back in high school, for God's sake: if you weren't part of the in-crowd you were nothing. And Jill was definitely not in. Being single, attractive and not-interested-thanks didn't automatically count her out, but it didn't help.

But it was Jill's last case that had simultaneously seen her promoted to sergeant and dumped to schoolyard-reject in the popularity stakes. Her bust of an amphetamine ring in Wollongong had sent five bikies to gaol, one of whom was the brother of a cop in her unit – Eddie Calabrese. He was supposed to have been all over the drug trade in the area, and had never forgiven her. When she sent his brother to gaol, Calabrese looked like a fool, and worse: suddenly he was all wrong in the eyes of the powers that be. Nicknamed Elvis, because he thought he was king, he'd sent word everywhere that Jill was a man-hating bull-dyke who couldn't be trusted.

When she flew into Maroubra Road, Jill became aware of a breeze on her neck, cooler each time she glided into the deep shadows cast by the unit blocks that lined the street. The light changes became hypnotic, shadows and brightness, the rhythmic pumping of the pedals and her heart all she could hear. Suddenly Jill was back in the basement. She smelled her flesh burning as the big one pressed the cigarette into her nipple; saw her twelve-year-old self open-mouthed and screaming.

Jill's foot slipped off the pedal. She almost veered into an alarmed postie and caught her balance just in time to see Scotty's bulk, hunched over his handlebars, streaking past her right shoulder.

'Oh shit,' she breathed, pushing her foot back through the pedal. She saw Scotty's familiar smirk over his shoulder as he accelerated ahead, and she realised she was safe and alive in the present.

It was David Carter's favourite spot: warm, safe and up high, out of harm's way. He unrolled his colourful beach towel and unpacked his backpack, placed his lunch, hand moisturiser and can of Coke on the rock to his right, and put his new digital camera in his lap. He liked the computerised whirring sound the camera made as he scrolled through the images he'd already taken. He always left his favourites on the camera after he'd downloaded all the pictures to his laptop.

He settled down expectantly, hoping that Red Girl and Stumpy would be here today. He was a little early, as usual, but he liked the wait.

Cross-legged and comfortable on his towel, he peered through the overhanging branches of the shrub that partially surrounded him; he noted that there were only two older teenage girls swimming laps of the 50-metre pool. No-one at the wading pool yet. He opened his fly and used the waiting time to caress himself as he studied the pictures. It was going to be a hot one today; there'd be plenty of kids.

He wondered about the meeting The Owner had called tonight. Usually they met just once a month for the game, swapping photos, police statements, movies; hell, sometimes someone even brought a kid to trade for an hour or so. Calling a meeting mid-month had never happened as far as he could remember. He felt a lick of anxiety: what if someone knew about the meetings? What if his wife found out? He knew she already suspected, but not even she would put up with hard evidence of his favourite games.

Worrying was killing the moment, he decided. The meeting was probably just about some new delights on offer, maybe an organised tour to Malaysia. Just the thought of it chased the fear away, and he concentrated on his erection.

A noise alerted him to someone making their way through the undergrowth behind him. Probably surfies or dole-bludgers, up here to smoke pot or fuck in the bushes. Animals. He wasn't concerned. He'd never been discovered here before. Plenty of bushes to go around.

When the first blow struck the base of David Carter's neck, he was temporarily paralysed. There was no sound and no pain for a moment, and he watched, troubled, as his camera tumbled from his lap, disconcertingly leaving his penis completely exposed against his white thighs. The pain smashed in with the second blow; he felt his left eye socket shatter, shards of bone ripping through his eyeball, and he saw one of his teeth fly from his mouth, landing near his sandwich. He didn't feel the third blow, which cracked his skull open and spattered globs of brain matter into the bushes and onto his towel.

'Is your arse getting fat?' Scotty asked, as Jill towelled off after their swim in the waves at Maroubra. 'It was all I could see when I was letting you lead up Arden hill. I hung back for a while so it could shade my eyes from the sun.'

Jill hid her smile with her wet hair. Casually, she swung her towel into a rope, then spun fast in the sand and cracked the towel across Scotty's tanned ribs.

'Ow! Truth hurts, huh, Jackson?'

Scotty caught the towel when she whipped him a second time. He used her momentum to wind it back around her wrist and swing her arm up behind her back. Jill tucked her head and rolled forward across the sand, easily getting out of his hold. As she tumbled, she kicked the side of her foot into the back of his knee and rolled out of the way, leaping to her feet before his two-metre-tall body crashed down into the sand.

'Poor Scotty,' she said, as he squinted up at her, grinning. 'Can't get any, so you have to get off checking out your partner's arse. Bet you did the same when you were working with Elvis.'

Jill left Scotty to the bikini girls beginning to arrive at the beach and wheeled her bike in the direction of home. When they'd first met, and were trying to work together, ten bikini babes trying to sit in his lap wouldn't have distracted Scotty from Jill. Unexpectedly, she'd felt the attraction too. Typically around men she had to fight her first urges to run or attack. Their smell, voice, maleness, usually triggered a threat alarm.

Scotty was different. For some frustrating reason, her body would draw closer to his any time he was near. Standing next to him and trying to think during a work meeting had been maddening. Jill noticed the baleful glances of a couple of her female colleagues and the knowing smirks of the men in the squad room. She hated it. She'd promised herself while still in the academy that there'd be no romance with her peers and she'd never found herself tempted. On her rise through the ranks, she'd watched others trying to work with people they'd slept with and now hated. And conquests were always fair game for lunchroom conversation. Dumped, broken-hearted, ashamed or disgusted, if you slept with another cop, for the rest of your career you could expect to be periodically reminded of it over your ham sandwich.

Jill's rule had always been easy for her to stick to. Until she was assigned to Maroubra. Until Scotty. Within a week of working together, she'd been more conscious of the sound of his breath than his voice. Her breathing had seemed to slip into the same rhythm. Passing him a pen caused a pulse to thrum in her ears. She'd never been much good at making small talk, but there'd been no uncomfortable silences with him. When she'd caught herself swapping outfits three times before work one morning, she knew she had to do something.

It wasn't until her third week as his partner, however, that things came to a head. They'd just interviewed the victim of an armed robbery. The Coogee fish and chip shop owner wouldn't leave his café to come in, so they'd gone to him to take his statement. Scotty had taken him up – of course – on his offer of battered calamari, fish cocktails and chips. Jill denied herself the pleasure – of course – and smirked at him over her Pepsi Max as he hoovered them down.

Their footsteps were in sync as they walked back to their car. He smelled delicious.

'Good thing you're not worried about that double chin,' she smiled up at him as they waited at the lights. The bright Sydney day faded around her as he stroked a strong finger slowly from her forehead down her nose. It stopped under her chin.

'And that you're not worried about your scrawny . . .' He trailed off, speaking to her lips, raising her face with his finger. She broke away just before his mouth touched her own. Her heart scudded in her chest as she realised how close they'd come to ruining their partnership.

By the time they reached the car, her walls were back up. The numbness had taken over.

'Just to let you know,' she told him, her hand on the door before she got in, 'nothing will happen between us. I just want to work with you. That's all.' Even to her ears, her voice sounded dead.

Scotty had seemed hurt and confused for a couple of weeks, but, to her relief, had allowed their relationship to become comfortably platonic. Except when they were working out together, in which case each tried like hell to thrash the other.

Right now, Jill was looking forward to her day off, and on the way home she picked up the newspaper, a mango, and half a litre of skim milk from the corner shop near her apartment. She locked her bike in the garage under the units and jogged up the stairs, grimacing as her thighs protested. Her two-bedroom flat would be cool and quiet. She planned to use the day to work on a couple of reports.

She swung her shopping up onto the granite of her kitchen benchtop and surveyed the room critically; nothing caught her eye to cause concern. All the surfaces were clear and clean. Regardless, with a small sigh she walked through her flat to check.

I have to stop these rituals, she thought, entering each room, pushing the doors flat against the walls when she opened them, leaving nowhere anyone could hide. Logic told her that there could be no-one else in here – her building was a high-security block and the wall facing the ocean was unscaleable. Her front door and the doorframe were steel reinforced, with three two-inch steel rods simultaneously interlocking when the handle was activated with the key. She'd caught the men who'd installed the $3000 door laughing when they thought she was out of earshot. They were used to putting in doors like this for jewellery shops and mansions on the North Shore. What was in this two-bedroom flat in Maroubra that was so special, one had asked. His mate, with a lewd laugh, had obviously made some crass comment she was glad she didn't hear.

A single petal, fallen from a bunch of roses her mum had brought over yesterday, marred the blonde beech of the dresser in her bedroom. She absently picked it up and palmed it, continuing her reconnaissance. Her moves were perfunctory, the path familiar. She let her thoughts roam as she padded through her flat. Scotty's advice regarding Elvis was uppermost in her mind.

'Jill, the more you react, the worse he gets. He sets you up, and you bite every time,' Scotty had told her. 'He's a splitter – he's gathering his crew around him, telling them how you're going to respond, and when you overreact, exactly as he predicted, he looks good and you look like a dickhead.'

Jill knew he was right, but there was something about the macho posturing of Elvis that she couldn't fail to respond to. It wasn't just his set-ups and put-downs; she felt he was too close to the Wollongong bikies they had taken down. Her investigations had led to his little brother, Luca Calabrese, at almost every turn. Calabrese Junior was a made member of One Percent, the outlaw motorcycle group that ran amok on the South Coast. Witnesses had told her they'd made police statements about assaults, rapes, drug deals, all related to the gang, but nothing had ever eventuated; for the most part, police had not contacted them again. Elvis and his brother had grown up in the area and still knew everyone in town. A couple of their local mates had also joined the service. They knew her bust had made them look bad, and she felt their knives poised at her back.

She hadn't told Scotty about the dildo left on her desk last week, but he'd seen the crude phallus inked onto her locker in black marker. She knew that formal complaints were just what Elvis wanted – to make her look overly sensitive, a whinger who couldn't take a joke, who might put in a complaint about any member of the team. Scotty had offered to back her up with a complaint to their commander, but she'd seen his relief when she'd brushed the suggestion aside. They'd stayed late one afternoon, cleaning the locker door with solvent.

Tour complete, Jill walked back to the kitchen. She poured the carton of cold milk into the blender and then peeled the fat mango, dropping globs of it into the milk. She planned to drink the smoothie, tidy the mess and catch a shower before settling down to the reports.

Her mobile pealed. 'Shit.' Sucking mango juice from her fingers, she flicked open the phone with one hand.

It was Scotty. 'Yo, J. Dead one. We're up.'

Scotty was running, she could hear him breathing hard.

2

Jill let herself smile, watching Scotty striding up the sand-hills, sunglasses on, joking with the uniformed cops who were almost running in their attempts to keep up with him. He was on his way to a murder scene, but for Scotty this was still a trip to the beach.

Her mask slipped back into place when she reached the cordoned-off homicide site, regaining her breath quickly after the hike up the hot beach track. She took in the scene around her. The colours were exaggerated – opal blues of the ocean and sky, blinding white sand dunes, the wet red and purple smashed face of the man lying in the dirt. An ill-looking couple of kids stood a few metres away, looking everywhere but at the body.

'Gordon,' Jill acknowledged the uniformed cop who worked downstairs in their unit. 'What've we got?'

Gordon was overweight and bright with sweat. Jill took the smallest step backwards when he spoke. His breath smelled like cigarettes and constipation.

'The kids over here found the body about half an hour ago,' said the officer. 'They called it in. Looks like he's forty-ish. Killed this morning. We interviewed the kids. They didn't see anything.'

He averted his eyes from hers and Jill detected something unsaid. She waited. When nothing was forthcoming, she decided to look around for herself before she spoke to the witnesses. A chopper droned above the scene, circling lazily, a massive buzzard. She squinted into the glare overhead. Channel Nine. She tugged the rim of her baseball cap lower and walked through hot sand to the body.

She took in the camera next to some neatly packaged sandwiches on the ground; a cling-wrapped bunch of grapes. It was like a child's packed lunch. She stood next to, but not disturbing, the blood-spattered towel on which the dead man had been sitting. There were already numerous sets of foot-prints leaving and leading to the towel. Some of the sandy indentations were blood smeared. She needed to find out how close the kids had come to the body. Glancing at them through her reflective glasses, Jill thought they now looked as if they wanted to be as far away from it as possible.

Movement below the cliff face caught her eye. Kids, swimming and playing in the wading pool at the edge of the ocean. Their giggles bubbled up with the breeze. On the rocks by the side of the pool, a woman changed a baby's nappy; another slathered sunblock over the plump belly of a toddler. She squatted carefully next to the towel, her head now at sitting-height. Perfect view. Sick fuck. Her disgusted glance at the corpse revealed that his fly was undone.

Jill straightened, tasting bile, and swayed for a moment. Telling herself it was just the heat, she made her way over to where Scotty was talking to the kids who'd called in the body.

They appeared no older than seventeen. Locals probably. It looked like the girl's nose had been sunburnt a few times already this summer; her skin peeled over her freckles. Right now, she looked pale under her tan, white around her eyes and mouth. She wore long board shorts, a bikini top, and no shoes. Her boyfriend's arm hugged her shoulders. They seemed to be holding each other up. He was tall, but he still had to look up at Scotty as he spoke.

'Jill, this is Adam Harvey and Tamara Wade. They live down on Clovelly Road. Came up at about eight this morning for a walk and found the body. Tamara's not feeling too good, and I told her she could go home and have a shower before they come in to make their statements.' Scotty turned to the boy. 'Before you go, Adam, I'd like you to meet Sergeant Jillian Jackson. Could you tell Jill about the car you saw before you found the body?'

'Yeah. All right.' The boy's voice sounded like he looked, thin and shaky. 'When we got to the car park around the back of here there was this new Mercedes. Red. A coupe? Tamara said she wants a car like that, and we just checked it out a bit, looked in the windows, you know.'

'Was anyone in the car, Adam?' asked Jill.

'Nah.'

'What about other cars?'

'Ah, yeah, like we were saying before, it was pretty quiet. Surf's shithouse, you know. But there was a van, surfer's van, probably. No-one was in the van either,' he said.

Jill asked, 'Did you see anyone around, Adam? Who else was around here?'

'We didn't see anyone up here, but when we were coming up from the beach we saw two guys with their boards heading down. We can't remember anyone else.'

'Do you remember seeing anyone, Tamara?'

'No. I've already told four people that.' Tamara was teenage-indignant, but her lower lip trembled. 'Can we go now? It stinks here.'

The sun was high and hot now. A sheet of blowflies surfed air currents over the body. The smell filled Jill's mouth and had permeated her hair. She nodded, and Scotty directed the kids away, ensuring he had all their details, then came back to where Jill was standing with the uniformeds.

'Did you see the camera?' Scotty wanted to know.

'He could've been an artist.' Jill didn't believe it.

'With his pants down? This guy's a squirrel.'

Jill's silence indicated her agreement. Together they watched two men draw closer. The man leading was older, his shiny head already scorched by the sun. The officer behind him, a boy in comparison, offered his hand when the man's footing slipped in the sand. It was slapped away.

'Finally. The ME's here,' Scotty said.

Scotty and Jill walked over to join the police medical examiner and his assistant. The kid dropped the heavy bags he'd been toting.

'Could you be any more rough with that equipment, Jarred? Honestly!' The medical examiner wiped at his forehead with a lavender handkerchief. Scotty smirked at Jill while the man leaned on his assistant and emptied the sand from his shoes.

'Let's get everyone away from this area,' he snapped, motioning Jill and Scotty to follow him. 'This is a crime scene.'

No kidding, Jill sighed inwardly. She fell in behind the bristling doctor. They'd be in the sun for a while yet.

Mercy Merris didn't notice the driver of the courier van screaming 'Crazy bitch!' as he over-corrected and almost lost control when she sped past. Already two lanes away from him on the freeway heading southwest, her black curls streamed with her cigarette smoke out the window of her red Mercedes CLK. Belting out Aretha Franklin, she half-read one of the files propped open on her passenger seat; files she wasn't supposed to have removed from the psych hospital. She expertly flipped open her phone when it rang and overtook two cars in the left lane. Late again. They'd want to tell her her 11 a.m. appointment had arrived and her 10 a.m. patient was becoming impatient.

She recognised the voice of an ex-patient, Lisa, crying, halfway through a sentence that didn't make sense.

'. . . and I wasn't there for her and I said I would be . . .' The voice on the phone sounded fractured, slightly hysterical.

'Lisa. Calm down. What's wrong?' Mercy was surprised to hear her so distraught. Their therapy had been over for months now, and the last time they'd talked Lisa had been functional, rational. Mercy hadn't thought she would regret giving Lisa her private phone number.

'Calm down, Lisa,' she said again, suddenly tired. 'What's happening?' She glanced at the dash clock. Shit, she swore inwardly as she saw the time. She pressed the accelerator a little harder, then noticed a cop car ahead. Great, she thought, that's all I need, another speeding fine on the way to work. She jabbed the CD off and swerved her car into the breakdown lane. She braked hard and the files from the passenger seat flew forward, merging into a mess on the floor.

Mercy heard Lisa's voice from the mobile still in her hand.

'It's Carly Kaplan,' Lisa sobbed. 'She killed herself last night. You weren't there for her either.'

Mercy felt, rather than heard, a high-pitched whine begin in her head. Guilty thoughts of her last session with Carly, one of her most troubled patients, stabbed at her consciousness.

Carly had threatened suicide in her last session, as she did almost every session, but Mercy had helped her consider other options, refusing to give in and admit her again to hospital – Carly seemed to deteriorate further when in hospital. She'd seemed calm when the session ended.

When Carly hadn't shown for her appointment yesterday, Mercy had been relieved rather than worried, kicking off her heels and reclining in her chair to read. She knew she should've called her, but she had been so tired, and she'd felt angry that Carly was manipulating her again by failing to show up. She'd told herself to discuss this resentment in her next supervision session, at the same time knowing she wouldn't – she'd already decided to skip supervision again.

And now Carly was dead. Mercy felt her racing thoughts slow, becoming syrupy and hard to grab hold of. Her patient had committed suicide and she had breached at least five hospital rules regarding her care. She hadn't written up her file notes in weeks, and she had the file off the hospital grounds; she hadn't brought Carly's case to the team supervision session for two months, and she hadn't mentioned to the team that Carly had threatened suicide again, even though the threat would be clearly recorded in the session audio tapes. The hospital would be looking everywhere for the file by now. There'd be a formal enquiry.

Mercy found she'd disconnected the phone with Lisa still speaking, but she hadn't registered any words since she'd heard that Carly had killed herself.

When she realised her pager was sounding, Mercy calmly picked it up and stared at it blankly. She pressed the pager into the dashboard with the heel of her hand until the plastic casing snapped, a shard slicing into her skin. She didn't flinch as blood welled up in her palm.

3

JILL GOT BACK TO HER apartment with a headache that felt like sunstroke. She let herself in and went straight to the fridge, opening its stainless steel door and leaning into the cool interior. She grabbed some water, drinking half the bottle as she kicked off her shoes and pulled her socks off. She padded barefoot across the pale granite tiles to the medicine chest over the sink. She reached for the Panadol and downed two capsules with the rest of the water.

She tipped her now warm breakfast smoothie into the sink. The orange pulp of the mango triggered images of the smashed head in the sand. Even the hot, sweet smell was evocative of the death scene on the beach; the effect was disorienting. She placed a sweaty palm on the cool benchtop and directed her attention to the muted colours of her apartment. Her mum said the unit was too plain, that she should add decoration, but Jill loved the all-white and beech interior, colours broken only by cool steel.

After her ritual tour of the unit, she buzzed open the motorised vertical blinds in her loungeroom and let the daylight in. Although the surf could barely be heard through the double-glazed balcony doors, right now its blue brilliance was too bright. She used the remote to shut it out again.

She stripped down to singlet and briefs and entered the laundry, pleased with the shining newness of the German appliances. She sorted clothes to be washed, soothed by putting colours with colours, whites with whites, taking back control. The flashback on her bike had been so real that morning. It had been months since she had felt like she was actually back in the basement. It usually took hours to still her mind after an intrusion that real. Her head still thumped.

What a day. Not what she'd been expecting. The hour with the ME had paid off already; fingerprints identified the body almost immediately. David Carter. He'd done twelve months weekend detention for teaching his seven-year-old stepdaughter how to insert tampons. Just trying to teach her, he'd offered in his defence in his police statement.

The photos on his camera could all pass for innocent if they were of your own kids – children paddling, some of them toddlers, too young even for swimming costumes. Close-ups of their wide smiles, round bellies, short, fat legs. Scotty had taken a call from the cops going through Carter's home, now also a crime scene – they had found a library full of child porn, much of it movies of him with Asian girls under ten.

Jill hadn't seen the movies, but she knew what they'd look like. She'd had her own mental film projector playing for twenty years. Mostly she could keep the curtains drawn, but she was always aware of the tape running.

She felt hatred burning her diaphragm, a metallic taste at the back of her throat. Head throbbing, shoulders knotted, she tried to slow her breathing. She couldn't catch her breath. She tried to focus again on the washing, but felt her throat closing, her chest crushed. Grey spots danced in front of her eyes.

'No, not again,' she moaned. Waves of anxiety rolled over her, washing nausea up from the pit of her stomach. She tried to distract herself, to listen to the front-loader rhythmically turning her clothes, but her heart was pounding louder than the machine.

She stumbled from the laundry as angry tears began. She hadn't had a panic attack in two years. Now, gasping for air, she ran to the balcony, pushing through the blinds, fumbling with the locks, sliding open the doors. She leant on the railing. With nothing in front of her, it felt like she had more access to air. She held on tight, dizzy. A salt-soaked breeze dried the sweat on her forehead and played with her hair. The panic began to subside.

Watch the waves, Jill. Slow your breathing. She tried to match the rhythm of the ocean with her intake of breath. Her vision began to clear. She could breathe again, but her chest felt bruised, like someone had been standing on it for half an hour.

She stepped back into her lounge room, furious with herself. Why am I letting this stuff back in my life? It was the case, she knew. A paedophile with his head caved in. The real-life manifestation of a fantasy she'd had for years had not been as satisfying as she'd thought it would be.

She lay on the sofa for a while with her eyes closed. She would love to sleep, but knew that was never going to happen feeling this way, so she picked up the phone to call home. Talking to her mum usually helped when she felt like this.

Her sister, Cassie, two years younger than Jill, picked up the phone. Great.

'Hey, Cass. It's Jill. What're you doing home?' She kept the tears from her voice.

'Jill. Hi. I'm just back from Morocco. I came home to eat some real food before I'm off again.'

Jill mentally snorted. Her sister was a fashion model, and she knew Cassie ate just enough to keep herself out of an anorexia ward.

'Wow. Morocco. Sounds amazing.'

'It was boring. Horrible food. Dirty,' replied Cassie.

'Yeah? Where to next, then?' Jill felt the distance between herself and her sister more than ever. The effort to find common ground was beyond her right now.

'Just Cairns this trip. Swimwear shoot.'

'Lucky you.' Jill tried to convey enthusiasm.

The conversation faltered, and then Cassie spoke up; it sounded like she was scrambling for something to say. 'So, are you still seeing what's-his-name?' she asked Jill.

'Huh?' Jill paused. 'Oh. Joel. Forgot you met him that night. No. That's history. Listen, Cass, is Mum there?'

Cassie had been ten years old when Jill had been kidnapped. Their family had been transformed by the incident, their best-friend relationship severed forever. For years their father, Robert, had withdrawn into himself, ashamed that he hadn't been able to keep his family safe, unable to look his daughters in the eye. Their mother, Frances, had spent much of her time helping Jill battle the terror that lived inside her like cancer. At first Cassie had been bewildered by Jill's anger, anxiety and nightmares. As time had marched forward she'd become hurt, lost, invisible.

By the time they'd reached high school, Cassie had developed a defensive shell, a sardonic superficiality through which she interacted with the world. Despite her scorching putdowns of almost everyone and everything in their hometown of Camden, people lined up to be looked down upon by the beautiful Cassie Jackson. She'd kept her most scathing opinions for her kickboxing, social-phobe sister. By the time Jill was well enough to mourn the loss of their closeness, her own protective shield had seen her incapable of thawing the ice between them. She had no vocabulary for her feelings any more.

When her mum came on the line, Jill relaxed a little more. Her calm voice had been there through many of the hard times.

'Hi, baby,' she said. 'How was your day?' Jill smiled. No-one else ever called her that.

'Oh, okay. Foul actually, but I don't want to talk about it. What'd you do?'

Eyes closed, she listened as her mum ran through a Tuesday in semi-rural New South Wales; gossip about the neighbours, all of whom Jill knew, and minute details about her immediate family, cousins, nephew and niece. By the time she hung up, she felt exhausted.

She needed rest, and wished she could bypass her gym for once, but she'd never sleep without following all her routines.

She trudged into her spare room, set up as a gymnasium, floor to ceiling in weights and machines. She wrapped the blindfold around her eyes and began kicking the heavy bag suspended from the ceiling.

When Mercy Merris had first heard about paedophile rings operating in Sydney, she'd thought the reports far-fetched. She had then been a clinical psychologist for five years, specialising in working with survivors of childhood trauma, and hadn't come across any evidence for such goings-on. However, one afternoon about five years before, a colleague had invited her to a late evening gathering of psychotherapists at a local hospital, where she'd heard tales of satanic cults and organised kiddie-porn groups that had supposedly existed in Australia for years. She'd listened, incredulous, as members of the group spoke about links between these groups and their overseas counterparts, who, they said, had been breeding children for abuse for generations.

The aim of the meeting had been to discuss therapeutic methods to try to counteract brainwashing techniques that these groups were said to use upon some victims to stop them escaping from the cults. At first, she and a couple of other therapists had asked sceptical questions to try to clarify what they were hearing. Finally, one member of the group spoke to silence them.

'Look, it's great that we have new members at this meeting, and everyone's welcome,' the man began in response to the last question, 'but we're not actually here to prove to anyone that organised paedophile rings are operating in Australia. That's someone else's job. The people who established this group are working with the victims of these groups. We know they do exist, and we need to help each other find ways to de-program the victims.'

The relatively young man, dressed in an expensive, although crumpled, suit, ran his hand through mussy light-brown hair. He looked more like a lawyer than a therapist, thought Mercy.

'If there are people here who'd like to do some reading about these activities, we can give you some references to follow up, but I'm getting tired of the curiosity factor tonight, and I want to get back to focusing on therapeutic techniques to help these people.'

Chastened by his earnest exasperation, Mercy had sat back and listened for the remainder of the meeting. It was like sitting in while a group wrote a horror movie. She heard the young man speaking about one of the patients in his hospital having a 'call-back' activated during one of her admissions to hospital. Mercy gathered that this meant that the therapist had inadvertently triggered some pre-programmed message to return to the cult. He explained that the woman had presented for treatment, but once her therapist had approached a topic that could have identified the cult, an alter-personality, programmed by the cult for just such an eventuality, had surfaced. The woman had switched from sobbing victim to malevolent aggressor in five frighten-ing seconds. She'd picked up a phone and thrown it at the therapist's head, then had run from the room, discharging herself without heeding any of the staff or other patients.

Mercy had mentally blocked a lot of the rest of the meeting, internally asking the questions she longed to ask out loud. Oh come on! she'd wanted to protest. Surely police would have discovered evidence of organised kidnapping, paedophile cults, humans bred to be sex slaves. Why hadn't she heard this stuff on the news? Still, she'd thought, police had never managed to stop her father bashing the shit out of her and her mother and little brothers every night. Lots went on behind closed doors that people didn't know about.

Mercy had later done some reading on the subject, learning that the paedophile rings purportedly contained members of the judiciary and police service, some of whom had supposedly grown up in these cults, and had been selected to be placed in positions of power to further their ends.

But as her reading had widened, Mercy also found literature for therapists treating patients who'd supposedly been abducted by aliens, or who could not let go of their past lives as Roman kings or African slaves. At that point she'd put the material down in disgust and had not returned to the meetings. It was easier to lump the whole lot in as a bunch of loonies, or at best as over-involved counsellors who'd been carried away by some sort of group hysteria. Sure, she knew there were plenty of sickos who preyed on children, but organised gangs of paedophiles running amok in Sydney sounded like a paranoid delusion.

But that was then.

4

WHEN MERCY ARRIVED at the private psychiatric clinic at which she worked, Carole Dean, Programs Director of the Sisters of Charity Hospital, caught her before she'd made it past the marble reception desk. The receptionist was already waving a fistful of messages at Mercy.

Carole, flawlessly groomed, took in the sight of their foremost psychotherapist with anxiety. A mass of uncombed black curls, a too-tight designer suit and tottering heels had always been delightfully unconventional when paraded with confidence by Dr Merris, but lately she was just looking unhinged. Smelling of smoke and heavy perfume, there was a vacant look in her eyes and lipstick stained her teeth. File notes, unlawfully removed from hospital grounds, poked from a large tote bag; some of them, Carole noted with alarm, smeared with what looked like blood. Carole then noticed a blood-soaked tissue pressed into Mercy's palm. Without doubt, this woman looked more like her patients every day.

'Dr Merris – Mercy – I'm glad you're here,' Carole found herself speaking in the soothing tones she usually reserved for the clients. 'It looks as though you've cut yourself. Let's go to my office and see to that. I'd like to catch up with you before you start your day.'

Mercy allowed herself to be steered from the lobby through the halls of the beautiful hospital. Her head still hummed, but she felt comfortably disconnected from the scenes around her, unaware of the CEO of the hospital headed purposefully in their direction, or of Carole's smooth, non-verbal deflection of him. She sank gratefully into a deep armchair in Carole's office, feeling comforted, as intended, by the beautiful architecture, deep carpeting, fresh flowers and family photos.

'Mercy, you look tired. And you're hurt. Here, let me look,' Carole unclenched Mercy's palm and saw the bleeding gash that had been caused when Mercy had crushed her pager in the car.

'That's deep. What happened? You may need a stitch. Let me call Kim.' Carole reached for her phone and asked one of the nurses from the closest unit to come to her office with a first-aid kit. Mercy watched her serenely.

'Are you okay, Mercy? We've a lot to deal with today. I had to cancel your first few appointments this morning, as we have some important matters to sort out.' Carole was growing increasingly worried by the placid demeanour of this usually extroverted woman.

'Mmm, fine. Just tired.'

'Mercy, I'm not sure whether you know yet . . . One of your . . . one of our patients, Carly Kaplan, died yesterday. I'm sorry to tell you, Mercy, she took her own life.' Carole paused, waiting for Mercy's reaction.

Mercy gazed back with a look of polite interest.

'And,' Carole continued slowly, 'there will be an inquest. As you know, Carly was having outpatient treatment with us, having been discharged just last month. We have a lot of paperwork to do, and we can't place this client's file. Mercy, do you have the file?'

'Mmm.'

Mercy reached down and pulled a mass of bedraggled notes from her tote bag, the cluster of which had also caught up a parking ticket, pharmacy script and a broken hair clip.

Carole stared for a moment at the mess on her polished side table and then opened a drawer beneath it and slid the paperwork in. She'd have to straighten that out before the CEO arrived.

She turned anxiously when a knock sounded at her door, but it was just Kim from St Brigid's unit, first-aid kit in hand. Carole ushered her in and closed the door.

'Shit, Mercy, how'd ya do this?' grinned Kim. Dr Merris was a favourite with most of the ward staff, working long hours, helping out on the units, and always taking the hardest patients.

Mercy looked perplexed as she stared down at her hand.

Kim threw Carole a glance; Carole stared flatly back, and Kim was suddenly all professional nurse, firm and gentle, tending to the wound.

'You know, Mercy, this needs a stitch or two. I have what I need right here. Let's fix this up properly.' The nurses on St

Brigid's unit were more than used to suturing wounds like this; there were at least two and up to ten self-harm incidents each week.

Kim cleaned the wound on Mercy's hand and after applying some anaesthetic spray began to stitch the skin together. Mercy was silent during the first two sutures. Then, without warning, she screamed, and Kim jumped. Her first-aid kit crashed to the floor.

Kim stared at Carole as Mercy scuttled into the corner of the room. She squatted there, rocking, holding her hand and sobbing.

All day Wednesday, Jill and Scotty worked almost exclusively on the murder of David Carter. No-one in the unit was co-operative when they needed help investigating the case, with Emma Gibson even suggesting that they lose evidence so the killer would never be found.

'You're not seriously going to try to catch whoever took that arsehole out, are you?' Emma asked Jill and Scotty as they pored over the murder book. They were adding details from people they'd talked to about Carter's life and activities in the lead-up to his death. 'You know it's just going to be one of his victims all grown up and back for justice. It always is in these cases.'

'Really, Emma? Damn. We hadn't thought of that,' Scotty said sarcastically. 'And we're just loving that we caught this case. You think we want to help this shitbag? I just want to get it done, so could you back off a bit?'

Emma flipped her straight black hair over her shoulder and shot Scotty a sneer, but she looked stung by his tone as she sashayed back to her own desk. Everyone was used to Scotty being a good-natured clown, and Jill knew that Emma rarely took her grey eyes off him when they were in the same room.

Jill knew it was probably her fault Scotty had no patience left for any more negativity on this case. She'd been making smartarse comments since they'd escorted Carter's body to the morgue, intimating, just as Emma and half the unit had done, that they shouldn't make any real attempt to find the killer. At first Scotty had laughed along, but when it became clear that Jill was serious, he'd seemed worried – Jill was usually the most conscientious on the job. By now though, he seemed fed up with Jill's constant comments that she was glad Carter was dead.

'Don't you say anything,' he warned her as she stared at him when Emma walked away.

'Huh? No,' she said, distracted. She'd been searching the database for new crimes in the metro area. 'Scotty, look at this. There are two other bashing deaths with similar MOs in here. Both male, alone, head beaten in with a blunt instrument. The cops who caught the cases thought there was something off about each of these guys,' she said thoughtfully.

'They're rock spiders too?'

'They could be. Listen to this.' She read: '"Victim: Dennis Rocla, River Road, Lane Cove, DOB 11/11/1955. Victim's wife reports finding victim near garbage bin in front of garage, deceased with head injuries. Victim's wife reports that they had been separated and victim had not been welcome at their home. States she was not aware that victim had apparently come to the home the night before when assault took place. Victim's details known to police."

'And this one – "George Manzi, a.k.a. George Marks, 56." Again deceased, assault, head injuries. Says here, "Items of interest to police recovered from scene."'

'Well of course they've recovered items from the scene. It's a freaking homicide investigation.' Scotty stretched and yawned, his limbs sprawling, his elbow almost taking out a pot plant on a desk behind him.

'Exactly. So why even add that bit in there?' asked Jill, pensive. 'They've got something on him.'

She rocked back on her chair, its front legs in the air, her feet up on the desk. Scotty knew better than to tell her to be careful, sitting like that. The one time he'd tried, Jill had smirked at him and balanced the chair on just one leg, using a toe to steady herself as the chair swayed slightly, three of its feet in the air.

'And in both of these they also got no prints,' she read on, chewing her pen. 'Killer wore gloves; they got smooth glove marks from each crime scene. Don't you think that's unusual?' Jill and Scotty both knew that bashing deaths were usually crimes of passion or, more often, were committed by drunken youths in gangs. Gloves weren't typical in such cases.

'Yeah, well, we've got enough to do with Shitbag here,' said Scotty, indicating the murder book, pulling his hand through his thick blond hair. 'We've got a couple more fathers of his past victims to talk to. Could be one of them got sick of waiting for us to lock him up. And we've also got to interview that shrink, Dr Merris, who was treating Carter's daughters from his first marriage. She might have something to say about them or someone they're involved with. The oldest daughter, Hailey, is nineteen now.'

'Yep, okay.' Jill still felt distracted. She stared unseeingly at the flyspecked, dung-coloured wall of the squad room.

'Let's go get lunch, Jackson. I'm starving. I swear I'm gonna die if I don't eat soon.' Scotty half-lifted her from her chair with one arm.

'Yeah. You're fading away, fatso,' Jill laughed, woken from her reverie. She manoeuvred from his grasp, and in the same fluid movement aimed a roundhouse kick at his flat abdomen, deliberately just missing.

'Cut it out!' shouted their boss, Inspector Andreessen, as Scotty tried to lunge at Jill again, knocking over a chair as she easily sidestepped him. 'Go do some work for godsakes!'

Pushing each other through the office, Jill paused when she heard her name.

'. . . you watch. Everything will get buried with that Carter case anyway. Deviants like that always stick together. Jackson would think of him as part of the homosexual scene, like a brother.'

She stopped dead; blood suffused her face. She couldn't care less about Elvis spreading rumours that she was a lesbian, but she couldn't believe that he could even joke that she would somehow protect a paedophile. She didn't hear Scotty say her name, couldn't feel his hand on her arm. She didn't try to think of a comeback. Elvis had his back to her as he talked to two of his cronies, obviously aware that she was just then walking past. With no warning, she exploded into movement, shoulder-charging Calabrese. The heavy man sprawled forward, his gut connecting with a desk corner before he dropped to his knees, sucking air.

'Oh shit! Sorry, man,' Scotty offered his big hand to Elvis, who stayed where he was on the floor, his face black with rage. 'No really, sorry, man, and I'm sorry for pushing you like that, Jackson. Andreessen's right, we gotta stop mucking around.'

He steered Jill, who was standing rigid, out of the office.

'Just keep walking, Jill,' said Scotty tightly. 'You're gonna get a bullet in the head in some laneway one day, I swear.'

5

MENTALLY EXHAUSTED, JILL was tired of fighting the nightmare that started rolling as soon as she slipped into sleep. She gave up trying and walked, eyes closed, down the hall towards her gym. She was used to nightmares, but they were so real lately; last night she'd woken screaming twice, her pillow sour with sweat.

Jill had spent two years after the kidnapping waking every night from these dreams. She'd stayed hidden in her home, her mother by her side day and night. She wouldn't sleep alone and stopped eating. She was racked by paralysing panic that left her hyperventilating and sure she was going to die. As a way of blocking the pain, she took to scratching deep welts in her arms using her fingernails, and progressed to a Stanley knife on her thighs. She hated the burn scars left by the rapists, but revelled in the blood-red warrior marks she made herself.

After three days in the basement, Jill had learned how to turn the physical pain off, mentally leaving her body when the two men were in the room. Sensory deprivation had heightened this ability to disconnect from reality – in the dark she could not see her attackers and they never spoke. After the police had brought her home, she'd found this capacity to become numb would take over involuntarily, and would smudge its way over everything, leaving her feeling empty, like a puppet.

At fifteen, Jill had given in to her mother's tears and agreed to see a counsellor. To her surprise, this time something clicked, and she began clawing her way back into her life. She returned to school, swapped cutting for tattoos, and starving for exercise. She swapped crying for control and order, and set about harnessing her ability to numb any pain. She found that ignoring fatigue meant that studying all night was nothing for her. She quickly caught up with her peers in her schoolwork, and soon overtook them.

She then set about finding a method to defend herself, vowing that if anyone ever again tried to hurt her, she'd make them bleed too. She took up kickboxing, and found a gym that taught the sport using full-contact, gutter fighting. At first her instructors were bemused when Jill insisted on fighting others blindfolded. She was beaten constantly, and soon most at the gym refused to fight her blind and defence-less. She would inwardly curse as those who did get in the ring with her tapped her lightly, instead of connecting properly, or told her verbally where they would strike next.

One afternoon, blindfolded in the ring, Jill was sparring with one of the trainers. The woman was walking through her moves, easily dodging most of Jill's strikes and, every now and then, half-heartedly throwing a light kick. When the trainer began a conversation with an apparent bystander, Jill swallowed her frustration. She wanted a focused, determined enemy. She remembered the helplessness of being blindfolded in the basement, and she was determined to conquer her fear of the dark. The grunting and panting of her speechless abductors also taught her a lesson; by the time she'd been released, after three days, she was excruciatingly aware that sound and movement could predict future agony.

The male voice at the side of the ring was scornful. 'If she wants to get flogged, Kaylene, you should give it to her.'

'Yeah, righto, Price, there's nothing to see here. Just use the other ring will you,' Jill's sparring partner responded.

'She's the one with nothing to see. What a friggin' waste of time.' Jill heard the man moving closer to the ring. 'Use the force, kid,' he called derisively.

Jill didn't respond; she continued to try to make contact with her blows, trying to anticipate where Kaylene would move next.

'Give us a go, Kaylene. I'll partner her for a while.'

'Just forget it, Price,' Kaylene began.

Jill stopped. 'Yeah, all right,' she said, removed her blindfold, and faced the man outside the ring. 'Thanks, Kaylene. I want to get some practice with different people.'

'This is not a good idea,' responded the trainer. 'Jill, it's dangerous trying to fight like this.' In a quieter voice, just to Jill, she said, 'Not this guy. You're not training with him.'

Jill reached a hand down to the man standing by the ring. 'I'm Jillian. Two-minute rounds okay with you?'

Kaylene shrugged in disgust and got out of the ring. The man took her place. He was about 170 centimetres tall – a little taller than Jill – with thinning brown hair and a slight beer gut.

'Ron Price,' he ignored her hand. 'So what's with the blindfold? Kinky?' he asked.

'So are you okay with two-minute rounds?' Jill repeated.

'Yeah, whatever. This should be fun.'

He threw his towel over the ropes in his corner and Jill went to her own, her heart pounding. Although she'd wanted a serious opponent, she knew she wasn't ready for this. She took a deep breath and pulled her blindfold down, put her mouthguard back in. I'll never be ready unless I find someone to fight me, she thought.

Over the next two minutes, Jill hit the ground five times. When she sat back in her corner, her head was ringing and each breath felt like a stab wound to her ribs. She could hear Price sniggering in his corner. Five more rounds, she thought, this is gonna kill me. The blindfold felt suddenly stifling and she raised her hand to rip it off, a wave of fear and disorientation rising up to swamp her. She swallowed, pushed the fear back down and felt the numbness kick in. She heard Price breathing in his corner, eager to go again.

About fucking time, she told herself. I'm finally gonna learn something.

Over the next eight months, Jill sparred regularly with Ron Price, and soon found there were others happy to partner her in the ring. She learned to tune out the background noise of the gym and to concentrate solely upon the sounds of her foe – their footsteps, subtle movements, even their breathing, taught her where they were and the moves they would make next. These sounds began to replace the need to see, painting for Jill a mental image of her opponent's position, and she began striking accurately, pre-empting their next blow. She learned to use their punches and kicks to set up her own, increasingly accurate with her judgment of the time it would take for their balance to be regained, and striking before they could reposition.

She practised daily, at the gym at six when it opened, and fitting in two hours after school every day. However, when the number of people watching outside her ring increased, and their taunts became cheers, she left the gym and took to training at home.

Jill walked into her home gym and filled a cup from the water dispenser near the door. She glanced at the clock. 4.20 a.m. The alarm would've gone off in forty minutes anyway. She started her routine again, her headache forgotten as she punished her body for the weakness of the day before.

6

LATE THE NEXT MORNING, at her desk in the squad room, Jill tried to apply herself to paperwork on the Carter case. She and Scotty had decided to split some of their work to try to progress things faster. Neither of them wanted this to go on any longer than it had to.

Scotty was out interviewing the father of an eleven-year-old girl who'd been molested by David Carter five years previously. The case had only gone to court last year, and Carter had been found not guilty because of insufficient evidence. Although two children had testified that Carter had sexually abused them, his highly paid barrister had torn their evidence to shreds, arguing that if they had been mistaken about exact dates and times, they could have been mistaken about being abused at all. It was an outcome the police and DPP saw all the time, with crushed victims and devastated families walking away from the process feeling that the justice system was a sick joke. Little Madison Lee's father had been particularly vocal in his threats to castrate Carter. Scotty would be sympathetic interviewing him.

Jill stretched and took another sip of her Pepsi Max. She couldn't settle into this case. With her feet up on her desk, she ignored the muscle pain from her workout that morning and tapped into the COPS database, searching for updates on the murders of Dennis Rocla and George Manzi, also known as George Marks.

Within moments, she found what she was looking for.

'I knew it,' she breathed, sitting up straight in her chair, bringing her face close to the computer screen. She looked up from the database and punched in Scotty's mobile number.

'The dead guys in Woolloomooloo and Lane Cove' – Jill was speaking before Scotty had even said hello – 'Manzi and Rocla. I told you they were squirrels. They've both got sex offender sheets. This is the same killer. The same person killed them and Carter. I know it. Someone is getting payback.'

Scotty sighed. Then there was silence for a few beats. 'Shit. Yeah, maybe. Who knows? But if you're right, Jill, we're talking about a mass murderer now, not a simple bashing at the beach. This is gonna be big. Bigger than us.' He sounded tired. 'Who's working the Rocky and Manzi cases? I guess we'd better go talk to them.'

'It's *Rocla*, Dennis Rocla, not Rocky,' said Jill. 'And Harris and Jardine are working both cases over at Central.' She tried to keep the last part casual.

'Aw, fuck! Why'd it have to be them?'

'Yeah, anyway. How's Madison's dad?' Best to change the

41

subject. Scotty had a history with Harris and Jardine. Elvis's cronies.

'Let's just say he's not in mourning for Carter,' he answered. 'You wouldn't believe it, J. He shook my hand when I told him Carter was dead. He actually offered me champagne – at ten in the morning.' Scotty laughed. 'He's still pretty cut up about what happened, but the whole family's in the clear. They arrived back from a trip to China yesterday arvo. Couple of bags were still in the hall.'

'So when are you coming back?' asked Jill. Alibi or no, she and Scotty had thought it unlikely Jiang Lee would have carried through his threats to kill Carter. An accountant from Strathfield in Sydney's Inner West, Lee was a Buddhist with two young kids and a wife. He might have wanted Carter dead, but he just wasn't the type to kill him.

'I'm coming in now. You want to go for a swim and get some KFC?'

Jill smiled. 'Yeah, whatever. See you when you get here.'

Within thirty seconds of re-scanning the database, she'd dropped the smile. Manzi and Rocla had both been investigated for separate alleged sex offences dating back at least ten years. The three victims had not come forward until they were young adults. She noted the COPS event numbers that linked the complaints to the men, and typed one of the numbers into the computer. The database accessed a 2001 complaint by a then 18-year-old man who'd claimed that eight years earlier Manzi had raped him in a caravan. She copied down the complainant's name and address – a home in Castle Hill. She copied the contact number into her notebook and picked up the phone. Travis O'Hare.

Ten minutes later, Jill's blue eyes were wide. O'Hare no

longer lived at the Castle Hill address, but she'd managed to speak to his older brother. He didn't have a lot of time for Travis, but his diatribe against him had thrown up an interesting detail. A coincidence? Maybe. Jill accessed the database again and located contacts for Rocla's two victims.

'Scotty, where are you now?' She had the phone tucked under her ear, leaving her hands free to shove her notes into her briefcase. 'We're driving out to Richmond this afternoon to interview the shrink. You're not gonna believe this.'

7

WAYNE CRABBE HAD TRIED singles clubs and got lucky a few times, but he found it was a lot of work to get to the action in the end. The women were more careful these days, and would usually expect to be taken out a few times before you got to meet their kids. Then they'd be watchful for a while, and before you knew it you were spending half your life with a fat, ugly hag waiting for moments that might never come. And the longer you were with these bitches, the more they could learn about you. He hated the waiting. He wanted to be in and out. Minimum of fuss. No harm done.

Wayne had come up with the job offer idea while with a western suburbs troll who had a beautiful nine-year-old boy. She'd desperately wanted a job and all she ever did was whine about how hard it was to find one. When he met another mum one morning in a doctor's surgery, scanning the job ads, he came up with the plan on the spot.

'Excuse me,' he smiled at Rose Deloso, a dark-haired woman wearing a neat tracksuit. 'You're not looking for a job, are you?'

The woman looked him over, her brow furrowed, and said nothing. He nodded at the columns in the paper she was poring over.

'It's just that I'm having trouble filling a job.' He smiled reassuringly, trying hard not to look at the boy playing with Lego at her feet. 'You're not by any chance interested in casual work at a café, are you?'

'Really? Are you serious?' She was smiling now too. 'I mean, yeah, I'm looking for work. Are you for real?'

'Yep. You wouldn't believe how hard it's been getting someone to work the hours we need.'

'Well, I'm only looking for school-hours work.' She looked at him doubtfully, 'I've got to pick the kids up at three. Well, except for Fridays, when their dad's got them.'

'It's hard, isn't it, when you're on your own?' Wayne tried for empathy. 'I've just got one son. Me and his mum thought it would be best to have him a week each. It's working out pretty well, but only because my mother can drop him at school. I'm right to pick him up. You don't have anyone to help you out?'

'Nope. My parents still work themselves. It's just me, I'm afraid.'

Bingo.

Wayne smiled again, warm, but professional. 'Well, I can't promise you the job now, but we actually need someone ten till two, for the lunchtime crowd. Monday to Friday. If that suits, we could both be happy.'

'Oh my God, I can't believe this,' she laughed. 'This is the last thing I thought would happen here.' She self-consciously smoothed her ponytail, sat straighter, and shushed her delicious five-year-old boy, who was playing with the germ-infested clinic toys. 'Well, what should we do? How can I apply? Should I give you my mobile number?'

As easy as that.

'Look,' he said, thinking fast. 'You should have a look at the place first.' He gave her the location of a Burwood café he frequented. It was next to the railway station and was popular with the after-school rush.

'Listen though,' he added, leaning forward slightly, 'I'm the owner, not the manager, and the manageress is a bit, well, territorial. She likes to do the hiring and firing.' He smiled with chagrin, shrugged his shoulders. 'Would you mind not saying anything about the job when you have a look? Save me any conflict with Cath? I'll speak to her and call you in for a formal interview if she hasn't found anyone. What do you think?'

'Yeah, okay. Sure. I'll go have a look. And you'll call about an interview?' Rose was standing now, hurrying her son. Her name had been announced by the receptionist; it was her turn to see the doctor.

'I'll call you tomorrow,' he said, tucking her number into his pocket. Now to get into her house.

Wayne called Rose the next morning. Could she come in for an interview? Eleven tomorrow? Great.

Another call that afternoon. So sorry. A last-minute appointment in Brisbane had come up. He'd call her on his return.

Wayne's tone was polite but friendly when he called Rose the third time.

'Rose, I've spoken to Cath and she'd like to meet you. It's busy at work, though, and it'd be easiest for her if we stopped in at your house for a coffee after work tomorrow. Do you think that's okay? She knocks off at six. We could drop 'round at 6.30, and be gone by seven. What do you think?'

Rose seemed hesitant, somewhat puzzled, but was eventually won over. She wanted the job, and when Wayne arrived, alone and apologetic, bearing chocolate mud cake with Rohypnol-laced icing, she let him in.

Wayne made sure she had the biggest slice, and fifteen minutes later, with Mummy sound asleep with her face in the cake, he went to play birthday parties with the five-year-old.

8

CAROLE DEAN HAD FINALLY HUNG UP. Standing at the base of her winding gravel driveway, still in her pyjamas, Mercy dropped the phone handset into her dressing-gown pocket. She should've let the call go to the answering machine. When she'd realised it was Carole on the line, she'd resignedly taken the phone and her cigarettes out the front door. At least she could distract herself with the sky and trees as she reassured Carole that she was fine.

Mercy had been proud of her saccharine chatter throughout the call. She'd worked with this woman for years, and knew that Carole would never back off if Mercy couldn't convince her that yesterday had been an anomaly, that she just needed a good rest.

Wrapping her gown closer around her body, Mercy went back inside and looked around guardedly, almost as though she expected to see something unusual there. As it happened, this was not an ordinary house. Perched on the precipice of a cliff dropping to a deep ravine in the Blue Mountains, almost the entire back wall of the split-level house was glass. The effect was of living in the sky above a vast bush canyon; indeed, at the moment, clouds on the balcony whorled insistently as though indignant at being denied entry. Two galahs scratched at the jarrah decking, calling occasionally for more seed to be scattered.

It was always at least ten degrees cooler at Mercy's home than anywhere else in Sydney, and she shivered slightly as she stepped down to her sunken lounge, reaching automatically for the remote to play some music. She nudged the volume lower and the Japanese harps soothed her somewhat.

What the hell was happening to her? She stared down at her bandaged hand, fascinated by the white gauze marked by the bloom of red blood.

Her clinical supervisor, Dr Noah Griffen, had been warning her for months that she was taking on too many abuse cases, that she was at risk of burning out. She'd listened impatiently, resentful at having to spend more time at the hospital to attend these sessions. Regular clinical supervision was a requirement of her employment, though, and if she missed more than six of the weekly sessions in a year she had to answer to the Clinical Director.

She had been attending supervision with Griffen for ten years now, and had, in fact, decided to consult at the Sisters of Charity Hospital because of her mentor's practice there, but she'd grown increasingly intolerant of his admonitions to reduce her caseload. It wasn't like he wasn't doing the same kind of work.

Mercy's expertise with survivors of childhood sexual abuse had led to a lengthy waiting list for her services, and she felt unable to turn down the individuals who sought her help. But as the years had passed working with this population, she found herself in tears more often than not as they told their stories. She was increasingly unable to stop her imagination from conjuring images of the abuse they had endured, which would vie for space with memories of the beatings from her own childhood. A flame of hatred for the offenders was stoked with each new tale of suffering.

One sleepless night, after speaking with an eighteen-year-old girl slowly dying of anorexia nervosa, she had realised that this patient's file was still in her bag. Snapping on her bedside light, she had pulled the thick hospital folder onto her bed, hoping to find something within its contents that could help her with this young woman.

The girl had been repeatedly hospitalised since she was twelve, when she had tried to kill herself by taking every tablet in her home, washed down with disinfectant from the laundry cupboard. It wasn't until the year before, however, that she'd disclosed that her father had been selling her to his mates for beer for as long as she could remember. Although she'd now made a police statement against him, the DPP was still struggling to gather sufficient evidence to bring him to trial. In the meantime, this man was at home while his daughter fought for her life in hospital.

Impotent rage engulfed Mercy as she flicked through the file. Suddenly something snagged at her consciousness, and she stopped. She turned back a page, then another. There. An address. The father's address. The place where he was probably even now sleeping drunkenly while his daughter was nourished through a naso-gastric tube.

It wasn't far from here, actually. Windsor. She felt a thrill of surprise that she could drive to the house of a monster right now and knock on his door. She could see what such a man would look like, could speak to him; throw a brick through his window if she wanted to. She could tell this man what he had done to his child. Make him listen. Sit him down and force-feed him tales of the horror that she listened to every day. He wouldn't care; she knew that. He'd rationalise his way through what she was saying; he'd call the police, make her out to be the crazy one. He'd get away with it. They always did.

Windsor. She had his address.

It had not been difficult to access the identities of her victims' attackers once she'd started looking. In the past, Mercy had skipped these people's names when she came across them. They had no meaning for her; they did not help her to assist her patients.

When she decided to pay attention, however, Mercy found it surprisingly easy to gather facts about the offenders. They were identified in police statements, court documents, Apprehended Violence Orders – many of these documents were in her patients' files. Often the perpetrators' addresses were right there, their pseudonyms, sometimes even the names of other accusers. Sometimes officials had gone through and blacked out such details, but this would most often happen with one document and not another. Mercy soon had profiles on several men.

She began to work on these files late at night, also incorporating information she'd gleaned from her patients during therapy. She'd found herself specifically asking questions during the sessions that would fill holes in her knowledge about the offenders. She'd jot the missing details in her work notes, and then transfer them to her offender files when she got home.

Mercy began to notice patterns. Carly Kaplan had said that her abuser had made her dress as a fairy and a princess. He'd made Carly and her friend Brianna touch each other, and had taken photographs. Kathy Lin, another patient, had been abused by her father, but one evening he'd entertained a friend who'd also had Kathy and her sister dress as princesses while he photographed them. Kathy's description of this man – when Mercy had asked during their last session – had been very similar to the one given of the offender in Carly's police statement.

Then there was John Jacobs. One of Mercy's most damaged patients, he was able to work on memories of his abuse maybe only once or twice a year. Otherwise he spent months on the acute psychosis ward of the hospital while doctors tried to stabilise his medication. Both of his arms, from fingertips to shoulders, were a mutilated mess. He would carve and burn them, trying to release the demons he believed lived inside his body. He'd also mutilated his genitals, sure that the devil had control of his sex organs, and once, after stabbing himself in the stomach to punish himself for becoming sexually aroused, emergency surgery had been necessary to save him from dying.

John's file told a harrowing story. Removed from his parents as a mute and unresponsive toddler, bruises covering his body, he'd been placed in a group home. Made a ward of the state because of his parents' neglect, he was eligible to be adopted, but staff waited until they could determine whether he would improve and what legacies he might have been left with. His DoCS case notes indicated he'd rapidly responded to care and attention, learning to talk and walk, and endearing himself to staff. He'd been adopted by a family who already had two sons, and no significant entries were made in the file for several years. At age ten, he'd been temporarily returned to the care of the state. His adoptive parents had complained that he was aggressive, wouldn't shower, and was non-compliant. One caseworker had labelled the adoptive father as 'controlling' and 'aggressive'. Another had said that John was 'attention-seeking' and had 'deliberately sabotaged his placement' because of 'an inferiority complex'. The same writer had noted and dismissed John's claims that his adoptive father had molested him.

Although repeatedly exposed to it, Mercy never ceased to be horrified by the ineptitude of some of the departmental carers these children were entrusted to. The department claimed to have lost the remainder of John Jacobs' file, but he'd told Mercy that he'd been repeatedly sent back to the same family until he ran away at the age of fourteen and lived on the streets.

John's account of his time with the family was disjointed and blurred by delusional thinking, but one theme predominated. He claimed he'd been a prize in a game played by a group of men. His adoptive father played the game and John had been a 'party favour', swapped around amongst members of the group. Because he also spoke of the Secret Service using his brain to create a supercomputer that would one day control the world, Mercy had always only half-listened to him, aware that his words were distorted by mental illness.

Now, however, she scavenged through his account, foraging for potential truths amongst the chaos that was this patient's reality.

Her files were growing daily.

9

'I DON'T SEE WHY we had to come out here this arvo,' grumbled Scotty, steering the car with one hand, nursing a Pepsi with the other. To accommodate his long legs, he had adjusted the seat back as far as it would go; he was practically sitting in the back seat.

Beside him, an open street directory lay on Jill's lap. Her feet were up on the dashboard.

'Are you serious?' she asked. 'Don't you think it's kind of significant that Mercy Merris has counselled victims of all three dead men? We've got to talk to her – she could be a link.'

'Yeah, but it's boiling. And we're going to Richmond, for God's sake. We could've just called her.'

Jill had called Mercy, and she knew they were coming.

They'd been driving west for just over an hour. The built-up shopping strips and unit-blocks had given way to huge, blank-faced factory estates as they made their way through the afternoon traffic. It seemed like half of Sydney was heading home to the western suburbs.

Reading the map while travelling left Jill feeling queasy. She pressed her forehead against the window. Parched bushland bordered the two-lane road. The scrub was broken every now and then by a ranch-style house, or a service station.

'Another friggin' speed camera! Can you believe this shit?' Scotty backed off the pedal a little. The car's dashboard display still registered 41 degrees outside, even though it was now after 3 p.m. Scotty had been bitching for the past thirty minutes.

Jill tuned out and thought about the last time she'd met Dr Mercy Merris. A psychodynamic psychotherapist in private practice, Dr Merris used to do some work for the New South Wales Police Service. She'd counselled cops who had problems at home, with the boss, or who, like Jill, had attended a fatal, or a shooting incident, and had been sent to a shrink for a mandatory debrief.

Like most cops, Jill hadn't wanted to go to counselling. In fact, having spent a year in therapy at fifteen, she was even more reluctant than most. So she'd been surprised when she found the obligatory three meetings helpful. She'd gone to the sessions determined to say as little as she could and get out as soon as possible, but had found it easy to talk to Mercy. Dr Merris had recommended more treatment; but hey, she didn't like it *that* much.

An approaching intersection snapped her from her thoughts.

'Turn left here, Scotty.'

*

'Finally,' he grumbled five minutes later, steering the car into the drive of the private psychiatric hospital.

The wheels of the Subaru crunched gravel as they rolled down the two-kilometre, palm-lined private road. Hills of waving grass poured down to meet a river and in the distance were the mountains. In the foreground to their right, a few cattle grazed stupidly, sun-addled, tails swishing at flies; on the left four bored horses ambled. Jill wound the window down and took a long sip of the hot, clean air. A bellbird whistle-cracked.

'Worth going nuts for, this is,' said Scotty, taking in the peaceful surrounds. He turned completely in his seat to watch a young woman in pyjamas, clutching a teddy bear, walking with a young man in suit pants and a shirt.

The car rolled to a stop in front of a long, low, sandstone building. The bulk of the hospital sprawled behind this building, across beautifully manicured grounds. A sprinkler thwacked water across an emerald lawn, and Jill did a double-take when a peacock on the grass angled to catch the overspray. She noted a sign near the sprinkler commenting that it was run from a rainwater tank – drought-stricken Sydneysiders hadn't been permitted to use sprinklers for a couple of years now.

Before she had time to remind Scotty of their agenda for this meeting, a beaming woman was at her door, welcoming them to the Sisters of Charity Hospital.

Carole Dean, well-groomed in skirt-suit and heels, had come to greet them while Dr Merris was with a client. Would they like a late lunch while waiting? It was seafood day. Could she show them the grounds, or to the library to collect themselves after the drive? She smiled as she ushered them into a plush, cool foyer more resembling a five-star hotel than a psychiatric hospital.

'Lunch sounds great,' boomed Scotty at the same time as Jill stated, 'Actually, Carole, we'd like to have a look around while we're waiting.'

Jill wanted to see the hospital. It could be a possible link to a serial killer; hell, the killer could be here right now.

She ignored Scotty's disgusted look and his mumbled 'Don't see why we can't do both' as she led the trio from the foyer in the direction that looked like it could lead to patient wards.

Carole caught up quickly and, gracefully overtaking Jill, her smile glued on, she guided the group across the deep carpeting.

Jill noticed Carole's smile slip as they turned into the hallway ahead.

Scotty had managed to convince Jill that a tour of the hospital grounds would be helpful, and he had slipped away well before they reached Mercy's rooms. She was certain that this would first lead him past the hospital restaurant. She looked around the room and recalled the sense of refined warmth she had experienced the last time she was in this office. The squashy armchairs squatted around a low table bearing a water jug and platter of fruit. On three walls, framed photography depicted single flowers in exquisite, almost erotic close-up. Along the fourth wall, full-length glass bi-fold doors opened onto a terracotta-paved courtyard framed by flowering shrubs and trees. Birds foraged familiarly across the lawn.

Today the room was less carefully arranged than she remembered. A pile of books had spilled from the desk and lay splayed across the thick carpet. An ashtray near the computer overflowed with lipstick-rimmed cigarette butts, and a pile of unopened mail and magazines threatened to join the books on the floor. The afternoon sun speared in through the glass doors and cast parts of the room in a garish glow, while shadows waited in corners.

'Jill, it's so lovely to see you,' smiled Mercy, walking towards her from the glass doors. She took both of Jill's hands in her own and brushed her cheek with a kiss.

'You too, Mercy. It's been a while. I hope you're well?'

'Fine, fine, always busy, of course, but aren't we all? And you, Jill? Are you taking care of yourself?' Mercy's brown eyes scanned Jill's face as she guided her to one of the armchairs.

Jill felt herself drawn into the cocoon of caring she had experienced when she had consulted Mercy two years before.

'I'm well. I'm trying.'

She felt suddenly defensive under Mercy's searching gaze. She didn't need anyone probing her feelings right now. Besides, this is my investigation, she thought. She straightened her back in the chair. Mercy might be a skilled psychologist, but Jill knew a bit about interviewing too.

'Mercy, as I mentioned on the phone, I want to speak with you about some of your clients.'

'Of course, of course, darling, but first we must have a coffee, a glass of wine? How is your sister?' she said over her shoulder as she walked towards a sideboard.

Mercy's tangle of curls was more unruly than usual and hid half her face as she fussed around an espresso machine in a corner of the room. She turned to face Jill with a coffee cup in one hand, a wine glass in the other, wearing a questioning smile.

'Coffee, thanks, Mercy. Black. No sugar. And Cassie's fine.'

Mercy dropped the smile when she turned back to the sideboard. She sloshed red wine into a huge glass, then attended to the espresso maker.

'I've no more clients today. Might as well,' Mercy chirped brightly as she took a deep sip of her wine. 'Sure I can't tempt you? Just a glass. I picked this up in the Hunter last year. It's a gorgeous pinot noir. You have to try–'

'Mercy, I don't want any wine. Thank you.'

'Of course. No problem. I know you're working. Sorry.'

'Don't be sorry, Mercy. I appreciate the offer.' Jill curbed her impatience. She knew that interviews, unlike interrogations perhaps, should always remain positive. A collaborative atmosphere was required when gathering information from someone. She smiled. 'I really appreciate your time. You look like you've got a lot to do.' She gestured around the room.

Mercy looked at her office as though seeing it for the first time. 'It is a mess, isn't it?' She giggled nervously.

'You should see *my* office!' Jill knew most people would be happy to eat straight off her desk, it was so clean, but she wanted to join with Mercy, reduce some of her defensiveness.

Mercy finished preparing Jill's coffee and brought it over to the low table. Jill noticed half of the wine Mercy had poured herself was already gone. Oh boy, she thought. Better get on with this.

'Mercy, I've got some news to tell you that could come as a bit of a shock,' she began, when Mercy had taken a seat. 'I'm in the middle of an investigation. Three men have been killed. Believe it or not, Mercy, each of these men was connected to patients you've treated in the past.'

'Are you serious? How extraordinary.'

'That's what I thought.'

'How can I help, Jill?'

'Well, I don't know. The thing is, in an investigation you look for patterns, anything that seems to link things together, and then you follow them wherever they take you. It's probably a little like your work, Mercy, searching for reasons why people have particular problems, looking for things that could have happened in their past.'

'Quite. Yes, I see what you mean.' Another deep sip left little wine in Mercy's glass.

'First I thought I'd tell you the names of the men who've been killed. Maybe you've heard your patients mention them.'

Mercy waited.

'Dennis Rocla, David Carter, George Manzi.'

Nothing.

'Mercy, have you heard those names before?'

'I don't believe so, no, Jill.'

'You're sure? Give it some time.'

Mercy finished her wine, set her glass down on the table. Too hard. The delicate stem of the glass snapped in two.

'Shit!' Mercy looked as though she might cry. She and Jill both stood.

Jill tried a small laugh to dispel the awkwardness. 'Flimsy bloody things. You know, my sister bought me six Riedel wine glasses. Supposed to cost a hundred dollars each or something. She got them duty-free. I've got two left! I'm going to have to go out and replace them before she comes over.'

Mercy took the broken glass to the sink. She seemed to draw herself together as she walked.

'Jill, I'm sorry you've had to come all this way. I don't think I can help you. I don't know these men.' She walked back towards the armchair, but rather than taking a seat, she fussed around with a potted plant, absently breaking off leaves, snapping them under her fingernails.

'I do not associate with men like that,' Mercy continued. 'I'm afraid there's nothing I can tell you.'

'Men like what?'

Mercy's face coloured; her eyes narrowed.

'Well, Jill,' she said, 'if these men are connected to patients of mine, I'm assuming that they had no positive influence in their lives. You know the people I work with are mostly victims of abuse.'

Jill let it slide, but she was puzzled. She'd come out here because she thought that Mercy could have an unwitting link to the killer, might unknowingly have some information she could pass on. But the psychologist was obviously very rattled; this was not the calm woman she'd consulted two years ago, and her last comments revealed she was hiding something. Or someone.

'Yep, well, you guessed correctly,' said Jill. 'Four of your patients have made complaints against these men. Let's see . . .' she consulted her notepad, although she knew the names by heart. 'Hailey Carter, Travis O'Hare, Giselle Forest and Carly Kaplan.'

'Ah.'

'I thought maybe if we talked about your patients a bit,' Jill continued, 'you might think of something that could help us find some sort of connection between the deaths of these men.'

Mercy walked to the glass doors and opened them. Scented warmth wafted into the room, soon obliterated by acrid smoke when Mercy lit a slim dark-brown cigarette. Gitanes. Jill remembered her smoking the French cigarettes in the courtyard during one of their sessions.

'Jill, I did tell you on the phone that I won't be talking about my patients. In fact, I can't. Unless I believe they, or someone else, is in direct danger because of something they have told me, I am obliged to maintain confidentiality about everything we might have discussed.' She blew a long stream of smoke into the courtyard. 'I'm sure you can understand my position. I can assure you, however, that I don't know anything about the deaths of those men.

'I can say though, Jill,' she continued after a pause, turning and looking Jill in the eye, 'that I'm not particularly perturbed about them having been killed. And to be honest, I don't know why anyone else would or should be.'

Jill leaned back in the armchair and studied her hands. She looked up at Mercy, framed in the doorway, arms held close to her body, her posture reflecting both anger and anxiety. This wasn't at all the way she'd thought this interview would go.

On the drive home from the hospital, Jill was quiet. She told Scotty she had a headache, and while this was true, the main reason she wasn't speaking was because of the confusing thoughts chasing each other through her mind.

She couldn't shake the ridiculous notion that Mercy Merris might have actually killed these men. But this didn't seem to make sense. First of all, female killers did not typically bash men to death. And Mercy was a wealthy professional woman. Why would she do it? It had to be something else. Maybe she knew the killer, or suspected one of her patients and was covering for them. Maybe Mercy was just burnt out, and Jill was reading culpability into her exhausted anxiety. She could relate to that feeling. She chewed on skin around a fingernail.

Mercy had articulated the question Jill had not been able to rid from her mind all week – why was she investigating these deaths at all? Why was anyone? Before the interview had ended Mercy had said that someone had done the world a big favour, and it was pretty difficult to argue with her. Wasn't someone out there doing what Jill had signed up to do as a cop? Stopping child molesters?

She shifted in her seat, faced the window.

Was the killer planning more deaths? If another paedophile were killed, how many children would that save from being raped? She'd read once that one paedophile might molest up to seventy children in their lifetime. What was the right thing to do here? Jill didn't know any more.

10

IT'S UNUSUAL FOR SO many to be here, thought Wayne Crabbe, darting glances around the room. He used a mirror beside him to surreptitiously observe his peers; he knew well that people here did not like to be stared at. An eclectic mix of men were scattered in heavy leather armchairs around what had been built as the ballroom of a sprawling harbourside mansion.

A clutch of three over-fed banker types laughed conspiratorially over their clinking drinks. They sat near massive glass doors that in daylight revealed a twelve-million-dollar view. Two men in running shoes hunched together in chairs by the unlit fireplace, whispering over a book placed on the low coffee table in front of them. The rest of the guests – six or seven men – like Wayne, sat or stood alone, heads down, occasionally shooting quick looks at the huge entryway to the low-lit room, obviously waiting for The Owner. Two uniformed waiters moved quietly through the room, delivering drinks and collecting glasses.

Wayne sucked in his gut when he caught a glimpse of himself in the mirror. Gotta do something about that, he thought, the ladies don't like it. He smiled, remembering Rose Deloso's flattered embarrassment when he'd shown up at her house alone. He'd counted on her assuming that he was interested in her for more than just the job. Lonely ladies are your forte, he told himself in the mirror, straightening his shoulders. And the job offer is genius.

Behind his reflection, he noticed a new arrival to the festivities. Wayne was always amused when 'The Judge' showed up; he loved watching the famous Sydney QC slide from loud and pompous to slurred stupor, having to use the wall to hold himself up. Eventually his driver would half-carry him from the room, semi-conscious and drooling. Just last month, Wayne had found him on the bathroom floor lying in his own piss. The country's finest. He'd lifted The Judge's wallet before he left the room.

Wayne sipped his strawberry milkshake. The waiters here were used to unusual requests and were hired for their discretion. He knew he too was being watched. He was relatively new here and The Owner kept a close eye on everyone who showed up. Not that Wayne had yet spoken one-to-one with The Owner, but they'd all seen some of his best work. His rape movies, in which he was always masked, were the hottest trade and hardest to get. Wayne had one prized copy, and to get it he'd had to trade 150 points, two of his Asian films, and ten mobile phone shots.

He moved over when he saw Tadpole making his way to

his table. Fit, fair and forty-one, Tadpole looked more like he was thirty. With hardly any facial hair and a permanent smile, Tadpole was the most popular teacher at Carrindon College, a $4000-a-term school for boys in years five through twelve. Tadpole had got him in here. He was everyone's friend.

Wayne pasted on a smile for the smarmy bastard. Wayne had no friends.

'Hey, Crabbe. Staying alive?' asked Tadpole, sliding onto the couch, invading Wayne's space, smiling of course. 'Someone doesn't like us. Hear about Dennis the Menace?'

'Is that Rocla? I've heard people talking, but I don't know what happened,' said Wayne.

'His wife found him last week with his head caved in. The Owner's pissed. Word is Dennis had a copy of one of The Owner's rape movies on his hard drive. Yuck. Who'd want to watch that stuff, anyway? All my boys love playing with me. You just have to use a little sugar. The world needs more love.'

Wayne tuned out from Tadpole's theories, and thought about these deaths. That was three in a month or something. Everyone was talking about Carter, Rocla and Manzi getting killed. Apparently they'd been members here for years, and Dennis Rocla was a playmate of The Owner. There were rumours that the killer was a cop, but Wayne knew their biggest threat was always the discards. Kids who grew up and didn't like the games they'd played. That's why Wayne stayed away from relationships. By the time a kid talked, he was long gone. He didn't have the money a lot of these guys had to travel to Asia whenever they liked, or to pay their way out of anything. He'd waited ages to join this little club and now it looked as though the members could be targets. Screw this, he thought. I've been doing this long enough on my own. He decided this would be his last meet.

Pity, he thought, I never got a chance to bid for a live trade. Still, I'd never have the money to outbid some of these old farts anyway. Back to being alone. In and out. No harm done. He could just as easily score Rowies, his date-rape drug of choice, off the internet.

11

JILL HADN'T EVEN reached her desk the next morning when she was told to see Inspector Andreessen.

'There's a rape case asking for you,' he grunted, gesturing out his office door to a very tall, dark-skinned girl who was drawing a lot of stares from the males in the squad room. She wore thigh-high, black PVC boots, white micro-shorts and a lime-green cropped jacket. She perched on one of the government-issue chairs in the waiting area, all legs, her back to the wall.

Jill wasn't surprised this girl had asked for her. Most of the working girls told one another to ask for her if they needed help. She didn't know whether it was because she didn't judge them, or because hers was the only name they knew. She suspected that some asked for her because she was partnered with Scotty.

'Name's Honey Delaney,' said Andreessen, head down now, looking at papers on his desk. 'She's had a rape kit done, and the hospital sent her over. Like I said, she asked for you.' He turned a page and started writing. It was clear she was dismissed.

Jill made her way over to the waiting area. As she drew nearer it became clear that Honey had not been given that name at birth. She was stop-traffic gorgeous, but her hands and jaw gave away the fact that she'd been born a boy.

When the woman looked up, Jill masked the shock she felt at seeing her eyes. They were a plastic, lolly-green colour, shining too brightly. The effect was momentarily frightening, until Jill realised that Honey was wearing cosmetic contact lenses. There was no attempt to make her eyes appear natural – the lenses were like something shock-rocker Marilyn Manson might wear.

Well, we all have masks, thought Jill. She sat down with a chair between them to give the girl space.

'Honey, I'm Jill Jackson. I understand you've been attacked. I'm sorry to hear that,' she paused, and when Honey said nothing, continued. 'Do you want to come with me to a more private room and you can tell me what happened?'

In a voice devoid of all emotion, her shark eyes staring ahead disconcertingly, Honey told Jill that the night before she'd been anally raped by two football players at Moore Park. The attack had taken place near the cricket grounds, in a particularly isolated region of the vast parklands that traversed several inner city suburbs.

Jill led Honey to another room and formally took her statement. Before she ended the interview she offered to get her some help. When describing the attack, Honey's voice had been so flat, lifeless.

'Did the hospital arrange for some counselling for you, Honey?' asked Jill.

'I'm not interested,' Honey replied, staring unnaturally from the synthetic eyes. She looked around the dingy room with a look of distaste and then down at her acid-orange talon-like fingernails, flicking her thumbnail against her pinkie.

'Tell you the truth,' she continued in a raspy voice, 'I'm only here because I can't claim Victims Compensation unless I've made a statement. We all know you guys aren't exactly gonna bust your arses trying to catch the guys who raped the trannie.'

Jill inwardly winced. Honey's cynical resignation that her treatment would be unfair probably reflected the truth. She took a deep breath.

'Anyway,' Jill said, 'I really think you're going to need some help. You've been through a terrible experience. I'm going to check that someone comes to see you within the next couple of days.' She leaned forward, concerned.

'You only want to make yourself feel better, Sergeant. I said I'm not interested.'

Honey paused, and Jill reached her hand forward, to comfort, reassure.

'Don't fuckin' touch me.' The tall woman suddenly stood, towering over Jill, screaming down at her. Her eyes looked crazy now.

Her voice cracked, saliva frothed in the corners of her mouth; she was standing between Jill and the door. 'Do you think some fucking social worker is going to take away all the shit that's happened to me in my life?' she screeched.

Jill knew that to avoid escalating the situation she needed to be calm, but authoritative.

'You need to SIT DOWN,' she ordered in her police voice. 'I said, sit down, Honey,' she repeated, waving away a uniformed colleague who'd obviously heard the shouting, his face questioning through the clear panel in the door.

She watched Honey register where she was and crumple back into the chair.

'Just don't fucking touch me,' she said quietly now, her voice almost dead again, but with a tear sliding through the make-up on her face. 'I have to be wasted before anyone can touch me. Speaking of which,' Honey wiped her manicured finger down the trail made by the solitary tear, 'are we done here? I've got to go score.'

Jill couldn't get Honey out of her mind for the rest of the day. She followed up with the hospital and collected all the information she could, but there was little to go on, and she doubted they were going to get these guys. They'd worn condoms, according to Honey, and had pocketed them before they left. It sounded to Jill like they'd done it before, and that the crime had been planned, rather than opportunistic.

She didn't feel she could send the mental health team around to Honey's home after she'd been so insistent she be left alone, but she also didn't want to just leave her like that, without any help. She decided to go to Honey's house and make sure she was okay. Leaving Scotty to do some paper-work for a South Maroubra break-and-enter, she made her way over to the address Honey had given her that morning.

Honey had a bed-sit in a large housing commission

block at Malabar. This beachside suburb, home of Long Bay Gaol, also housed an uncomfortable mix of long-term public housing tenants, pensioners and retirees. A handful of new millionaires had built self-conscious mansions on blocks left to them by their parents. Waterfront was waterfront in Sydney, even when the suburb had one of the highest break-and-enter rates in the state.

Jill jogged up three flights of graffitied stairs, her hand over her mouth to block the piss-stench that permeated everything. A woman cursed in a singsong heroin whine. She heard a door slam, and a child crying. From behind a screenless window, a radio played J.J. Cale's 'Cocaine'. She'd be using that too if she had to live here.

She reached Honey's door and knocked. Nothing. She tried again. There was no-one home. Jill felt guiltily relieved. She had turned to leave when the door opened on a chain.

'Yeah?' the flat voice was also slurred now. This was a bad idea.

'Honey. It's Jillian Jackson. I just came to make sure you're all right.' The room beyond the crack in the door was dark and smoky.

The door shut and then re-opened. Honey stepped back and stood there. Jill was supposed to go in.

The two rooms that made up the entire unit were visible from the entry. The kitchen, laundry and sitting area were all part of one room, and Jill could see the tiny bedroom, with a double bed draped in a purple spread. Dark curtains covered the only window in the sitting room. The place smelled of stale smoke, but the surfaces looked pretty clean.

She swallowed and walked past Honey into the flat and waited for her eyes to adjust so she could look around.

'I'm not going to pretend I'm here with good news, Honey,' she started, watching the tall woman walk towards a Formica dining setting that took up most of the room. She perched on a chair at the table opposite Honey. 'It's going to be hard to catch these guys unless we get lucky or you remember something else.'

'Oh I never get lucky, Jill,' Honey took a drag of her cigarette, 'and they never get caught.'

Her hair in a ponytail, and the lolly-green contacts removed, Honey looked more like a fourteen-year-old schoolgirl than the pimped-out prostitute who'd come to the station today. Jill could see she was stoned, but she seemed calmer than that morning, and her speech was slow.

'It sounds like you've had it pretty hard,' said Jill cautiously, wondering what she was doing here, why she was inviting this woman to tell her a story she wasn't going to want to hear. She didn't need this right now.

God, it's hot in here, she thought.

Honey laughed flatly and leaned back in her chair, an appraising look on her face.

'You know I never asked you to come here, Sergeant Jackson,' she said, 'and I don't need your help.' She took another drag of her cigarette. 'So what do you want from me? Last cop in here got a blow job. The two before him wanted me to rat out the speed dealers in 31A. So what's your thing?'

Jill felt stupid. Her head had started to thump again and the smoke was making her throat dry. She realised she hadn't eaten anything since a banana at breakfast.

'Look, I'm sorry, Honey. You just looked really bad this morning and I wanted to make sure you hadn't done something silly. I knew if I sent mental health over here, you'd freak out, so I came myself. I'll get out of your way now. I'm glad you're okay.' She stood to go, hoping Honey would stand too and let her out.

Instead, Honey stayed seated. Her head on a slight angle, her eyes showed she was still obviously weighing Jill up. 'Can I get you a coffee?' she asked, finally.

'Water. Water would be great,' said Jill, sitting again, 'and do you have any Panadol?'

12

OVER THE NEXT TWO HOURS, Jill learned that Honey had run away from home twice by the age of ten. The second time she'd left, her mother had not even tried to find her, furious that her latest boyfriend spent more time watching Honey than her.

Watching Honey's every move was not the only thing her stepfather had done, though. At least three nights a week, he would stumble, drunk, into Honey's bedroom and perform oral sex on the frightened little boy. The other four days of the week, apparently cleansing himself of feelings of shame, the man would subject Honey to beatings and verbal abuse. When the nighttime visits escalated to sodomy, Honey fled, living in a park with other children who felt safer sleeping under a bridge than in their own beds.

One wet and freezing Sydney winter's night, Honey was

huddled in the dirty stairwell of a supermarket, eating a barbecue chicken pilfered from a fat shopper's trolley. Her new friend Mia, a beautiful Vietnamese girl who looked around Honey's age but was actually fourteen, was sharing the meal. Honey had been wearing girl's clothes whenever she could for as long as she could remember and now that there was no one to interfere, her black hair was curling down almost to her shoulders. She knew that no one she met for the first time would think of her as anything other than the girl she believed she was.

'What would you say if I said there was somewhere we could stay tonight?' Mia had asked Honey, trying to wipe her chicken-greasy hands on the inside of her jeans so the stains wouldn't be so obvious. She glanced at Honey sideways from underneath her long, black fringe.

'I'd say what the hell are we doing here?' Honey laughed. 'Let's go. Now!' And she'd dragged Mia up from the filthy stairs on which they sat. Honey told Jill that she could tell even then that Mia was scared of the place they were going, but she didn't really care. Nowhere was safe anyway, right?

Mia and Honey had caught the train from Parramatta to Auburn and jumped down onto the tracks to avoid the ticket collectors. They'd scrambled up to the soggy street above the station platform and looked around. Kebab shops and amusement centres spilled coloured lights onto the wet roads, but the rain, and the dinner hour of 6 p.m., meant there were few people about.

'Um, I think it's this way,' Mia had said, holding onto Honey's cold hand as they made their way through the darkening streets. The shops alternated with houses and unit blocks now, and Mia eventually stopped in front of a block of flats, pushing the hood back from her sweatshirt, revealing her dark eyes. 'Shit,' she muttered, 'I know it's one of these.'

While they stood there shivering, a fat black car glided into the gutter in front of the units. A tall, skinny man with a scarred face and broken nose exited the front passenger's door. He threw them a hungry look, and opened the back door of the expensive car. Mia pulled at Honey's hand.

This was Honey's first sight of Mr Sebastian – a man in a dark suit. He stepped from the rear seat, pushing aside the thin man who was trying to offer him an umbrella. He smiled widely at Honey and Mia, his eyes on them from the moment the door had been cracked.

'What are you children doing out here in the rain?' he had asked them, covering the ground between them alarmingly quickly. 'Are you lost?'

Honey had expected Mia to make a typical smart-arsed reply to this stranger, and was taken aback by her head-bowed silence and the white knuckled grip of her hand.

'Ah, I see it's little Mia,' he said when they didn't answer, 'and a friend. Lovely. Lovely,' he beamed, smiling down into Honey's face. 'I'm glad you've come to visit us, Mia,' he said, still looking at Honey. 'Let's get inside.'

The man had placed his big hand in the small of Honey's back, and marched them forwards towards the unit block. Honey noted that she and Mia were suddenly flanked on three sides by the men who'd got out of the car.

Although the apartment block was unprepossessing from the outside, the unit into which they were steered seemed amazing to Honey. The heavy front door opened into a wide room and Honey told Jill she'd later learned that the apartment had been rebuilt from the inside and took up the entire floor. Shiny white floors stretched towards several closed doors at the back of the large room. Huge potted palms filled the corners, and low leather lounges were wrapped around coffee tables and two huge television screens. A small boy in pyjamas was asleep on one of the lounges, sucking his thumb. Another boy, who looked about Honey's age, did not look up when the door opened, intent upon the joystick and video game in front of him. A white cat snaked out of a shining black kitchen and slinked around a corner before Honey could bend to pat her.

Honey and Mia stayed at the apartment for three days, helping themselves to food from the walk-in pantry and huge refrigerator, watching TV, and playing video games with Ethan and Andrew, the two boys sharing the unit. Honey slept curled up on one of the lounges with Mia and the white cat, occasionally waking when men came and went at odd hours.

On their second day at the unit, Mia had left with one of the men. She did not want to talk to Honey when she returned that evening, instead sitting with her knees under her chin, playing video games for hours.

Honey didn't see Mr Sebastian again until the morning of their fourth day. She was sick of being inside and she and Mia had decided to go shoplifting for clothes at Westfield in Parramatta.

She and Mia were trying to figure out how to open the front door of the unit when it was opened suddenly, sending her sprawling backwards. There hadn't even been a sound to indicate the heavy door was about to open. She looked up to see Mr Sebastian smiling down at her, offering her his big hand. The smile didn't reach his eyes.

'You *girls* going somewhere, are you?' he asked, as Honey

scrambled to her feet, ignoring his hand. Neither she nor Mia said a word.

'I'm going to need you today, Honey, Mia, so I don't want you going anywhere you could get lost. I'm hosting a dinner party tonight, and I'll be requiring your assistance.'

He walked past them into the kitchen, filling a glass with filtered water from the specially fitted tap on the granite benchtop. He spoke rapidly in another language to the hook-nosed man who'd entered the unit behind him, then turned back to the girls.

'Jamaal has some clothes for you to wear tonight. You can try them on now, please.'

Later that night Honey discovered the price of a warm place to sleep and food whenever she wanted it. Within a month or so she learned that being 'nice' to Mr Sebastian's friends also meant that she was given enough money to buy herself new clothes, jewellery and make-up. For the first month, although disgusted by the groping, fondling old men she was expected to kiss and cuddle, she'd thought that she could tolerate these weekly evenings for the exchange.

One night, however, a flabby white man, older than most of the others, had tried to push his penis into her bottom. She had run from him into the small bathroom that was attached to the bedroom they were in. Crying, she'd locked the door and hoped the man would get tired of waiting and leave.

Within ten minutes, she'd stopped crying and was plucking her eyebrows in the mirror when the door was kicked in. Mr Sebastian slammed the back of his hand across her mouth, splitting her lip and loosening her tooth. Jamaal picked her cowering body up from the floor and held out her arm. The thin man was smiling with stained teeth as he clenched his thumb and forefinger around her tiny bicep to restrict the blood flow. Flicking her arm a few times, Mr Sebastian then slid a thin needle into a vein in the crease inside her elbow. Both men stood back as she vomited into the bathtub, and then, her sobs subsiding, they led her back into the bedroom and left her with the old man on the bed. None of the men spoke or looked at one another.

Honey spent the rest of the night in a dream-like state, and had been seeking that sensation ever since.

13

IN THE PRE-DAWN GLOOM, MERCY groped for her Ventolin, heart thumping, tasting bile. The sweat was drying on her skin, but her pillow was still damp. Another one. Another nightmare.

She felt for a cigarette and put down the asthma inhaler. She saw her hands tremble in the flare of the lighter. As she dragged in smoke she felt her heart slow. Stupid really; she knew nicotine was a stimulant, told her patients that every day, but she felt her nerves settle slightly nevertheless.

There was always so much blood; that was the problem. She'd have to find a way to do it without all the mess. Not for the first time, she pictured a huge gas chamber, herding them all in and letting them go to sleep in there.

She took a final shuddering drag of her cigarette and stubbed it out. She closed her eyes and settled back into the pillows, though she knew sleep would not come again tonight.

14

UNTIL IT WAS RIGHT behind her, Jill didn't notice the patrol truck that combed the sand every morning at Maroubra Beach. The unshaven driver motioned to her from his cabin to move over. She must have been running up and down the sands for more than an hour now; she realised that it was almost completely light.

Other features of the morning also began to register – she could hear seagulls fighting and playing, dive-bombing the waves. She saw some sandy adolescent surfers struggling, still half-asleep, into wetsuits, and an elderly Asian man was up near the pavilion, performing tai chi. She suddenly became aware that her thighs were trembling with exhaustion and she dropped onto the wet sand, her chest heaving.

She sat there for a while as her breathing slowed, and looked down at her raw, peeling hands. After she'd left Honey's unit yesterday she'd gone back to her own and embarked on her most obsessive cleaning frenzy in years. She'd ignored her mum's calls through the speaker of her answering machine, and her door buzzer sounding twice. The white-eyed girl from her dreams was haunting her while she was awake now, and even kicking the bag until her lungs were burning didn't distract her from her memories of herself in the basement.

Twice she'd gone to her large stainless steel refrigerator and rested her head against the cool exterior, her fingers on the freezer's handle.

'Open it,' the white-eyed girl had called inside her head. 'Make it stop. Please.'

Jill knew that if she'd opened the freezer at that point she would have remained standing there barefoot in her underwear until she'd drained the 750ml bottle of vodka that was hidden right at the back. The bottle had been unopened in her freezer for ten years, moving house with her three times. Her sister, Cassie, forced by their father to help her move once, had found the bottle and cracked the seal.

'Well, the night's not a total loss, then,' she'd giggled, holding the bottle aloft, while with her other hand she'd removed a carton of grapefruit juice from the fridge. 'Who'd-a-thought you'd have vodka in the house, sis?' she said, kicking the fridge door shut with her foot.

In one gliding move, Jill had removed the bottle from Cassie's hand, opened the freezer door and returned it, before her sister had even fully registered what was happening. Cassie had looked down at her empty hand.

'Hey!' she'd sounded shaken. 'What was that? Don't do that karate shit on me.' She flicked her hair back from her face. 'God you're weird, Jill. If we're not allowed to drink in your temple, why do you keep that bottle here?'

Jill couldn't explain it, but she knew that if she had one sip of the colourless liquid, her carefully maintained world would slide into the abyss. She wouldn't be able to stop herself a second time.

Now, sitting in the foam at the edge of the ocean, Jill wiped her surf-wet hands across her face, tasting salt. She'd had little sleep, but she had a lot to do today and needed to get going. She stripped to her bikini and ignored the surfers' calls as she strode out into the waves, letting the fizzing water wake her fully.

Twenty minutes later, she jogged out of the water, smiling.

'I'm just not seeing it, J. I really don't see how she could've killed three men. Not like that, anyway.' Scotty and Jill were on their way to speak with the last group of parents who could have had an interest in seeing David Carter dead – the last group they were aware of, anyway. 'I mean, that MO is not really the way that women kill men.'

Jill sighed and stared ahead, eyes on the road. Scotty had voiced her own doubts about Mercy being involved in the murders. She took one hand from the wheel and rubbed at some skin peeling from her sunburnt nose. She knew that female serial murderers were rare, and that those who existed usually used poison or a firearm.

'I know. I know that. But, Scotty, the three deaths have got to be connected, and she's linked in some way to all three,' she said. 'And to be honest, no, I don't really think she killed them, but there's something really odd about her lately, you know? She seems . . . well, a bit cracked.'

Scotty turned sideways to view Jill's tanned profile. Her white-blonde hair looked tousled, not as in place as usual. He took in her set jaw and the cold sore on her lower lip. He turned his eyes back to the road when he caught his own face staring back at him through the mirrored lenses of her aviator sunglasses.

'What?' she asked, voice flat.

'Nothing,' he said, and then paused. 'It's just that you're looking a bit tightly wound yourself lately. You're not sleeping well again, are you?'

Silence from the driver's seat.

'Are you eating, Jill?'

She focused on the road.

'Right. Well. Anyway,' said Scotty, giving up, looking down at some notes in a folder on his lap. 'Let's go through what we know about these cases. If we're going to convince Andreessen that they're connected, we're going to have to find more to go on.

'Okay – George Manzi, AKA George Marks,' he continued, 'found in a car with another guy on Elizabeth Bay Road at the back of the Cross.'

'The other guy they found with him – do they know his name yet?' Jill asked, changing lanes to take the right turn that led to Bondi Junction.

'Yep. Jamaal Mahmoud, found unconscious in the back seat, single blow to the back of the head. He's still recovering – they've got him in the Brain Injury Unit over at Prince of Wales.'

'What'd you say his name was?' A bubble of recognition floated up from the tangle of thoughts in Jill's mind.

'Mahmoud. Jamaal Mahmoud.'

'Jamaal . . .'

'Yep. A hooker found them last Sunday morning. Manzi was in the driver's seat, but he wasn't doing much driving when he died.' Scotty read from the notes in his lap – he had an updated version of the file Jill had read a couple of days ago. 'His pants were round his ankles. You reckon he was getting serviced by the killer?'

'Mmm. Maybe, but what would Mahmoud have been doing?'

'Watching? Waiting for his turn? Who knows?'

Jill was distracted. Where had she heard that name?

'Harris and Jardine found no sign that entry to the vehicle had been forced, or even that they'd fought the attacker off,' Scotty told her. 'They've guessed that Manzi and Mahmoud let the killer into the car with them. Also says here that Mahmoud was probably drugged. Hospital tests found Special K in his system, but too much of it for just a night on the town. It could've been an accidental OD, but they reckon that amount would've knocked anyone out.'

This information was new to Jill. The man in the back seat had not yet been identified when she'd read the file. So maybe the killer had drugged Mahmoud. Why? It would make sense to wait for the drug to take effect on the man in the back seat before striking – it would be difficult to fight two men off within the confines of a car. Eight holes had been punched through Manzi's skull with a claw hammer, the left side of his temple caving in completely; the killer would have been covered in blood and brains. The killer had then struck the man in the back seat. This awkward position, or a passer-by, had probably saved his life. He'd been hit just once.

A car horn sounded behind them, and Jill noticed that the lights were green. She accelerated forward.

'Jamaal!' she exclaimed, suddenly remembering. 'What if it's the same Jamaal?'

Earlier that morning she had briefly told Scotty about her visit with Honey. He'd asked first thing about the girl who'd come in to report a rape. Half the squad room – the male half – had told him about her. Now Jill filled him in a little more on Honey's past, telling him about Mr Sebastian and his driver Jamaal and their private parties in Auburn.

'We gotta turn left back there, Jill – where are you going? I told you I should've driven.'

Jill cursed and pulled into a driveway. She'd have to do a U-turn.

She decided that tomorrow she was going to see Honey. It couldn't hurt to take her on a visit to the Prince of Wales Hospital, check out the patients in the Brain Injury Unit.

Jill shaved her legs in the bath that evening. She knew she was too thin, but she felt vaguely pleased with the muscles of her thighs, stomach, arms. At least her body felt strong. She rested her head against the back of the bath, let the steam relax her. Interviewing the Kaplans that afternoon had been awful.

The glare of the late summer day had respectfully kept its distance from verdant Woollahra. Red brick and sandstone mansions rested sedately in the shade of huge Moreton Bay fig trees. Jill had removed her sunglasses at the last moment when they made their way up the flower-lined path of the Kaplans' three-storey home.

Carly Kaplan was eight, and captain of her softball team, when she begged her mother for horse-riding lessons at Centennial Park. Her parents, Marie and William, gave in quickly, using the two hours each Sunday morning to take a walk and have coffee in the park while their daughter rode, under the instruction of a man who'd advertised in an Eastern Suburbs community newspaper. When Carly had wanted to quit the lessons five weeks later, however, William had put his foot down.

'We've paid for six months,' he'd told her, 'and you can't just go from one activity to another without seeing things through.' He told Jill and Scotty hollowly that he'd been determined not to let their children take their life of privilege for granted.

Marie Kaplan had been alarmed by her daughter's change in demeanour that year, but because Carly had seemed to lose enthusiasm for most things, she had not honed in on the riding lessons as the source of her misery. Besides, she'd tried to reason with herself later, Carly's best friend, Brianna, also took the lessons, and the girls were out in the fresh air. It had seemed the right thing to do to encourage her to continue.

But the girls hadn't spent all of their time in the fresh air. Their instructor, David Carter, had told them that he had to take some photos for their horse-riding licences. Marie and William learned years later that Carter had taken the girls into a disused cricket stand in the grounds of the park. Under the isolated bleachers he'd encouraged them to dress in their riding clothes and later fairy outfits, snapping away as they changed and posed, giggling, in the costumes.

Face grey, eyes dead, William Kaplan told Jill and Scotty that even when Brianna had quit the lessons he had insisted that Carly see out the six-month contract with the riding instructor. His wife stared at the carpet as he spoke.

Under the bleachers one week, David Carter had convinced Carly that he could kill her mother any time he wanted to. He told Carly where Marie Kaplan shopped, the name of her best friend and their next-door neighbour. He knew where Carly's mum swam three mornings a week, and that she volunteered at the school canteen twice a month. If Carly ever told anyone what they did under here, he'd told her, he would kill her mother before anyone could do anything to save her. And it would be all Carly's fault.

Her parents recounted how Carly's marks had declined steadily from that year. She showed no respect at school any more, especially for male teachers, and she became a nightmare at home – harassing her sisters constantly and lashing out in fury when chastised by her parents. Their formerly quiet home was constantly ringing with the sound of Carly swearing and slamming doors. When Carly was eleven, Marie Kaplan found cigarettes in her daughter's backpack. At thirteen, Marie and William had been called to Carly's new high school, enduring an hour with an excruciatingly embarrassed principal who finally choked out that Carly had been caught having sex behind the gymnasium. Later that month they were back at the school to take her home, suspended for arriving back to class drunk after recess; vomit in her hair. School counsellors and changing schools twice hadn't helped at all.

It wasn't until Carly's fourteenth birthday, after yet another screaming row, that Marie and William Kaplan had found out what David Carter had done to their child. A sobbing Marie told Jill and Scotty how she had walked into the bathroom to find Carly slimy with her own blood, razor-blade in hand, carving at her thighs. In the emergency department at midnight she and Carly's father had learned that their daughter had been self-mutilating for two years, and that this was a commonly observed behaviour in child sexual abuse victims.

Jill understood too well that a door to a nightmare world had opened that night at the hospital; Marie and William Kaplan walked in, and had never really come out. They learned that Carter had raped their eight-year-old child once a week for four months while they'd been walking in the park. They'd driven her there, taken her home – forced her to keep going when she'd asked to stop. William Kaplan held himself more accountable for the abuse than the man who'd actually committed these crimes. In her deepest heart, Marie blamed him too. They became strangers in the same house.

Over the next six months, Carly had made a one-hundred page police statement that required the most explicit, exhaustive minutiae of every encounter she'd had with Carter. Carly had come home from each appointment with the police beyond exhausted, her stomach cramping, unable to sleep. She missed weeks of school at a time, beset by nightmares and bouts of tearfulness and anxiety attacks. She'd had to tell the same story to doctors, counsellors, and the Department of Public Prosecutions over the remainder of the year.

Marie told them quietly that Carter had finally been arrested and charged. Carly had prepared herself for the agony of going through the details again in court. The matter was deferred every time it was listed, and the process continued for two years. The case had finally gone ahead last month. The court found Carter not guilty and he was acquitted.

Jill and Scotty already knew that Marie had not been fast enough to stop Carly bleeding to death in the bath. In the living room in Woollahra, Jill had watched Marie mentally replaying the bathroom scene. She knew that movie would be screening the rest of her life.

15

After her bath, Jill stood on her balcony in boxer shorts and a singlet, watching the beachside afternoon becoming evening. She loved the sounds and smells of the ocean, and watching the cars and the people below left her with a sense of community. This connection from a distance was as close as she got to being neighbourly.

The sunset bled into the horizon, and a chill breeze puckered Jill's bath-warm skin. She hugged her arms, unable to rid her mind of Marie Kaplan's thousand-mile stare.

Time to cook, gotta eat, she told herself firmly. She stepped back into her living room, relishing the thick carpet under her toes.

From a rack next to her lounge, she selected a glossy food magazine and walked with it into the kitchen. Her mum had bought her the rack, and the twenty or so magazines had been home-delivered monthly via the subscription she'd also bought. Jill smiled. More than one way to tell your daughter to eat properly, she thought.

Hmm. Poached chicken breast with rocket pesto. Easy, and she had everything she needed. She pulled produce from the refrigerator, lulled by the rituals of cooking.

A glass of wine would work well right now, said the white-eyed girl in her mind. Jill tuned her out.

She thought about Jamaal.

She knew that the inspector would be reluctant to let her take Honey out to the hospital. Mahmoud was a witness in the Manzi case, ostensibly not related to the Carter killing, but the cases had to be connected. Besides, she had to know if he was the same man who had ensnared Honey a decade ago. Was he still in business? Was Mr Sebastian still around? Somehow, these questions seemed far more important than who had killed David Carter.

Convincing Honey to come along to the hospital hadn't been easy. She'd been sullen when Jill had shown up at her door the next evening. She was dressed in low, low-rider jeans and a pink halterneck top that left the creamy skin of her back completely exposed; her acid-green contact lenses glinted like gaudy beads, still freaking Jill out a little.

'I'm going out tonight. A girl's gotta work.' But Honey moved backwards to allow Jill into the flat.

Jill stayed where she was. That place was too small.

'Come on, Honey. I'll get you back here by nine, I promise. You wouldn't have left before then anyway,' Jill wheedled.

'We can grab something to eat. What do you want to eat? I'm paying.'

Honey stood silent in the doorway a few moments longer, her eyes giving nothing away; then she turned and walked back inside.

'Shit,' Jill muttered, moving to leave.

'God! Give me a minute,' Honey stood in the doorway again.

She threw Jill her handbag, juggling her keys and a canary-yellow cowboy hat while she locked the door. 'I want Lebanese food.'

The corridors of the Brain Injury Unit of the Prince of Wales Hospital were haunted by the relatives of patients who fought for life behind the doors that flanked it. Their wraith-like presence contrasted with the bright efficiency of the hospital staff manoeuvring around them. Jill needed to show her badge twice before the Nursing Unit Manager gave them permission to visit Jamaal Mahmoud, the nurse's eyes on Honey the whole time they talked.

'He's popular tonight,' the woman commented, finally returning to her notes. 'He's just down the hall,' she said, scribbling a number on a piece of notepaper and handing it to Jill.

Honey and Jill made their way through the disinfected corridors and looked for Jamaal's room. Even if this is the same guy, thought Jill, what does that mean? What am I going to do about it? She decided that she was just following a potential lead in the triple murder investigation, but she was more interested in finding out any connection between the three men in life than in their deaths. If their deaths were connected, could they have been part of some sort of group? Were there more of these guys out there? Her breathing quickened when she saw the room number ahead of her.

Jill had been hoping that she and Honey could just identify the man in the bed unobserved, but, as the nurse had intimated, he had visitors. Through the open doorway she could see a heavy-set man in a dark suit.

Before she could suggest they hold back, Honey had sauntered straight into the room.

'Honey, hang on a sec . . .' She trailed off as Honey, smiling, offered the suited man her cheek to kiss.

'Mr Sebastian, this is a friend of mine, Jill.' She still smiled broadly. 'We're here visiting her aunt, and she came up with me to see how Jamaal was going.' The man in the bed stared flatly at the wall, not even turning towards them at the sound of his name.

Honey seemed to have taken charge of the encounter, and although her eyes gave little away, glistening madly, her body language seemed to imply that Jill was to remain in the background. This was fortunate, as Jill could not have said a word if her life depended on it. What the fuck was going on here? Mr Sebastian – the man who had drugged and pimped Honey into child prostitution. Jill had no idea he was still part of Honey's life.

'Jill, is it?' Mr Sebastian extended a large, manicured hand. 'It's always nice to meet Honey's friends.'

He didn't introduce the other man in the room, a hulking tattooed figure with Mediterranean features, wearing sweatpants and a singlet. The contrast between the men could not have been more stark – Sebastian in his sixties, carefully groomed and tailored, offering an urbane smile; the other maybe early thirties, battle-scarred, staring flatly at nothing in particular. Jill thought maybe she'd seen him before.

'So nice of you to come and see Jamaal, Honey,' said Sebastian in his unctuous voice, turning away from Jill. 'As you can see, he's resting now. The doctors do not feel there will be any permanent damage, fortunately. He should be able to leave tonight or in the morning. The blow rendered him unconscious, but he's now left with little more than a headache, unlike the poor devil he was with.

'Did you hear, Honey, what happened to the other man?' He waited while she muttered her assent.

'It's hard to imagine the world has grown so violent, is it not?' he asked, looking at Jill. 'It's a terrible shame. The police seem to have no control over the streets anymore.'

Honey said something in reply, but it didn't register with Jill.

'We were just on our way out, Honey,' Sebastian said, sidling past Jill. He pressed his body unnecessarily close as he passed. Jill felt dizzy, ill, and leaned as far back against the doorframe as she could manage. He then turned to kiss Honey, who had followed him out.

'We'll see you at the club soon I hope, Honey?' he said, motioning his minder to follow. 'We've all missed you. Bring Jill and have a drink, something to eat. In the meantime, take care.

'I hope your aunt recovers, Jill.' He smiled down at her, and the two men strode off along the corridor.

Jill didn't know whether she was more surprised by Honey's behaviour or by her own – she couldn't believe she was walking with Honey out of the hospital; that she hadn't just left her there to find her own way home. She said little as they traversed the sterile corridors, and didn't speak a word on the drive to Surry Hills.

She glanced at Honey's profile in the car and realised she didn't know this woman at all.

Honey didn't try to break the silence, staring expressionlessly into the night. Jill didn't feel like food, but she'd promised Honey dinner.

They had circled the block several times for parking, and now sat in a crowded restaurant, more than a few dishes of Lebanese food in front of them. While waiting for their order, the sky had hurled spears of rain without warning, stopping as suddenly as it began. The hot Sydney footpaths steamed.

'So?' Jill started.

'So what?' Honey matched Jill's glare. 'I never told you that I escaped from Sebastian and never saw him again, did I? And you never asked me if I knew Jamaal's full name,' she continued. 'You never even asked me if the guy in hospital could be the same Jamaal. You just asked me to come with you and check him out. I knew he got fucked up last week. Heard it out there.' Honey gestured to the street.

Jill couldn't trust herself to speak. She instead selected some pickled vegetables, flat bread and yoghurt from the dishes in front of her and arranged them on her plate. She waved Honey's hand away when she tried to pour her a glass of wine, still not looking at her.

After several moments of silence, Jill said to the tablecloth, 'Obviously I haven't been asking you the right questions. I would like to know more about Jamaal Mahmoud and any connection he has to George Manzi, the man who was killed. Two other men have also been killed in a similar way, and I'm interested in whether they knew one other. If you know anything about that, I'd love to hear about it.'

She used the Lebanese bread to wipe up yoghurt and vegetables from her plate. She ground a mouthful into paste.

'And while I'm asking questions,' she continued evenly, 'I really wouldn't mind knowing . . .' she took a deep breath and continued in a forced conversational tone, 'how the fuck you could kiss a man who sold you for sex?' She finally looked up.

'Look, Jill,' Honey said, green eyes glittering, 'you have no fucking idea what it's like to grow up the way I did. I do what I have to do. Who was going to help me? The police?' Her laugh turned into a cough. She took a sip of wine.

Jill stayed silent, waiting.

'I tried going to the police. Twice, when I was a kid. Great help to me. First time, I got put in a foster home, where I was made to sleep in a kennel three or four nights a week.'

Honey's face was curdled. She drained her wine, reaching for the bottle as soon as she put the glass down.

'Second time – I tried to tell them what Sebastian was still doing to the street kids in the Cross. Got a beating for that. They nearly fucking killed me.'

Honey paused and stared out at the night, the streets wetly malevolent. 'Anyway, he's still there, I'm still here, and when I see him I'm fucking *polite*.'

The bread caught in Jill's throat. She reached for some water.

'Honey,' she said levelly, searching for eye contact, 'if that freak is still hurting kids I'm going to do something about it.

I'm sorry that you went through the shit you did. No kid should have that happen to them. If you could help me – if you could show me and tell me what you know about what is still happening out there – I promise I'll do something about it.'

Honey finally met her gaze, but there was no way to tell what was going on behind her lightless eyes.

16

JILL PULLED AGAIN AT the black rubber skirt, trying to inch it further down her thighs. What the hell was I thinking, she thought, letting Honey dress me? When Honey had agreed to show Jill Sebastian's club in the Cross, it was on the proviso that she not look like a cop.

'I don't even wear a uniform,' Jill protested.

'You might as well,' responded Honey dryly. 'And where we're going it'll help if you show some skin for once.'

And here she was. Tottering towards Kings Cross in spiked black boots, mini-skirt and sheer black shirt – these were the most conservative clothes in Honey's acid-splashed wardrobe.

Honey had gone into pyjama-party mode, squealing and exclaiming as Jill had tried on and rejected most of her clothes. She had insisted on doing Jill's make-up and hair, and because she hadn't let her look in the mirror until she was done, Jill had ended up with kohl-rimmed, black-lidded eyes and teased hair glittering with beads and pins. She left the hair clips on Honey's bathroom sink before they left the apartment.

She glanced to her right and took a deep breath. Honey wore a bright orange slip dress with spaghetti straps, her surgically perfect breasts just restrained by the fabric. Beneath her cowboy hat, her long black hair hung in a fluid sheet down her back, and her strappy stilettos put her at just over six foot.

The traffic never moved at this time of night in Kings Cross, but tonight even the foot traffic had stopped to watch them walk past.

Although she felt only half-dressed, Jill's skin shone with sweat. The heat of the day had not dissipated with the onset of darkness, and humidity left the air thick and glue-like. Green–grey thunderclouds smudged across a full moon above the lights of the Cross. Cars crowded the streets, but there was no sense yet of the dirty-glamour gaiety that usually infused Kings Cross by midnight. Silent black bats winged over the throbbing lights.

Jill felt her gut clench as they got closer to the Bluegrass Club. Up to fifty parked motorcycles, mostly Harleys, curved in a shining path around the front of the venue. On the pavement before the wide glass entry, shark-eyed girls draped themselves over leather-clad, bearded men in club colours. Her jaw tight and senses wired, Jill wanted nothing more than to walk as far from this scene as possible. Too late, she was only now listening to the nagging voice that told her tonight's trip with Honey was a very bad idea. As this was an unofficial outing, she had no badge, gun or radio, and no-one knew she was here. She had half reached forward to grab Honey's arm, ready to tell her that she was going to leave, when she recognised one of the women watching them approach.

Working undercover in Wollongong two years ago, Jill had several times bought small amounts of speed from this girl. The sullen nineteen-year-old uni student did some small-time drug sales for the local bikie gang that provided the South Coast with its significant amphetamine requirements. When Jill's crew had busted their operations, the girl copped a two-year suspended sentence and was kicked out of her science degree. Her boyfriend got four years in Goulburn Gaol.

Jill saw the girl's eyes narrow with recognition and she leaned forward to whisper to the huge man seated next to her at the outdoor table. Jill couldn't see any change in his expression, probably because almost all of his face was concealed by hair, but he looked up and stared directly at her.

Her feet moved forward of their own volition. Honey entered the dark club ahead, Jill about eight paces behind her. She felt as though she were completely naked, in one of her slow-motion nightmares where she couldn't stop herself walking straight into danger. She moved closer to the outdoor table, all senses alert. She turned her head and flatly met the gaze of the bikie staring at her. He smiled, but Jill could feel hatred emanating from the whole group.

Half a step ahead of the table now, the darkness of the club was suddenly a refuge. It seemed to be too far away; she felt completely exposed. She kept her eyes angled down to the bikie, now at her right.

To her horror, Jill saw his hand coming up from under the

table; she felt ice drop into her stomach. There was nowhere to hide. She prepared herself to hit the pavement, throw herself to her belly, sure she was about to be shot.

Just as she steeled herself to dive, the bear-like arm rose above the table, the bikie's hand empty. His fingers formed the shape of a gun, aimed at her head.

With one more step, Jill walked into the haven of the dim club and waited for her eyes to adjust. She swallowed hard to push her heart back down into her chest.

Honey was already leaning on one of the two long bars in the crowded club, her yellow cowboy hat keeping her visible. It also got her served quickly, Honey assured Jill, as she drew alongside her at the bar. Watching Honey leaning forward towards the bartender, Jill thought there were probably other factors involved in their swift service. She nursed iced lemonade, hopeful it might settle her stomach a little, and took in the room.

Most of the people in this club were at least a decade older than those who would, seven hours from now, stumble into daylight from the dance clubs on Oxford Street. There were more bikies and their wannabes inside the venue, alongside mid-week office alcoholics, using anybody's birthday as an excuse to get pissed, and groups of thirty-somethings here to meet their next ex. It was smoky and sweaty and the rhythm-and-blues was too loud. Jill turned to ask Honey if she saw Mr Sebastian or his cronies, but two hopefuls trying to buy her another drink already flanked her. Jill elbowed her way closer.

'Honey, do you see them?'

She managed to push past a guy in a bright red shirt covering a burgeoning beer belly; he looked pleased that she'd done so.

'Now, where are we going, princess?' he asked, reaching for her arm to pull her back towards him. Jill slid from his reach in an easy side step, quickly appraising and discounting any threat from the half-drunk man.

'Honey, can you see them?' She shouted to make herself heard over the music.

'Relax, Jill. They won't be here tonight,' Honey said, flicking her hair, flirting with the man next to her.

'What? What did you say?' Jill couldn't believe she'd heard right.

'Mr Sebastian will be at *his* club tonight,' Honey said, still smiling and sipping at a cocktail as colourful as her dress.

'I thought *this* was his club,' Jill tried to keep her voice level. What was going on here? Once again, Honey was playing her own game.

Honey laughed, and leaned in to answer something the balding man next to her had said out of Jill's earshot.

'Jill, darling,' Honey finally answered, 'we couldn't get anywhere near that place. Not at our age anyway.' She smiled, still seemingly unaware of Jill's shock at her words.

'Then why,' asked Jill, her voice hard, 'did he invite us to come to his club? And what the hell am I doing here?' This time her voice carried, and a cluster of women, all sequins and cleavage, laughed at her question and raised their glasses towards her in a toast. A group of three men wearing ponytails and leather jackets also stared hard.

'Jill, don't flip out,' Honey smiled at her, this time giving her more attention. 'This is the club he was referring to, but he's never here before two or three. He doesn't own this club though. He only comes here to talk business.'

'So where is *his* club, then,' Jill asked slowly; this was like some kind of guessing game, and she didn't know the rules. She tried to calm down, simultaneously bringing her foot down hard on the instep of Mr Red Shirt, who had tried to cop a feel in his attempts to gain her attention. She ignored his slurred yelp of pain.

'Well, he has a youth drop-in centre just down the road from this club,' Honey said. 'For recruits,' she added mildly and Jill's eyes widened, horrified. 'But his play den is on the North Shore somewhere.'

Jill felt suddenly very tired. Did Honey think this was fun for her? She probably did – she looked to be enjoying herself, although it was hard to tell with those contact lenses.

She couldn't imagine spending much longer in this place. She looked at people laughing and talking, at couples obviously forming, and it reminded her how empty her love life had been since Joel. Not that it had been that full-on then. Joel had been impulsive and spontaneous, physically affectionate. She pushed the word needy from her mind; that wasn't fair. He loved to drop by unannounced. She disliked this habit so much that she would sometimes drop to the floor when the doorbell sounded, spending the next two hours in the dark so her caller wouldn't know she was home. Even when he'd phone from his mobile in the lobby Jill would maintain the ruse. It was the principle – she needed time to prepare herself for visitors.

Joel, twenty-eight, a scientist from the University of New South Wales, had never really left college. He admitted that he loved the lifestyle and was happy to combine lecturing with his marine environment research projects. When a floater had washed up on a beach in Wollongong, Jill had travelled to the university to seek an expert opinion on the body's rate of decay, trying to better place the time of death. He asked her out, in front of her uniformed partner, within ten minutes of her being in his office, and although she shot him down in her best cop voice, she'd been impressed by his audacity. When he called her office the next day and offered his services – more advice on the body, to take her scuba diving, to cook her a lobster dinner – she'd surprised herself by accepting the latter.

She'd agreed to meet him at the uni; running late she had rushed to find the lecture hall he'd nominated. When she finally located the building, she entered and, amused, realised he'd timed their meeting so that she'd catch him finishing a lecture. By that time the students were filing raucously out and she stood at the back of the hall to wait. She watched Joel at the lectern, surrounded by five students who'd stayed behind to ask questions. All female. He seemed to answer their questions distractedly, his eyes darting around the large hall. Jill slipped a little further behind a pillar at the back of the room. When Joel finally noticed her, she watched his face light up. Following a couple of words to the students, he bounded up the tiered theatre and was by her side in moments. The resentful stares of the girls down the front followed them from the building.

Joel had tried to make Jill go out more: movies, parties, art exhibitions, dancing, bungee jumping, shopping. He was endlessly enthusiastic about events happening in Sydney. He was puzzled when he finally figured out that Jill was uncomfortable in crowds and small group situations alike, and that she was perhaps most uncomfortable when they were alone. He grew quietly impatient with Jill's difficulties with intimacy and touching, and was easily hurt, taking personally her silent withdrawals at night. Joel had wanted to discuss their relationship endlessly, try couples' counselling, commit to one another by moving in together. And he was silently jealous of Scotty. After six months, Jill had told Joel that she was no longer interested in a relationship. Watching Joel's heart break had wrenched at her own. Until the numbness kicked in again, of course.

Walking through the bar in search of the toilets, Jill caught sight of her mini-skirted profile in an amber-tinted full-length mirror. She laughed at the thought of Cassie's face if she ran into her now. Her sister was also always telling her to get out more.

'How can you be that happy when you haven't met me yet?' A man in his late twenties who'd bravely gelled his thinning blonde hair into a faux-hawk stood smiling in her path.

'I'm just thinking about my lover,' she spoke loudly over the music, while gesturing to one of the leather-clad bikies playing pool nearby. She laughed again as the man turned away immediately, hurrying back to his friends.

After leaving the bathroom, Jill walked through the narrow alcove furthest from the bar. The corridor was quieter than the rest of the club, and seemed to be some sort of service access. A couple of busy staff members rushed by her on their way to the kitchen, and she leaned back against a fire hose mounted on the wall to let them past. She had made up her mind to at least go and check out the 'youth club' Honey had mentioned. Walking purposefully, and determined to get Honey to accompany her now she'd gone to all this trouble, she stepped out of the quiet corridor and straight into a leather-jacketed chest. The bikie from the tables outside pushed her back into the dark corridor.

'What's a rat-fuck cop doing here?' He walked her backwards; she couldn't coordinate her feet. Adrenalin pumping, she struggled to regain some control over her movements, looked for a way around him. He filled the corridor, twice her size, and before she could recover her footing, he pushed her into the wall. Pinned by the man-mountain, Jill's back crushed into something sharp behind her. He leaned in over her, dwarfing her completely.

She felt the familiar wave of panic when the breaths she took didn't seem to be deep enough; she couldn't get enough air. She struggled to position herself so that she could breathe, but just by leaning into her, this man had immobilised her arms and body.

'You know, you sent four of my brothers to gaol, you bitch.' Exhaled bourbon fumes filled her nose and mouth.

Her throat closed and she couldn't swallow. Dark spots danced in her vision. Keep it together, she thought. Do not have a panic attack in front of this pig. The thought of crying and gasping for air in front of him forced her to slow the panic.

She was trying again to manoeuvre for surer footing, when the bikie suddenly moved his arm backwards. She felt his body tensing and, too late, realised what was about to happen. She tried to clench her stomach muscles, prepare herself. His huge fist smashed into her gut. The pain exploded in her stomach and her back, where whatever pushed into her had jammed hard into her spine. She would have dropped immediately but his weight kept her pinned there. She coughed, tasted blood on her lips.

'You. Dumb. Fuckin'. Slut.' His lips skimmed hers as he breathed into her face. 'There's probably fifty of us in this place right now, and we sent word out that you're here for a good time. I'm gonna carry you out of here like you're wasted, and when you wake up you'll be in our clubhouse. You're gonna love how we party.'

Just one blow had rendered Jill faint, but she knew that staying alert was her only hope. She'd rather die here than leave this place with him. She felt his weight shift as he moved his arm back again and, terrified, Jill was sure she wouldn't be conscious following the next blow – with her back pressed into the wall, her internal organs would absorb the full force of his punch. She had to get out of there. She tried to scream, but even she couldn't hear the moan she just managed. When his fist slammed into her stomach again, through the white-hot pain she felt ribs fracture.

Jill's body buckled under the force of the next blow, but this time she felt no pain. She couldn't hear his voice either; it was replaced by a muffled sobbing sound that she did not recognise as her own. But with the pain and fear gone, Jill knew what to do. She closed her eyes and listened to her enemy. She heard his intake of breath as he prepared to pull his arm backwards to hit her again. She waited. One beat. Two. And with all the force she had, when his body was most open, ready to strike, she slammed her knee upwards into his crotch, full force. As his pupils were still dilating in agony, she struck the same place again, her knee moving before his hands could reach for his broken balls. He swayed, half-turned, and smacked face-first to the ground, his body filling the tight corridor.

Bent double, Jill sucked in air, her vision blacking in and out. The pain in her ribs threatened to return and she knew she had to get out of that place. Think! She could not walk back into the club. They'd be waiting for her.

Straight ahead lay the front door, but she'd have to traverse the dance floor to reach it, and she didn't feel up to getting past a drunken executive, let alone an angry biker or two. To her right were the toilets. She looked down the corridor and saw light spilling underneath double doors. The kitchen. There'd be a back route out of there. There was always a fire exit in a kitchen. There'd be a phone, staff, people to help her.

Between Jill and the double doors, however, lay the giant, making animal sounds on the floor. To get past him, she'd have to step on his back. She considered a running jump, trying to clear his mass to reach the other side. But even if she could manage the leap with the pain in her ribs, the thought of him grabbing her ankle in mid-air and hauling her back down terrified her. She couldn't make herself seriously consider it as an option. That left straight ahead then. Could there be another fire exit somewhere?

Fire exit. Fire. That's it, she thought, turning back into the corridor. She scanned the wall she'd been pinned against, and spotted the object that had dug into her spine. The fire hose. Next to it, a small perspex box housing the fire alarm button. She looked down; within sixty centimetres of the fire hose, the biker's meaty head rolled around the floor. Jill noted with revulsion that his cheek was lying in a pool of his own vomit.

Taking a deep breath that felt like swallowing crushed glass, Jill stepped within easy reach of the leviathan on the floor. She smashed the box with the heel of her hand, and instantly the fire alarm boomed unbearably loud from all sides.

Crouched forwards, more from pain than to hide, Jill shuffled towards the front of the club. Someone killed the music and hit the lights. Some of the blinking patrons shielded their eyes, while others held their ears. They lurched to their feet, trying to figure out what to do. The alarm made it impossible to hear anything else. She had to get to the door before any panic started. She couldn't bear to be immobilised again. Her heart was a budgie bashing around in her chest.

Staff in black aprons now moved through the crowd. Efficient and coordinated, they looked like they were herding cattle.

A female staff member with a face full of piercings motioned the group nearest Jill towards the front of the club. Jill managed to slip between some low chairs and a cluster of staggering suits, all clutching Coronas. If she could just keep moving quickly, she could negotiate a fairly clear path to the exit. She tried to jog a couple of steps, and stifled a scream when her broken rib stabbed her insides. She hunched a little lower, one arm across her gut.

Maybe thirty steps and she'd be out of here. The front of the club opened completely to the street now; the blare of the fire alarm and the lights and noises from the road merged at the doors, marking the threshold of safety.

Twenty steps, ten. Right behind her, the mob from the club surged forwards, some laughing, others complaining about having to evacuate. Almost there.

She stopped. Straight ahead, directly in her path, stood the speed dealer from Wollongong. The fresh-faced college fitness the girl had radiated just two years ago was long gone. Her arms were scrawny and marked with bruises; her eyes, locked with Jill's, were hooded with hate. She smiled coldly and looked to her left, showing Jill her fate. Three fat bikers leaned against the folded-back doors.

Jill knew what she'd do if she was them. One blow would knock her out; the movement of the crowd would cover the action, and no-one would notice a doped-out mini-skirt being poured into a waiting car.

She swayed where she stood, considering her options.

'Not feelin' the best myself.' The suits had caught her up, and a short, dark-haired man was at her side, an arm snaking around her waist. Even over the fire alarm, Jill thought she could hear his shiny suit swoosh as he walked. What remained of his hair was slicked back, gold flashed at his neck and wrists.

'I'll give ya a hand, luv.' He smiled at her. 'Let's get out of here and figure out where we're all going next.'

In the few seconds she'd stood immobile, the crowd had reached her. Jill looked around wildly, caught up in a wash of beer breath and cologne, heels and hairspray. The group carried her along, a human tide that spilled out the doors of the club. The wave swept her past the gorillas at the door and spilled onto the pavement, overflowing into the street.

Car horns sounded and people yelled and whistled. A tubby girl, heels in hand, climbed on top of a traffic signal box, gyrating in green Lycra, while her hooting girlfriends tried to pull her back down. Jill looked to the right and saw a group of young men kicking water at each other in the El-Alamein fountain. She saw the white helmets of four mounted police riding up Darlinghurst Road. The sirens of the approaching fire brigade joined the cacophony.

Jill walked left, away from what was fast becoming a street party, and within a hundred metres reached the front of the cab rank. She ignored the stares of the cabbies standing at the sides of their taxis, and got into the back seat of the first cab. When she sat down, her vision darkened as a bloom of pain burst in her chest. She put her head between her knees. She heard the cab door shut, and the world went blessedly quiet.

'You have money?'

She heard the cabbie from the front. She pulled a fifty from her purse and gave him her address, then let her head fall back onto the seat.

'You no do spew in my cab.'

Jill closed her eyes.

17

'HOW DO YOU KNOW Honey didn't set you up?' Scotty was sprawled full-length along one of Jill's chocolate leather sofas, his huge bare feet hanging over the edge, soles pointing towards the ocean.

Jill made a noise of impatience. 'Why would she?' she said. 'No, Scott, it was just the wrong place, wrong time. I could tell by their faces that they were just as shocked to see me as I was to see them.'

She was lying on the matching sofa, her feet pointed towards her kitchen. It was a damp Thursday afternoon; a warm drizzle rendered the Maroubra sands wet concrete.

'What's Honey's real name anyway?' Scotty wiped orange fingers on his board shorts, dropping his empty Twisties packet on top of the Mars Bar wrapper on the coffee table. Jill had to look away to stop herself getting up to clean the mess.

'She was born Matthew Hudson. Had a full sex change when she was eighteen, changed her name to Honey Delaney. She's now twenty-seven. Minor possession charges, solicitation, one assault charge.'

'Assault?'

'Yeah, a trick didn't pay. She put him in hospital. Broken jaw, fractured eye socket.'

'Nice friends you have. Now she can add two broken ribs to her list.'

Jill shifted, and winced with the movement. 'I told you I think I was just unlucky running into them. I saw the dealer recognise me.'

Scotty yawned and stretched, then propped himself up on his elbow, face serious. 'What are we gonna do about these arseholes anyway? I know you said you don't want to go after them, but we can't just leave it like this.'

He had been furious when Jill had told him that morning what had happened at the club. He was on his feet and half out the door to find the offenders, and she'd had to beg him to stop. How would she explain to the squad where she'd been and what she'd been doing there? She didn't want the inspector knowing she was out at night with Honey Delaney, and she didn't want Elvis to find out about any of it. Not that he probably didn't know already. She didn't believe Elvis's brother was the only member of his family connected to the bike crew.

Jill grimaced as she forced herself to sit up. Her ribs were taped. The doctor had told her there was little else they could do. She was not to run, ride or exercise, and he'd given her the week off. But it was time to work.

'So what's for lunch?' Scotty rubbed his stomach. He blocked the cushion she threw at his head.

*

Although Scotty had tried to put it off, Jill had insisted they travel out to talk to Detectives Richard Harris and John Jardine about the Rocla and Manzi murders. An hour later saw them bumper to bumper in traffic on Anzac Parade.

Harris and Jardine were plain-clothed detectives at Central police station. They'd written up the deaths of these men, and Jill had called them to let them know she and Scotty were coming out to talk. Jardine sounded as pleased as Scotty was about the meeting. He and Harris drank with Elvis. Jill had had to hold Scotty back at a work function one night when the three of them, pissed, had eyeballed each other across the room.

Scotty was scowling behind the wheel. Jill sat straight in her seat for once, her face white. She'd taken one of the tablets the doctor had given her for pain, and she felt muffled, dull. Scotty didn't seem in the mood to talk either, so Jill closed her eyes, relaxed into the seat a little. She slept.

Back in the basement. The little girl with white eyes was screaming again. The one with the big hands was burning her. When Jill had been kidnapped, and the pain and the fear had become unbearable, part of her had somehow shut off, or maybe separated. Suddenly it was like there were two girls in the basement – the white-eyed girl who took the pain, and a secret, hidden girl, who watched in muffled silence.

In the car with Scotty, Jill moaned in her sleep, trying to swim up through the waves of the drug, to wake up, break the nightmare, get out of the basement. Her thoughts were syrupy, her head too heavy. She couldn't rupture the dream. Resignedly, she looked around the basement. The perspective seemed different. She wasn't watching from the ceiling this time. For the first time she thought she could see the big one's face.

If I just move closer, she thought, get closer to the little girl.

Don't look at what he's doing, don't look down there.

His face. I think I can see his face.

Red eyes burned into her own. Jill stared into the horned face of the devil. She screamed.

Scotty pulled over on Cleveland Street. 'You okay?' He was smoothing her hair. She pushed him away and almost threw up with the pain.

'Sorry,' she croaked, her head in her hands. 'Nightmare.'

'No kidding,' he said, immobile behind the wheel.

'Why are we stopped?' she asked.

'I should take you home, Jill. You shouldn't be working today.'

Her tongue was furry. Even with all the drugs, her head still ached.

'I'm fine. Let's go,' she looked at Scotty. 'I just need another coffee.'

The meeting with Harris and Jardine had been brief. Scotty, perhaps realising that Jill was not up to coping with aggression, led the conversation with the two detectives in a cordial manner. There was little discussed about the murdered men that Scotty and Jill did not already know. When the meeting finished, they left their car parked under the station and walked the couple of blocks down to Chinatown for lunch. Jill took it slowly, but she found the walk cleared her head a little.

They took a seat at an outdoor table in a small restaurant.

The shopfronts provided some shade. The mall was full of office workers, locals and tourists.

Jill started summarising the case as soon as they sat down. She put her spiral bound notebook on the small table between them.

'Right. Let's run through the names we've got connected to these guys.' Scotty poured them each a green tea from the pot their waitress had brought over. He took a sip. 'Okay. Manzi was bashed to death by a claw hammer in the company of Jamaal Mahmoud.'

'And Mahmoud works for Alejandro Sebastian, who's been selling kids for at least ten years, and is number one on our hit list so far.' Jill circled his name in the notepad.

'According to Honey.' Scotty drank more tea.

'What's your point?'

'Well, you're putting a lot of faith in her version of events,' Scotty replied casually, his sunglasses reflecting back the red of a Chinese New Year flag hanging in a doorway next to their table.

Jill fidgeted with a menu. It was true that Honey had not always been completely straight up with her.

'Look,' she said finally. 'Sebastian's a squirrel. And I guarantee we're going to find he knows both these men.'

'So let's go talk to him,' Scotty was still looking at the menu. 'What do you reckon about Peking Duck?'

'I'm not really hungry.'

Jill felt irritated talking about food; the bitter medicinal paste of the painkillers still coated her tongue.

Their waitress stood a few paces from their table, smilingly trying to tempt others into the restaurant. Scotty cleared his throat, trying to catch her eye. She ran over to their table when he moved to get up from the tiny outdoor table. He ordered steamed pork dumplings, the duck, and deep-fried ice cream for both of them. Jill asked the waitress to swap her dessert for a ginger ale.

'I don't think we should talk to him yet,' said Jill broodingly, again bent over the notebook.

'Huh?' Scotty was chewing his coaster, watching the woman and two kids at the next table enjoying a huge spread of food.

'It's impossible working with you at lunchtime,' Jill gave a short laugh. 'I hope they hurry up with the food.'

'Yeah, me too,' said Scotty earnestly.

Jill smiled, and tried again.

'Scott.' Maybe using his real name would catch his attention, she thought. 'I reckon we should leave Mr Sebastian for now. He's clever and very guarded. I don't want him closing up shop before we can get anything on him.'

'Yeah. Okay.' Scotty tore his eyes away from the next table and studied the notebook. 'So what about Bobby Anglia? Known associate of Dennis Rocla. Rocla lived with him when his wife kicked him out. He's doing eighteen months at Long Bay.'

'Yeah? I'll set it up.' Jill already had her mobile out; if she hurried she could organise a trip to the prison that afternoon.

18

MERCY LEANED BACK in the chair and sighed, rubbed her gritty eyes. She looked at the others in the group. They all looked alert and pleased to be there. Most mental health professionals usually had to fight to get supervision; Mercy was forced to attend.

She used to enjoy these meetings. Conducted by clinical psychologist Dr Noah Griffen, they were attended by two psychiatrists, a psych registrar, another psychologist, and Mercy. Each member of the group discussed their progress in therapy for the week, and one person brought a more detailed case for group discussion. The group members offered suggestions for difficult patients. Also encouraged was insight into personal feelings, and reactions the clinicians might be experiencing in therapy with their clients. Members were expected to bring to the group their feelings of frustration, anger, sadness, even lust, elicited during treatment sessions. Most of the therapists taped their sessions and each week an excerpt of a session was played to the members, who dissected its content. Mercy had learned lessons of great value in past groups.

Today, she tried to hide. She shifted in her seat, pulling her suit jacket down over her bulging stomach. Under the cover of her jacket, she popped the button on the fly of her pants, and a roll of fat eased out. God, that felt better. Worry about her ever-increasing weight rose from the swamp of her consciousness, but she forced the thoughts back below the surface. Blocking such mundane concerns grew easier every day.

She became aware of the woman next to her nudging Mercy's foot with her own, trying to attract her attention.

'Dr Merris. Mercy.' Noah Griffen was staring at her expectantly. 'Do you have your presentation ready?'

Mercy nodded and handed around the single-page summary of the case she'd brought for discussion today. She presented the case with her head down. She'd deliberately chosen one of her few non sex-abuse cases. She gave intelligible responses to the comments and questions and stood to leave as soon as the session started to wrap up.

She was first at the door when she heard her name called.

Noah was waiting for her. She took a step back into his room; he waited until the last of the group members had said their goodbyes.

'Coffee, Mercy?' he asked.

'I've got a lot on, Noah.' She talked to the carpet.

'Are you okay?'

She looked up into his face and quickly down again. She felt short and frumpy next to her colleague; his hair was slightly greying, but his face nevertheless shone with health, tanned from weekly triathlon training in the sun.

Mercy now wondered what it was she'd previously found so irresistible about him. When he'd first asked her out some years ago she'd been ecstatic, certain they were destined to be together. But after two of the best evenings out that she could remember, they'd booked a harbourfront room at the Hyatt Hotel in Sydney. Mercy had been lighter then, her curves dangerous. She'd spent the day before the rendezvous in the city, having a massage and splurging three hundred dollars on black La Perla underwear. Squeezing her scented body into the teddy in the change room, she knew she looked hot.

Dinner in the suite had been exquisite. The harbour was magical; they'd shared a bottle of French champagne. Perfect. Everything. And then he couldn't. Nothing. Not even the hope of an erection. Mercy lied and told him it had happened to lots of guys she'd been with.

Maybe her feelings for him wouldn't have changed had he not become so strangely silent. He would not speak; his body seemed to almost vibrate with rage. While offering more reassurance to his closed, expressionless form, she had a sudden image of him striking her and she recoiled.

The affair had died then and there.

Atypically, Mercy had managed to remain cordial with a former lover, and they'd continued and then developed their professional relationship without ever again mentioning the Hyatt.

'Yeah, I'm fine, Noah.' She pulled her jacket over her open waistband and tried to keep her voice neutral. 'I just don't want to spend my whole life at work, that's all. I'll see you tomorrow.'

'Remember that we have an individual session in the afternoon.'

How could she forget? She avoided eye contact and left the room. She went to the hospital's nearest exit and lit a cigarette as soon as she hit the outside air. It was critical that she keep people out of her head, especially him.

19

JILL WAS UNABLE TO arrange a visit to Bobby Anglia until the next afternoon.

Great, she thought, driving to the correctional facility, he's in the MSPC. The Malabar Special Programs Centre of Long Bay Gaol catered for inmates with problems so severe that they were considered unsafe to themselves or others in the main gaol. A maximum-security facility, the MSPC was broken up into five sections, including a sex-offenders' unit, a psych hospital and a unit for inmates considered acutely suicidal or at high risk of self-harm. Inside the walls of the MSPC was also a unit for those offenders requiring twenty-four hour monitoring – the Acute Crisis Management Unit (ACMU) – the most secure unit of its type in New South Wales Corrections. She'd been out there before, and wasn't looking forward to the re-visit.

Jill sighed. Of course Anglia had to be in ACMU.

She had spent the morning on case notes and Department meetings. Scotty had a compulsory training session all day today, and she'd decided to make the trip to visit Anglia without him.

She'd had a swim at Clovelly at lunchtime; she was still feeling delicate, and a sheltered section of Clovelly beach ensured she could swim without being buffeted by waves. Problem was, she'd come straight from the beach without thinking to change her clothing for her trip to the gaol. Her first female supervisor had taught her never to wear anything the inmates could see through, down or up. She pulled the neckline of her T-shirt higher as she steered her work Commodore towards Malabar.

Jill turned the car stereo down as she drove up to the first security gates of Long Bay Gaol. She needn't have bothered – the prison officers saw her badge from their office, waved, and raised the gates. It was an unseasonable 38 degrees in the city today, and the guards would leave their glassed-in office as infrequently as possible. She drove past the main car park and up to the top section of the compound, parking in the area closest to the MSPC.

The MSPC was a gaol within a gaol; a walled compound located deep' inside the already secure outer prison. Jill approached the entrance – a towering wall of stone inset with a blank-faced iron door big enough to admit a semi-trailer. A metal intercom box greeted visitors. She buzzed the guards, gave her details, and leaned against the wall to wait. She forced herself to slow everything down, adjusted her need to keep moving and get things done. Nothing in gaol was rushed – it was like combat duty: hurry up and wait. Fortunately, her impatience was tempered today by the after-effects of last night's painkillers. Her tongue was stuck to the roof of her mouth and it felt like cotton wool blocked her dull headache.

She picked at the skin around her nails, thinking about dinner at her mum's this weekend, pretending her ribs weren't killing her and that she didn't wish she was at home in bed. The sound of footsteps on the gravel path caused her to look up.

'Hello.' A grey, tired-looking woman smiled at her. 'Bit slow on the gates this afternoon, are they?'

'So what's new?' Jill smiled back. 'I've buzzed them. Shouldn't be long.'

'I've brought you luck,' the woman said as the gates were opened by a male guard in mirrored glasses. He glanced at Jill, nodded at her companion.

Jill followed the woman around to a small alcove on the right. She signed her name in the visitors' book, checked in her firearm and jotted down that she was visiting Bobby Anglia in the Acute Crisis Management Unit.

'I'm on my way there too,' the woman said, looking over Jill's shoulder. 'Claire Walker, visiting chaplain.' She held her hand out.

Jill adjusted her shoulder bag and put her pen down. She shook Claire's hand. 'Jill Jackson. I'm a detective over at Maroubra. Got an interview with an inmate.'

'Yes I saw, Robert Anglia. A very troubled soul.'

Jill looked down rather than respond, and pinned her temporary visitor's badge to her T-shirt.

Claire clipped on her chaplain's badge. They walked over to another set of gates and waited again. By then, another couple of people were also waiting to walk across the yard that led to yet another set of gates. A guard accompanied them all across the hot concrete courtyard and let them into the next area. Jill and Claire walked straight ahead, as the others veered left.

Claire used her own set of keys to open still another gate that led into the small compound that was the ACMU. Jill walked in behind her. Claire had a smile and a word for the two men in prison greens sweeping the path near the gate. Jill kept her face impassive as they surreptitiously checked her out. Blah. She already felt she needed a bath. They walked up the path to the officers' room and into its cool interior.

Ordinarily when cops had to interview a prisoner, the inmate would be brought over to an interview room in another section of the gaol. Jill knew the senior officer at ACMU, however, and he'd told her just to come over to the unit. The gaol was often short-staffed, and Jill knew having even one officer off the unit to transport an inmate could mean the entire unit had to be locked down. Jill had been there during lockdown several times. The inmates were sent to their single cells, each monitored on CCTV. Their every move was on camera. The first thing that one noted in the small strongbox that was the officers' quarters was the bank of CCTV screens on the left when you walked in. The second thing you saw was the riot gear lining the walls. Jill knew there was another locker full of the vests, helmets, restraints and stun guns just outside the unit.

There wasn't much for the inmates to do in their rooms during lockdown. Since her first visit, when she'd caught a man masturbating for the camera, Jill tried not to look at the screens.

Claire greeted the two taciturn guards on duty and Jill introduced herself; she hadn't met these officers before.

'Anglia's in the yard.' The female officer nodded at the bank of video screens on the wall. 'Closest to the wall there. You ready to go now? Boss said to use his office.'

'Yeah. Thanks.' Jill followed the heavy-set woman from the room, giving Claire a nod on the way out.

ACMU housed a maximum of fourteen inmates. As usual, the unit was full, and the majority of its occupants were out in the small, dusty courtyard of the compound. Four men kicked a tennis ball against a wall, while others watched the game from the partial shade of a covered walkway. Two or three men talked to themselves, making listless hand gestures to the air. Although obviously heavily medicated, their hallucinations were evidently breaking though. This unit wasn't designed to house the mentally ill, but with the majority of the gaol's population suffering some form of mental illness, all units had to share. These men would be especially vulnerable, unable to survive in the main gaol.

'Did ya hear Finker's in here?'

The officer spoke without looking at Jill, nodding towards a heavily bearded man sitting alone near one of the guards.

Jill thought a moment before the name registered.

'You're kidding,' she said, unable to keep the disgust from her voice and face as she stared at the man.

Larry Finker was one of the state's most hated. When his wife had left him, he'd kidnapped their two children; a boy aged four, and a girl, six. He'd strangled his son the first day, but kept the little girl alive for 24 hours, raping her repeatedly before strangling her as well. Jill had heard he was trying for forensic status, appealing to the court on the grounds that he was mentally ill in an effort to keep himself out of gaol. Although there was no evidence that he was insane, it looked like his attempt would be successful – he'd be murdered within a week if not afforded protection.

'He's been here since Monday. We fought to keep him out for three weeks, but in the end we had to take him.' The officer's voice was flat.

'Looks like someone's got to him already,' said Jill, noticing the man's left eye was blackened.

'Yeah. We broke up the fight as soon as we could,' the officer said, sounding unconvincing. 'What're you gonna do?'

Jill laughed, and the officer half-smiled for the first time.

'I'll unlock the office for you and bring Anglia over,' she said.

'Thanks, Kellie,' Jill responded, reading the woman's name from her badge.

Kellie unlocked a door just inside the covered walkway, and began to walk back towards the yard. She stopped, and turned back to Jill.

'You know who that is, don't you?' Kellie pointed her chin at a relatively small, dark-skinned man pacing near the wall in the hot sun.

'Um . . .'

'That's Teddy, serial rapist. Attacked a female officer at Goulburn.'

'Nice place you got here, Kellie.'

The officer gave another small smile and left.

Jill put her shoulder bag on the desk in the tiny office, and stretched the kinks in her neck. She looked up at the camera staring down at her. Every room, every corner of this compound was monitored by a camera. While this should have been reassuring, Jill couldn't shift the heavy blanket of dread that settled over her shoulders every time she visited this place.

Sensing movement, Jill looked up to see Kellie approaching the doorway. A pair of thin legs in green shorts was visible behind her.

'Robert Anglia,' announced the officer, stepping aside. 'Buzz when you're done.' She pointed to a button at the door.

'Thanks, boss,' Anglia said, as Jill motioned the small, thin man to the only other seat in the room. She sat in the seat nearest the door. First rule in these places. The windowless room was painted the same dirty green as the inmates' uniforms. A bench secured to one concrete wall served as a desk. The phone and PC were both outdated and box-like. Only the omnipresent security camera in the corner seemed to have been made this century.

'My name is Sergeant Jackson,' said Jill, taking control of the interview. 'I'm investigating the death of a couple of mates of yours – David Carter and George Manzi or Marks.' She held her pen ready and looked at him expectantly.

Jill already knew that Anglia knew Rocla. She wanted to know whether he also knew Carter and Manzi. The small man shifted in his seat.

'It's not like they were mates of mine. I hardly knew them,' Anglia said, scratching unconsciously at a bandage taped across his forehead.

'Really. That's not what we heard.' She decided to change tack for a little while. She was already ahead with his easy admission that he knew the other dead men. 'So how did you end up in this unit anyway?' she asked.

Anglia looked down at his shoes. Gave her nothing.

'Not hard to find out, is it, Bobby?' Jill said turning slightly in her chair, typing purposefully on the keyboard of the ageing computer. It was a bluff – she didn't have access at the moment to the prison's record system, although she could get it if she needed to.

'Who gives a fuck who knows?' Anglia muttered. 'Took a header off the shithouse.' He kept his face angled at the floor.

'Whoah!' Jill gave a disparaging laugh. 'And that's all you got, that cut on your head? Doesn't look too bad to me.'

Self-harm and suicide attempts were one way to get into this unit. Spearing oneself headfirst into the concrete floor from a height, like a bed, or in this case the toilet, could cause serious head injuries or death. Given the small bandage on his forehead, it looked like Anglia was more interested in getting out of the main gaol than out of life altogether.

'What do you fuckin' know?' Anglia was sullen now.

'Sounds like you needed to get out of the main pretty bad.'

Anglia said nothing; his eyes darted towards the door.

'Come on, Bobby. You can tell me. Who's after you? You're an endangered species, you lot.' She gave a short laugh.

'I don't know what you're talking about.'

'Yeah you do. Someone's killing off members of the club. We've heard you're next.'

'What? I'm not even in their fuckin' club.' Anglia was on his feet.

'Sit. Down.' Jill stood too. Anglia sat quickly.

So there was a club.

'Look, whether I like it or not, Bobby, I'm getting paid to stop the next death, so it's in your interests to tell me more about the club. You can't expect me to catch whoever's taking you guys out if I don't know where to look.' Jill had her pen poised. 'Let's start with the members you know.'

'I don't know what you're fucking talking about.' Anglia's

eyes were back on the ground. 'I got nothing to say about no club. I don't even know of any club.'

Jill closed her notebook; put the lid on her pen. 'You know, Bobby, you should be a little more polite, swear a little less. I am a cop, and I can make a note in your file about your attitude. If you're in here for protection, doesn't your attitude have to maintain a certain standard?'

He raised his eyes, all compliance now. 'No problems here, boss. Sorry, boss.'

''Cause I can call Kellie back now if you really want to go. Tell the other guards you didn't feel up to cooperating today.'

'Nah, it's all sweet. I'm cooperating, boss. What did you want to know?' Anglia's feet had started to tap under his chair.

'Well, if you're sure now.' Jill paused a little, as if she was considering whether to go on or not. Finally, she took her notepad out again, tapped her pen on the paper. 'I just want to talk a little more about your friends. How long did you know Dennis Rocla?'

'He used to go out with my sister. I'd sorta see him around at times, you know. Then when he split up with his missus he stayed at the same pub I was staying at for a while.'

'Which pub was that?'

'Great Southern.'

Jill wrote it down.

'And then you moved in together, is that right?'

'Yeah.'

'What was that address?' She copied his answer into her notes. 'And how did you know George Manzi?'

'I didn't really know him. He was a mate of Dennis's. Him and that Carter came over once.'

'And when was that?'

'I don't know, a year ago? Something like that. I don't remember stuff too good. I got assaulted by police a few years ago, and since then I can't remember *shit*.'

'How did they know each other?'

'How the fuck would I know?' Suddenly Anglia's little attitude was back.

'You're going to watch your mouth, Anglia, or I'm gonna walk out of here right now and make a note in your file.'

Jill knew the officers on this unit tolerated no insubordination and came down very hard on anyone who tried it on. There had been several investigations into excessive use of force. Anglia had to know that too.

'Let's talk about the club.'

Anglia squirmed. 'Honestly, I don't know about any club.'

'But you know they were all into kids, don't you? You had to know that. What are you in for this time, Bobby?' Jill read from her notes. 'Says right here, "indecent sexual assault of a child under ten".'

'It was all bullshit.'

'Now, Bobby, come on. You pleaded guilty to this one.'

'I had to. They reckon I could've got ten years if I didn't. My ex-wife made it all up to get custody of my kids. All the dykes at DoCS stick together. Fathers have no rights. You don't see me in no sex offenders' unit do you?'

'Well you first have to admit that you're a sick fuck to get in there, don't you? So how did you get to know about the club?'

'I told you I don't know about no club.'

'No, you said you weren't in the club.'

'Whatever.'

'Well, tell me how long you've known Jamaal Mahmoud.'

Pause. 'Never heard of him.' Eyes up and to the left. Lying. Jill's first supervisor had taught her about visual accessing cues. When thinking about an answer, if someone rolls their eyes to the right, they're searching for a fact, accessing information they remember. When they move their eyes up and to the left, they're using their creativity, imagining an answer. Lying.

'Uh-huh, sure you have, Bobby. You know Mahmoud. Hired ape for Alejandro Sebastian?'

'Look, I don't know these people.' Anglia's eyes were a little wild now. 'Can I go? I'm gonna miss afternoon smoko.'

Scared. Jill figured he had shut down and she'd get little more from him.

'Yeah. Right. Go.' She stood and walked with him to the corridor outside. 'Stay safe, Bobby,' she said as he stood waiting at the gate for a guard to come and let him back into the yard. He didn't look at her.

Jill turned around and walked back into the office. She sat down and made a couple of quick notes. She stretched her neck again, kneading at the bunched muscles in her shoulders. Everything hurt. And this place did not help. The walls were oppressive, the air replete with pain rather than oxygen. The pain medication made everything feel muffled, the air stale.

She swapped chairs to be closer to the computer monitor; she wanted to check she hadn't unwittingly opened or closed any files when she'd used the keyboard earlier.

A sudden rush of movement left Jill no time to block or duck. The smell of male hair and sweat filled her nostrils. Struggling silently, her face squashed into the computer screen, her left arm wrenched high behind her back, Jill stopped moving when an intense pinpoint of pain stabbed at the side of her neck.

'Anglia?' she tried to speak.

'Shut up, you fucking slut.' The voice in her ear was restrained violence, and definitely not Anglia's. The sharp point at her neck pushed deeper, breaking the skin. She got her right hand up to it. Her pen. She tried to push it away.

Her throat closed on a scream as the man pushed his hand down her shirt, crushing her breast in his fingers, pulling her upwards. The pain forced her to stand. She was not close enough to hit the buzzer.

'Don't fucking scream, you cunt, or I'll kill you right now.'

Jill gagged with revulsion as the man pushed his tongue into her ear. Wet, panting. His fingers were now at her fly, tearing at the zip. One hand still crushing her breast, he used his other hand to rip down her pants. His body pressed into her back, crushing her pelvis against the table. She could feel his erection on the exposed skin at the back of her legs. Blind panic overtook her and she thrashed violently; the movement causing her broken ribs to rip at her insides.

The world went white.

20

'IT WASN'T ME!' Jerome Sanders screamed over his shoulder at his father as he was marched up the corridor to his bedroom. His brother, Nathan, took the opportunity to make faces at him behind their father's back.

'You arsehole!' he tried to jerk from his father's grasp on his pyjamas. He wanted to smash Nathan's laughing face.

'Nathan. Get to bloody bed now.' Jerome's father opened his bedroom door, 'And you. Get in your room.'

Jerome threw himself on his bed, hot tears of rage welling despite his best efforts to force them away.

'It wasn't me, Dad. It was fucking Nathan.'

'You will not speak like that in this house, Jerome. Your little sister can hear you. I don't care who did it. You're both going to bed. We can talk about this in the morning.'

'It's not fair! You said I could watch *South Park*. I didn't do anything.' The tears were now falling down Jerome's twelve-year-old cheeks.

His father pulled his door closed.

'It's not fair,' Jerome sobbed into his pillow. 'I hate all of them.'

Tonight's fight had started when Nathan had grabbed the remote control and changed the TV from the news to *The Simpsons*. Normally that would be great, and Jerome would be all for it, but tonight his best mate's brother was going to be on the sport segment of the news. Nathan knew it.

By the time his dad had changed the channel back again, the sport was over.

Jerome made their sister, Abby, cry when he flew at Nathan, knocking her over in the process, but it was Nathan who'd pushed him into the china cabinet, smashing the curved glass panel.

His dad didn't even listen to him. Nathan got away with everything.

Jerome was sick of it. He'd missed Logan's brother on TV and he was going to miss *South Park* again.

Suddenly he had an idea.

He slid open his bedroom window and popped the flyscreen soundlessly out, letting it fall into the garden bed below. He then took his pyjamas off and pulled on the shorts and T-shirt he'd been wearing after school. He put his Vans sneakers on without socks.

Logan's parents are so much cooler than mine, thought Jerome, perching on the windowsill above his bed. It's only 7.45. They're not gonna care if I come over for a while.

Still, he thought, looking out into his shadowy backyard,

it's going to take me twenty minutes to get there, and it'll be pretty dark by then.

Jerome listened to the sounds in his home. He could hear his mum and dad talking in the kitchen and the low murmuring of the television in the lounge room down the hall. Nathan was still watching TV!

He turned away from his bedroom and dropped down from the window ledge into the garden.

'Shit!' he exclaimed, landing awkwardly in the azalea bush below the window. He looked up at the light from his bedroom window. Would they have heard him? He crept closer to the house, favouring his ankle.

There was no movement in the window above. Jerome straightened up and brushed some leaves off his skinned knee. He limped quietly past the clothesline and the above-ground pool they'd got for Christmas last year. Logan's family had an in-ground pool with a wooden deck and an outdoor spa. Maybe they'd be able to go for a swim tonight. Manoeuvring around the lemon tree at the bottom of the garden, he let himself out through their back gate. He would ring his mum from Logan's and ask to stay the night. His dad would be pissed, but they'd have to say yes in the end. He laughed, imagining Nathan's face when the phone rang.

Cicadas screamed at Jerome as he trod gingerly along the newly mown grass behind his neighbours' houses.

21

JAMAAL'S HEAD POUNDED. He'd been out of the hospital less than an hour. The doctors had told him to rest for a week, but he went where he was told by Sebastian. For now. He had just to pick up some money from one of Sebastian's clients, drop off a video to another, and he could go home. He thought of his fat wife and daughters waiting there, and decided instead to play some cards when he'd finished for the day. He consoled himself with revenge fantasies directed towards the person who'd almost cracked his skull last week. He felt himself grow hard as he replayed the violent images in his mind.

'Can't you close your mouth when you eat?' Jamaal Mahmoud hissed, staring at his dining companion in disgust. He stood up from the plastic table, pushing his half-finished meal away from him. Other than the two of them and an ageing man behind the counter, the café was empty.

'Where are you going? I'm not finished yet,' whined the thin man, still at the table, but standing anyway, shovelling food into his mouth in resignation. 'Why you always gotta be in such a hurry, Jamaal?'

Jamaal kept his hands by his sides, felt his fists clench. He imagined grabbing this junkie by the hair and cracking his face into the corner of the table. He couldn't stand the way addicts talked, as if they were always begging forgiveness. He stared at the table rather than at the gaol-drawn, ink tattoos on the man's hands and face. He couldn't keep the snarl from his face however, and his companion, noticing his eyes on the diner's cutlery, moved faster.

Why does Sebastian make me ride with these low-life scum? thought Jamaal, stalking from the table out to the carpark. A young couple, walking together towards the diner, wordlessly parted to allow him to walk between them.

The sun was setting on Parramatta Road, but the street-lights hadn't yet clicked on. Peak hour was dying down, but there were still plenty of cars driving west, home from work. Jamaal climbed up into the driver's seat of the Ford Transit van, his face dark with anger. Sebastian has a Mercedes, a Range Rover and a Lexus, he thought, and he gives me this shit to drive while I do his bidding.

He watched the junkie walking towards him, watched him struggling with his skinny arms to pull himself up into the van, concentrating, like it was hard work. Sebastian had insisted this guy come along to pick up the money; the client wouldn't open the door for a stranger. He turned his head, repulsed by the sores around the junkie's mouth, and started the van.

It was then that something caught his attention, distracting him from his favourite feeling – hate. A small figure. There. On the other side of the road. A boy, alone. Jamaal scanned the street on both sides, the car yards, parked cars. He couldn't see anyone with him. His breath quickened and his eyes narrowed. He felt a squirt of adrenalin in the pit of his stomach.

'Christ! Can't ya wait till I'm even in the car?'

Jamaal ignored the nasal voice of his passenger, eyes locked onto the kid who had just turned left onto Broughton Street.

Can't be more than eleven or twelve, he thought. Where is he going? He eased the van into the westbound traffic, and pushed his way through to the right-hand lane. He got to the lights at Burwood Road, and indicated to turn right.

'Jamaal, we're supposed to be in Mount Druitt at eight o'clock. Where are you going?' the junkie whined from the seat next to him.

He turned with the traffic when the light changed and did an illegal U-turn back onto Parramatta Road, ignoring protesting car horns, absorbed by the boy's movements. The light was fading now, but there he was. Still alone.

Jerome was beginning to think this wasn't a good idea. What if Logan's dad got mad at him for showing up? What if they weren't even home? It was getting pretty dark too, and he was starting to feel creeped out. He'd never been out this late by himself. He tried to think about watching *South Park*. Jerome's mum would probably give them ice-cream.

That van's driving slow, he thought, his heart quickening.

Probably lost. Hope he doesn't ask me where to go; I don't know the names of the streets.

I wish I'd never come, he thought, as the van continued to idle along at his side.

He looked at his sneakers and kept walking.

22

'SHHH, YOU'RE ALL RIGHT NOW.'

Mum?

Something troubled Jill, batting around her thoughts like a blowfly. It's best not to notice, she told herself, unwilling to face the feeling. Just listen to the noises in the background. The page of a book being turned. Quiet breathing. Gentle repositioning noises of someone in a seat next to her.

Lying down or sitting up? I'm lying down. Must be night-time. But it doesn't feel like it. Smells funny in here. Kind of medicinal.

Jill felt the memory inexorably building at the edges of her consciousness, a far-away roar of knowledge gathering pace, drowning everything in its wake. Before the wave of recall hit, her stomach clenched in frightened anticipation.

She sat up, frantic. Wild-eyed. Where was he?

'Jill, it's okay.' A female voice, familiar, yet not. 'It's Claire. We met earlier.'

'What happened?' Her heart in her throat.

'The officers got him off you, love. Nothing happened. You're okay.'

'Who was it?' She already knew.

'Edward Pavey, I'm afraid. They call him Teddy,' said Claire.

'Where are we?'

'The clinic. The doctor's coming. Just lie back for a while.'

'I'm okay.' Jill bent down, fighting nausea, searching for her shoes. 'I passed out. I've had an injury. Supposed to be in bed,' she muttered. She felt so ashamed. What did the officers think of her? Attacked with her own pen. She just wanted to go home.

'You have to wait for the doctor anyway, Jill,' said Claire kindly but firmly. 'We have to fill in an incident report or we're all in trouble.'

Great. They'd have a record of her humiliation.

'Where's Pavey now?' She hoped she wouldn't have to see him. She didn't think she could walk past any of the men on the unit right now.

'Getting charged. He's over at the hospital. Got his arm broken when they got him off you.'

At least there's that, Jill thought.

Claire stood over near the sink. 'The unit's on lockdown, of course,' she said, walking back with a glass of water. 'Here.' She offered it to Jill.

Jill took it. 'Kellie said Pavey's a serial rapist?'

'He breaks into houses and ties his victims up. He likes to beat them with a dog chain.'

Jill drained the glass and leaned back against the pillows,

lightheaded again. After giving Claire a watery smile, she closed her eyes and resigned herself to the wait, to making the report, to the check-up by the doctor. It wasn't like she could just walk out of Long Bay Gaol.

Besides, she thought, I'm going to need to get something stronger from him to get to sleep tonight.

23

JAMAAL THOUGHT ABOUT snatching the kid now. Last time he'd brought in a boy this age, Sebastian had given him fifteen grand. He could use that right now. His wife was bitching about school fees, but he could probably use it to win twice as much at cards.

There was a park just ahead. On the other side of the road was a school. Perfect street really. The trees made it darker than others. He would just stop a little way ahead of the boy and pull him into the back of the van as he passed. He knew it would be easy. The kid would be in the van before he knew what was happening.

The junkie was on the phone. He had the thing permanently glued to his head, doing deals in his whiny voice. Could he trust this prick to keep his mouth shut? He listened to the lies he was spinning over the phone and knew he couldn't. The first chance he got to make some money from the story, the junkie would tell whoever was asking.

The boy was approaching the park. It was now or never. Jamaal felt his muscles tense. He was rock hard with the feeling of impending violence, mesmerised by the pulsing of his blood in his ears. He looked at the door handle, ready.

Reason prevailed. He had a witness. A witness that couldn't disappear yet. Sebastian had him by the balls. He let go of the door handle and watched the boy cross the road and walk up past a few more houses. Almost panting with suppressed rage, Jamaal watched the kid approach the gate of number 38; he saw him pause for a minute, then open the gate and walk through. As the boy approached the front porch, a sensor light tripped and he heard the doorbell ring. He waited until he heard voices, then accelerated a little and turned the corner.

Fifteen grand.

The junkie laughed at something said on the phone. Jamaal felt his blood boiling; he stared at the road through a film of wet red. He drove the van a couple of blocks, chest heaving, and pulled over at the first dark place he could find.

The junkie hung up the phone and looked around in surprise.

'What are we doing here, man?'

Jamaal didn't speak. He cracked his fist into his passenger's face, oblivious to his pleading; he could hear only his own blood, roaring in his ears like a great mob. He grabbed the junkie by the back of the neck and forced his head down to his crotch, his other hand freeing his erection.

The junkie only stopped crying when he nearly choked. He set to work getting it over with. It wasn't as if he hadn't done it all before.

24

'YES, HELLO, IT'S Peter Wheeler here. I'm Logan Wheeler's father. Is that Jerome's mum?'

Jerome looked anxiously up at Logan's father, on the phone calling his house. Mr Wheeler, listening to Jerome's mum on the other end of the phone, leaned against the kitchen wall and ruffled Jerome's hair. Jerome stuck his head around the kitchen door, hearing laughter from the lounge room. He was missing *South Park*.

'I don't know whether you've noticed yet, but you're missing a child.' Jerome was drawn back to the phone conversation. Logan's parents had been cool when he'd shown up, but when he'd told them he came over without telling anyone, they'd skitzed out. Logan's dad looked down at him, nodding.

'Yes, I know. I'd kill Logan if he did something like that too. But Jerome's right here, and he's fine. Logan's got him some pjs ready and it's okay with us if he stays the night.'

Yes! Jerome beamed up at Logan's dad. He positioned himself in the doorway and did a little victory dance in front of Logan and his brother. Logan pumped a fist in the air, grinning. Logan's big brother said, 'Faggots,' and went back to watching TV.

Brothers suck, thought Jerome.

'Yes, Narelle. I'm sure you do. I'll put him on.'

Logan's father handed Jerome the phone and Jerome stared from it to the man holding it and back again, horrified. He finally took the receiver, handling it as if it were burning hot, and head bowed, face miserable, he put the phone to his ear. Peter Wheeler smiled and shook his head, and walked from the kitchen back into his lounge room.

Jamaal and the junkie had completed their errands. Praise God, this night is nearly over, thought Jamaal, leaning against his van, his bandaged head resting on his hand. It was only when the junkie's whining had become unbearable that Jamaal had stopped the vehicle and given him a fix. Sebastian had insisted that Jamaal only give him heroin after they had completed their jobs.

Like I would be stupid enough to do it before, he thought, fuming at Sebastian's assumption that he was so ignorant. He intended to make his boss pay for his assumptions one day. Hadn't he proven his worth a thousand times over already? What about Mary – did she count for nothing? A slut who knew too much, and could speak too well. It had taken him just a week to find her after she'd gone underground. Sebastian had told him just to cut out her tongue. A lesson

to others, he'd said. It had been too difficult, however, for Jamaal to stop, once she had started to cry. Her bleating had excited him, had driven him to punish her further. Seven years, and still her body had not been found.

Jamaal took a few steps away from the van, walking a little way down the alley in which he had stopped to appease the junkie. From the wound at the back of his head, rhythmic flares of pain bloomed with his pulse. He took a small packet from the top pocket of his sweat-stained shirt. He popped two aspirin tablets from the blister pack and put them in his mouth, crunching them, dry. He ignored their bitter, vinegary taste. He lit a cigarette, inhaling deeply.

Under the only streetlight in the alley, he noticed a youth and his girlfriend parked in a car two vehicles behind his own. P-platers. They each looked away when his eyes met theirs. He noticed the female furtively use her elbow to push down her doorlock; her boyfriend's hand hovered near the ignition. He grinned, his yellowed teeth coated in the chalky residue from the painkillers.

He continued to watch the teenagers. Their eyes widened as the junkie performed his ritual, oblivious to all around him, absorbed in his communion with his one true love. Squatting in the gutter beside the van, a rubber tube was cutting the circulation to the lower half of the man's skinny arm, pumping up his veins. Jamaal had once watched him mainline into the fat blue blood vessel in his penis, frustrated with being unable to find a vein quickly enough in his arm.

The junkie was in the zone. He'd finished melting the white powder in a spoon. He drew it up, now a clear liquid, into the syringe and injected it. A moment. Then his body

lurched forward and he projectile vomited over his feet. He collapsed forward over his knees, in ecstasy.

Jamaal laughed in delight at the look of revulsion on the teenagers' faces, and walked back to his vehicle. He picked the junkie up by the shoulders and threw him in through the passenger's door, making sure to smack his head on the frame as he did so. He walked around to his own door and got in. The smell of vomit made him gag.

'*Kess emmak*,' he spat, cursing the man's mother in Arabic. He drove out of the alley.

Jamaal made his way back to the house in Hunters Hill. He promised himself that he'd go back to the street in Burwood in the morning.

The boy was a sign. Jamaal believed in signs. His luck was changing; he could feel it in his groin.

25

IT WAS THE WEAKNESS OF Australians he despised the most. The way they allowed their soft, white bellies to keep mushrooming over their pants; the way they couldn't keep their mouths shut, or the lust from their eyes. Jamaal watched another roomful of weak, white men being fleeced by his boss, Mr Sebastian.

They came from all over the state, some from interstate, drawn by word of mouth and by Sebastian's internet site, knowing that what they got here would be worth the trip, worth the premium price. The photos, jpegs and DVDs they could buy here could not be bought over the internet, on the street, nor from the backrooms of adult bookstores. Sebastian kept stuff you only heard about, stuff you dreamed about while lying with your ugly wife in the dark of night. He had all ages, different nationalities, rape films – some even said you could get snuff films. Jamaal knew the truth of the rumour.

'Ah, Jamaal, you're back. Things ran smoothly, I trust?' Mr Sebastian turned from one of his customers when Jamaal entered the room. 'I see you've brought our friend in with you.' He continued to smile, but Jamaal noted with satisfaction that Sebastian's eyes narrowed when he caught the odour the stupefied junkie trailed through the refined lounge room. 'Sometimes I wonder at you, Jamaal. Our friend looks to be unwell. Perhaps he'd be more comfortable at home.'

'I thought you'd want the delivery first.' Jamaal handed over a fat, dirty yellow envelope. Twenty-one thousand dollars. He'd counted. In addition to porn, Sebastian provided drugs to some of his customers. He was no big-time dealer – he didn't need to be – but men were used to getting anything they needed from him, and when one had the money, Sebastian could be a one-stop shop. Cocaine and ice had always been the most common requests, but over the past few years, Rohypnol, Special K and Fantasy were increasingly requested. Date-rape drugs. Jamaal could understand the attraction.

Sebastian took the envelope. Again, his face registered a look of distaste, directed at Jamaal. He fixed his employee with a final stare, and turned back with a smile to his customer, a slack-jawed sheep farmer from Wagga whom Jamaal had seen here before.

Jamaal looked around the room for the junkie and almost laughed out loud. He was on the nod on one of the designer lounges, no-one around him, regurgitated food still stuck to his shoelaces. Jamaal looked at his watch. Twenty to twelve. No time for cards. At least the fat bitch would be asleep.

And there was always Burwood in the morning to look forward to.

He'd intended to be out of the house before she woke up – God knows she usually slept late enough – but the five-year-old had been sick all night, and Jamaal was not able to avoid speaking to his wife the next morning.

'Where are you going already?' She was outside the shower. 'I need money for food. Money for medicine. Why do you spend all of our money on gambling? What kind of a father are you? What kind of a man? What time did you come home last night? God save me. My father told me you are no good.'

Jamaal got out of the shower. His head had ached all night. He reached up and touched the wound at the back of his head. The bandage had become wet in the shower and was peeling off. He walked into the bedroom of his small Lakemba townhouse and began to dress.

'I have to have money. There is no food.' His wife stood behind him. The baby cried. The sound bounced around and around in his aching head like a squash ball.

Jamaal moved to the bed, took a hundred-dollar note from his wallet and threw it on the floor. He continued to dress.

'That is not enough. I have the bills tomorrow! Medicine. I have passed by hell living with you! I wish God would take me now,' she wailed.

The baby's cries increased. Jamaal indulged himself in an image of slamming his fist into his wife's face. He did not enact the fantasy. He knew her father and brothers would finish him if he hit her again. Let them feed her, he thought, and left his house. It seemed as though everyone in it was crying.

The van started first time and he made his way towards Burwood. Saturday. There were few cars on the road. Every traffic light seemed to be green. Another sign.

Despite the pain in his head, Jamaal felt today was going to be a very good day.

26

'MUM SAYS I HAVE to go home before I can go to the beach with you guys.' Jerome sprawled on a mattress in the middle of Logan's bedroom floor.

'How come?'

'Gotta clean my room,' Jerome mumbled. 'She was absolutely spewing last night. She nearly wasn't going to let me come at all.'

Logan stretched on his bed, then hurled his pillow at Jerome's head. Jerome re-launched the pillow back at his friend, added his own pillow, and his doona, and then threw himself on top of the pile, punching into the pillow. Laughing and shouting, they ignored the thumping on the wall that came from Logan's parents' room.

'Get off, you idiot!' Logan managed to push Jerome off, toppling him back down to his mattress. 'You know Dad's gonna want to leave by about nine. What time is it now?'

'Shit! It's already seven o'clock. I told Mum I'd be back by now.' Jerome started pulling on his sneakers.

'I can ask my brother to give you a lift if you want,' said Logan doubtfully.

'Yeah, like he's gonna do that.' Jerome's voice was muffled as he pulled his pyjama top over his head. 'I can be back here in an hour if I leave right now.'

'Well, hurry up then.' Logan had already clicked on his TV and was surfing for the cartoons.

Jerome's stomach gurgled with hunger and excitement as he unlatched the gate at Logan's house. It was boiling hot already, he thought as he walked through, forgetting to close it behind him. It was going to be great at the beach.

He looked around. It was always quiet around Logan's house, he thought. No-one was ever in the street. Logan had told him his dad didn't even know their next-door neighbours' names. The idea was bizarre to Jerome, who'd lived in the same house all his life and knew every person in every house in his street. And they all knew him. Sometimes it was cool living there. Every few months or something, they'd have a street party at the bottom of the cul-de-sac, and he'd be allowed to stay up till whenever. At those parties, he could get away with practically anything, because his mum and dad didn't like to yell in front of the neighbours. And at Christmas everyone tried to have better lights and shit decorating their houses. In Christmas week, it was like there were street parties every night. Last Christmas they'd even closed half the street off at the top of the cul-de-sac, and his dad and

Mr Robotham had built a massive barbecue right in the middle of the road. Jerome had copped a hiding for nearly knocking it over when he'd come down the street on his belly on his skateboard. He laughed out loud now, thinking about it.

But at least Logan didn't have everyone knowing what he was doing all the time, he thought, staring at the neat houses. No-one was even mowing their lawn, or watering. Logan had told him his dad said everyone was too busy trying to pay their mortgage to talk to anyone else.

Jerome kicked a rock along as he walked, imagining he was Harry Kewell and the crowd was cheering his name.

Making a massive save from losing the rock down the drain, Jerome failed to notice the van stopped near the park.

27

JAMAAL HAD REACHED THE park at seven o'clock. The sun's rays had not yet reached this side of the quiet street. A seagull landed on his rear-vision mirror, hoping for leftover takeaway, begging for scraps. Disgusted by the creature's bright eyes, Jamaal smacked his hand on the glass and the bird flapped away.

There was no way of knowing whether the boy was still in the house. He knew he did not live there – the boy had rung the doorbell last night. Would he walk home alone? Had he left already? Would he leave with the owners of the house in a car? Jamaal knew the chances of seeing the boy alone again would be slim, but the feeling that had awoken when he had first seen him would not leave. Sometimes destiny provides.

So, when Jamaal saw the same blond hair and red T-shirt crossing the road straight towards him, he was not even surprised. The child had not seen him; he was busy playing with a stone on the road.

Jamaal felt the erotic throb of adrenalin that always surged through him before violence. He cracked open the door of his van.

'Excuse me, boy. Could you help me for a moment, please?'

Still no-one was around. Jamaal scanned the street and spotted nothing but the blond boy and the seagull.

Jerome looked up, a little startled. Shit, you scared me, he thought, but aloud he said, 'Huh?'

'I need some help for just a moment.' Jamaal smiled what he hoped was a friendly grin. 'My friend is not here yet, and I need someone to help me get some things out of my van.'

Jerome stood where he was in the middle of the road, his head on an angle. Was that the van from last night?

'They're not heavy,' tried Jamaal, sensing the boy's hesitation. 'I hurt myself.' He turned to the side, showed the still-wet bandage at the back of his head.

'Sorry, mister. I gotta go. I'm late already.'

Many of his friends would not have even answered this man, but Jerome's parents had taught him to answer adults when he was spoken to. But screw this, he thought. No way am I going to risk missing out on the beach to help this goose.

'Twenty dollars.' Jamaal had it in his hand, ready. 'It's just some tins and a ladder. It will take us five minutes, maybe less. Please, I am late for work already.'

Jerome had received fifty dollars for his last birthday and needed fifteen dollars more to buy the new PlayStation 2 game. Not even Logan's smart-arse brother had it. And

Nathan would shit if Jerome got it first. He could pick it up at Westfield tomorrow. Excellent.

'Yeah. Okay, then,' said Jerome, eyes on the twenty. He made his way over to the van. The back door was open, but it was shaded on that side of the road, and he couldn't see much inside.

Jamaal put his hand back into his pocket. He removed a wet cloth from a sandwich bag he'd positioned carefully. Within the five steps it had taken the boy to close the gap between them, he'd palmed the chloroform-soaked rag and was ready.

'It'll take two people to get this ladder out,' he said, as Jerome stepped into the shadows.

When he walked between the man and the open van door, Jerome smelt something real strong – fumes, like petrol, or paint. Must be a tradie, he thought, before everything went black.

28

JEROME'S MOUTH FELT ALL DRY and tasted funny. And shit, his head hurt bad. I'm not going to school today, he thought. Why is it so hot?

Eyes still closed. His head hurt too much to open them. 'M–Mum?' It came out a croak. 'Ma?' He tried again.

I feel so sick, he thought. It feels like I'm moving. He slept again.

The next time Jerome awoke, his heart was hammering, and he knew before he even opened his eyes that something was very wrong. He couldn't move his arms. He was lying face down on a carpet that smelled like petrol and something worse. Why can't I move? His heart thudded against the floor underneath him. That smell – chemical. Where am I?

It was then that Jerome remembered the man and the van and he knew where he was. He began crying straight away, sobbing into the carpet. The realisation that he'd been kidnapped crashed down on him like a huge wave, smashing into him like a physical blow. No-one knew he was in here. Would he ever see his mum again? What would happen to him? Horror stories he'd heard at camp of kids being abducted and chopped to pieces flashed through his mind before being whited-out by pure terror that robbed him of all thought. He lay in the van and cried until he was sick.

Jerome gradually became aware of a low keening sound. He stopped when he realised that he was making the noise. He must've been crying for half an hour, and no-one had come. Should he call out? But what if the man with the big nose came back? He felt scorching hot and so thirsty that his tongue had swollen and stuck to the roof of his mouth. He couldn't even moisten his lips. His throat rasped raw from crying, and his eyes felt scratchy and swollen shut. His hands were numb, and his shoulders gave off searing flares of pain where his bunched muscles pulled backwards. Dried vomit stuck to his cheek; he smelled hot urine and knew he'd pissed himself.

He decided to risk calling out. At first no sound would come from his dry throat. He tried again.

'Help. Help me. Is anyone there?'

No-one came. Jerome cried a bit more, his throat convulsing. He needed to sit up so badly that he tried to scream; the sound was feeble, even to his own ears. He lay there in complete misery.

Suddenly, noise. Outside the van. Someone was coming.

Jerome's heart beat so quickly he thought he'd probably die before the kidnapper even opened the door. But maybe it wasn't the kidnapper. Maybe it was someone else and they would rescue him. His mum and dad would be looking for him. It could be the police. He strained his neck and could just see one section of a steel rod that he knew was connected to the van's door handle. It was moving. The door was opening.

'Oh my God! Look at the poor thing!'

The voice was not that of the man who'd taken him! Jerome moaned – a sob of relief.

'Help me,' he croaked in little more than a whisper.

'Get him out of there. Quickly.'

Jerome felt someone kneeling in the van and hands gently lifting him to his knees.

'Are you all right?'

'My arms hurt,' Jerome managed.

'Look at his hands. They're white! He's been tied like an animal.'

'Be quiet, you're scaring him more, poor thing.'

Jerome let himself be lifted from the van. He tried to stand, to see his rescuers, but his eyes couldn't focus right, and his knees buckled.

'Let him sit! Get him water.'

Jerome sat at the edge of the van with his head between his knees. Sounds seemed muffled and he felt himself sliding sideways, unable to stay awake. He felt someone freeing his hands and a bottle was pressed to his lips. He drank, and his vision slowly cleared. He was in a huge room. It must be a garage, he thought, though he'd never seen one so large. Two men stood near him: one, a blond man, was smiling at him, friendly. He held the bottle of water out to him, and Jerome tried to take it, but it slipped through his fingers, still numb from being tied.

Dully, he watched the bottle roll towards a pair of feet. A hand reached down and picked it up. Another smiling man. Huge. In a suit.

'You must be very frightened, young man,' said the tall man, handing Jerome another bottle of water. 'I imagine you'd like to get home as soon as possible. We've called your parents and they're on their way.'

Jerome began again to cry again. Tears of relief. Thoughts of seeing his mum and dad again. Abby. Even Nathan.

'Th–thank you for helping me,' he said, sniffling.

The blond man ruffled Jerome's hair and smiled again. 'You're a brave boy. You'll have a story to tell at school later, won't you?'

Jerome needed more water. He was weakly lifting the bottle when a door at the side of the garage opened and the driver of the van walked into the room. Jerome froze with the bottle halfway to his mouth.

He wanted to shriek to his rescuers, to let them know that this was the man who'd kidnapped him, but he didn't know how the man would react if he did so. He stared wild-eyed at his rescuers, silently trying to alert them.

'Good, isn't he, Mr Sebastian?' he heard the hook-nosed man ask.

'Oh you've done very well, Jamaal,' said the big man in the suit. 'Very well indeed.' He put his arm around the skinnier man's shoulders and smiled broadly, looking down at Jerome as a starving man might view a feast.

Jerome didn't even notice the blond man placing his hand on his thigh. His brain struggled to register the sudden certainty that his mum and dad had not been called at all.

29

SCOTTY INSISTED THAT JILL stay out with her parents at Camden for a couple of days, and she was not up to objecting. She found it difficult to believe that two men had physically attacked her in forty-eight hours. Since she'd started investigating David Carter's murder, her carefully ordered life seemed to be unravelling.

At the moment, however, this thought was suppressed. Reclining on a sun lounge by the side of her parents' pool, her knees bent up – this position eased the pressure on her ribs – her hand shielded her eyes, blocking some of the late afternoon sun from her face. The cicadas chiming in the semi-rural neighbourhood nearly drowned out the sounds of her niece and nephew chortling in the pool.

'Girls, you should have a hit of tennis before dinner.' Robert Jackson stood at the barbecue, poking at the smouldering coals, beer in hand.

'Or, you could get me another white wine, Dad.' Cassie was on a lounge next to Jill, painting her nails. Their sister-in-law, Robyn, was in the shallows with Lily, Jill's niece and Robyn's three-year-old daughter. Avery, Jill's six-year-old nephew, was calling for his father's attention every minute or so. Tim, the children's father – Jill and Cassie's older brother – was touring the rose garden behind the pool with their mother, Frances.

'Robert, don't be silly,' called Frances, secateurs in hand, 'How is Jill supposed to play tennis with broken ribs?'

'And since when have *I* played tennis?' Cassie wanted to know.

Jill gave up trying to keep her eyes half-open and let the waning sunlight soak into her skin. She buried her hand in the silky fur of the cat pressed against her side. Fisher, her mum's blue-point Siamese, stretched full-length, upside down, drunk on the sun and Jill's attention. His purring chest moved against her own.

As usual when she was at home, she could feel herself healing. Here, in the scented afternoon light, she was suspended above her life, safe from the sharks snapping below.

Jill opened her eyes half an hour later to the clink of ice near her ear.

'Mango juice,' her mum said quietly. 'Sorry to wake you, darling. Dinner's almost ready.'

Jill stretched, and then winced; she'd caught herself before any real pain bit through her side. She opened and closed her mouth, rubbing her hand over her face. Her skin felt tight from the sun. I should've applied more sunblock, she thought. Cassie was just emerging from the pool in front of her, looking just as glamorous and skinny as she did in the magazines.

I can't talk, thought Jill, looking down at her own concave stomach. Gotta eat more while I'm here. She felt surprise that she had an appetite as she made her way up the stairs to the deck that surrounded the back of her parents' sprawling house. The cicadas were even louder now, if possible, and the smells of newly mown grass and orange-blossom filled the early evening air.

Lily wouldn't eat until Aunty Jill was sitting next to her, so Jill took her seat overlooking the pool and the ten acres of her parents' backyard. As the sun set over the horse paddocks, she wolfed down king prawns and lemon-crusted barbecued lamb cutlets, potato salad and roasted beetroot salad. She was certain that she wouldn't be able to fit in any of the tropical fruit salad and ice-cream, but over coffee she even managed a piece of Robyn's famous frozen Mars Bar slice.

She pushed her seat back from the table. Used to her silence, her family carried on their conversation around her, and she allowed their familiar noise to wash over her as she breathed in the hot, scented air. Funny that she forgot stars even existed when she was in the city – there were too many streetlights to notice them. Here, a billion tiny bubbles of brightness burst and reformed in the endless black sky above her parents' property.

Robyn lightly tapped her daughter's hand for the tenth time as Lily reached to touch one of the flickering candles that softly illuminated the table. Jill had watched the scenario, smiling each time Lily's face registered surprise when her mother or another family member tapped her hand. She was hypnotised by the dancing tea lights in the glass jars, the tiny flames reflected in her huge blue eyes. Rather than remove the candles and use artificial lighting, the family almost unconsciously attended to Lily's wandering fingertips, and she was beginning to learn to avoid the danger.

Tonight, the characteristic defensiveness of her brother's conversations did not disturb Jill. The elder by four years, he'd been sixteen when she was kidnapped, and she figured he'd taken on the same guilt as her father for being unable to protect her. She remembered her brother as open and boisterous; his teasing fun-loving and fond prior to her disappearance. Now it seemed he spoke to her as little as possible, with her own inability to initiate conversation compounding the problem. She had never discussed her ordeal with her father or brother, and the incident lay like an impassable swamp between them, the horror of the experience silently revived every time they met. Each of these men was overly sensitive to perceived criticism, quick to make cynical remarks about others' inadequacies, and could often grind family conversations into uncomfortable silences with their disparaging sarcasm or critical wit.

Tonight, perhaps the laden table, the soporific night air or the several empty bottles had soothed the men in her family. No-one had even told Cassie she'd had too much to drink. Jill watched her brother's hand on the back of his wife's chair, absently curling tendrils of her hair around his fingers. Together they watched their son swapping unopened Christmas crackers with his grandparents, trying to cheat to ensure he won each time.

She looked up and caught her mother smiling at her. She

smiled back sleepily; her face taut from sun and chlorine, her eyes grainy, like she'd been crying for hours. Fisher snaked around her ankles, angling for scraps.

Scotty's right, she thought. I'll stay another day.

Birds, rather than a nightmare, woke her. Nice change, she thought. She padded downstairs to the kitchen.

At 5.30, she thought there'd be no-one about yet, but through the kitchen windows she could see her mother standing barefoot on the deck outside, sipping a coffee. Jill poured some water from a jug in the fridge and joined her. Fisher was up on the table, sniffing the morning.

'Sleep okay, sweetheart?'

'Mmm, great. What'd you put in my food?'

'You just needed the sleep.' Her mum put an arm around her. 'So what have you planned for the day?'

'Thought I might hang around here actually. I'm still too sore to go back to work. What about you?'

'I've promised to help your Aunt Ro with food for Alyssa's engagement party. I'm going to do some cooking here.'

Alyssa was Jill's nineteen-year-old cousin; Aunt Rosalie her mother's sister. Jill's mother's side of the family was Italian – the wedding was to be a Big Thing.

'I know you don't usually come to these gatherings, Jill,' her mother began cautiously, 'but since you're down here, maybe you could stay for the engagement party tomorrow night. It's not going to be too big.'

'Yeah, right,' Jill laughed and gave her mother a careful hug. 'There'll be doves and smoke machines and shit, won't there?'

'I don't know, Jill, but you might enjoy a family get-together now. It's been a long time.'

After the kidnapping, large family parties had caused Jill to suffer panic attacks. Crowds of people who knew what had happened to her and stared at her with sympathy or curiosity was her idea of a nightmare. Still, it had been a few years since she'd seen her cousins. And what other plans did she have for this weekend?

'Well, we'll see, Ma, but in the meantime I wouldn't mind helping with the cooking.'

A big smile on her face, Frances Jackson began bustling around the deck, picking up the remnants of last night's gathering – mostly Avery's and Lily's toys.

'Great! Shall we have some breakfast now?' she said. 'Then I've got to go out to the fruit market. They're open at seven.'

Jill and her mum went back into the kitchen and plundered the fridge, bringing back to the deck bits and pieces of whatever they felt like. The morning was already hot, and Jill decided she'd make iced coffee for everyone. She poured a few shots of espresso, thick with sugar syrup, into a tall glass jug, splashed in a litre of cold milk, and added chunks of crushed ice and a slurp of vanilla extract at the end. When she carried it and some glasses out to the deck, she found her mother had arranged a platter of prosciutto and melon, ricotta and strawberries, and half a wheel of brie, already beginning to ooze as the sun rose behind the house. The toaster was set up in the middle of the circular jarrah table and thick slabs of homemade bread waited in a basket under a tea towel. Her parents had stocked up big time on food, knowing the family was coming down for the weekend.

Jill made some toast and slathered it with honey and ricotta. She poured the iced coffee, tucked her legs under her, and started munching.

'Jill, I know you said you didn't want to talk about it,' her mum began cautiously, 'but I'm worried about you.'

Jill brushed crumbs off her singlet.

'You've lost some weight, hon,' her mother tried again, 'and that usually happens when you're not coping.'

Jill sighed. Opening up about her feelings felt like trying to pry open an oyster shell barehanded, but she'd learned over the years that she usually felt better after she'd spoken to someone.

'It's a case, Mum,' Jill said, putting the toast down onto her plate and picking up her glass of iced coffee. She became aware of her body posture – she had squashed her knees up against her chest and she held the glass like a shield between herself and her mother. She forced herself to uncoil a little. 'It's brought the memories up a bit.'

Her mother took a sip of her drink, waited.

'The case itself is pretty rough,' Jill continued, 'but I don't know . . . it feels like more than that. I feel like something bad's going to happen.'

'Like getting your ribs broken,' said her mother dryly.

'My ribs are okay, Mum. Just a training accident. I told you.' Jill lied again. She stretched her neck from side to side, and looked at the marmalade sky ahead of her. The birds were a concert-hall choir. 'It's just that there are kids involved in the case. You know those jobs are harder for me, but they're also why I joined up.'

'I'm very proud of what you do, Jill, but it's hard on you getting these reminders all the time.'

'I keep getting the nightmare of the girl with the white eyes. It's like she's calling me, or warning me, or something.'

'Have you thought about having a bit more counselling? Who was that woman you saw through work a couple of years ago? You said that really helped.'

Jill gave a wry smile; her mother was suggesting that Mercy Merris help her deal with this case. Jill felt Mercy's help with the case would not be through providing counselling for her.

'You wouldn't believe it, Mum. I've seen that doctor recently, and she looks like she could use more help than me.'

'Oh dear. That's another difficult job,' her mother sighed. 'Good morning, darling,' she called, as little Lily came through the kitchen doorway, rubbing her eyes. 'Looks like the troops are going to start arriving,' she said to Jill. 'We can talk more while we're cooking. I'm so glad you're staying.'

30

WAYNE CRABBE LEFT THE CLUB about 1 a.m. and let himself into his half of the townhouse in Leichhardt. He couldn't wait to spend some time with the files he'd just traded. The boy in the last one looked about six. He slid his hand up the wall to flick on the light switch.

'Fuck.' A frenetic blur in the doorway near him. A punch slammed into his gut. He felt slow, strangely disconnected from everything.

Wayne's hand missed the light switch again as he slipped on something wet on the floor. What the fuck was going on here? Suddenly he was looking up. Someone's shoe filled the right of his peripheral vision. He felt, rather than saw, a person standing over him, everything blurry.

'Let me get up. I'll get money for you,' he said.

Wayne Crabbe screamed for the first time since he was ten when a boot kicked in most of his front teeth. Punches rained down into his body and he curled, like a slug doused in lemon juice.

Fuck, he thought, trying to stand, slipping again in the wet stuff.

'Stop,' he managed around broken teeth, and heard his attacker laughing, or maybe crying.

The blows continued onto his back, neck. He felt the weight behind them, but little pain. He raised a hand limply to try to defend himself, and felt a knife slice through the web of his thumb. When blood rushed up from his stomach and filled his lungs, mouth and nose, it occurred to him that he was being stabbed, not punched.

This wasn't how tonight was supposed to go, he thought, as he drowned in his own blood in the front hall.

31

ON THE TRAIN BACK to the city, Jill felt a growing sense of gloom with every station that flashed by. The weekend had been great, but already the peaceful feeling of the past two days was calcifying in her chest. She'd never felt so conflicted about a case before. Each time she applied her mind to discovering the identity of the killer, she felt guilty. Such an outcome could mean more child molesters left alive. Of course, she had no way of knowing that the murderer would kill again. Maybe all the scores had been settled.

Her eyes roamed the carriage. A huddle of high school kids, speaking in a language all their own, laughed intimately, secure in the belief that they knew more about the real world than the boring adults around them. The girls saw her staring and bent their heads together, whispering. Their giggles split the air. Jill turned her face to the window and thought about what Honey and Mia would have been like at their age. Maybe there'd have been no discernible difference – even kids living in hell could seem confident and happy when with their friends.

She hadn't talked to Honey since the club, and she realised that she kind of missed her. When had that happened? Mixed in with mistrust and wariness was respect for the girl who'd brought herself up through more adversity than most. Jill had also been experiencing a strange perceptual illusion with many people lately, and this had happened with Honey – she found that when she stared into some faces she could see through their adult features as though seeing the face of the child they had once been. It immediately endeared them to her, and it was hard to stay angry with someone after she'd imagined them this way.

What's happening to me? she wondered. Am I getting clucky? She'd been told about the maternal urge that could belt a woman over the head at about her age, and she'd been on the lookout for it for a couple of years. She'd once had a hard-arsed trainer at the police academy who'd been happily married for three years – until she turned thirty-four, and suddenly needed to be pregnant. The trainer had told her husband she wanted to have a baby, and had learned that he'd been growing increasingly disinclined to have children at all. Within twelve months, the woman had divorced and remarried, the intervening year spent like a heat-seeking missile, searching for a mate with whom she could procreate. Jill still saw the woman from time to time when she attended a training course. She had three children now, and was working part-time, fitting her job in around canteen duty.

Jill knew that it was the children involved in this case who kept her compelled to solve it. It was more like two cases really – the dead men could open a door that led to other men like them. She imagined that door opening and spiders teeming out, a roiling black mass of scrabbling predators. She shuddered, the feeling of gloom settling closer around her shoulders, wrapping her head in a blank fog. She consciously slowed her breathing, and deliberately changed her thought patterns, considering her next moves.

There was a lot more she could learn from Honey. It was time to get back in touch. Jill flipped open the cover of her mobile phone and reached into her bag for her palm pilot, containing the names and addresses of all of her contacts.

She felt him before she saw him, and didn't look up. Eight o'clock, or to her left and slightly behind her – she was being watched. The watcher was getting ready to move, and Jill felt a cold thread of adrenalin dart through her veins. She was on her feet before he'd moved. She sized him up. Twenty or so. Thin. Her eyes locked with his and she saw his face register surprise at her movement, and his conviction crumble. He looked down, and she knew he wasn't going to be a problem. She kept her eyes on him a few beats longer to make sure, but he knew she was not the easy road to a mobile phone. He kept his eyes on his shoes; probably made her for a cop. As she stared, his features morphed into those of a five-year-old, and she shook her head. What *was* that?

Although she no longer thought he was a threat, Jill got up and moved anyway. She made her way towards the guard's carriage. They were drawing close to Strathfield now and they'd soon be at Central. She thought about telling the guard about the guy back there, but what could she say? He hadn't done anything. Yet. She was sure someone else would be rolled for their phone before long.

Instead, she stood at the door intending to make a couple of calls. The first to Scotty. She smiled and moved into a corner as his voice boomed out of the speaker.

'J!' he yelled enthusiastically. 'Coming back?'

'Yeah. Hi, Scotty. You at work yet?'

'On my way.'

'Could you pick me up from Central in about ten, fifteen?'

'On my way. Meet you at the House,' he said, using cop speak for the police station. 'Had breakfast?'

'No,' she smiled. It was always about food with Scotty. 'I'll shout you to thank you for picking me up. See you then.'

Jill disconnected and then accessed Honey's number on her palm pilot, but reconsidered calling right now. It's nine o'clock on a Monday morning, she reminded herself. Honey would be asleep and not happy, although it'd serve her right for some of the games she'd played with Jill. Anyway, the train was at Redfern and would be pulling into Central any moment.

She worked her way through a smoothie for breakfast while Scotty downed two bacon and egg rolls and a chocolate milk.

'How's your mum?' he wanted to know.

'Great. It was good to get away. She says hi.'

'What about your ribs?'

'Fine. I'm all right. How was your weekend?'

They made small talk back to Maroubra, and as they pulled into the station, Jill told Scotty about her plan to contact Honey later that morning to set up another meeting.

'We going after Sebastian?' he asked.

'Soon.'

They entered the squad room and Emma Gibson caught them at the door. She slinked around a desk and moved to stand under Scotty's chin.

'Andreessen's looking for you.' She blinked up at him. 'You're always late.'

'Thanks Emma,' he said, turning towards the inspector's office.

'And you're always rushing away,' she pouted.

'But I always take my time when it counts,' he smiled down at her.

'Hmm, something to think about.' Emma gave him a half-smile and sashayed away, throwing Jill a satisfied smirk as she passed.

Jill and Scotty exchanged a look. Without saying a word, her eyes exclaimed, Oh for heaven's sake!; his returned innocently, What?

Inspector Andreessen looked tired, as usual. His shirt was already food-stained, and a button was missing. Other buttons threatened to pop at the waistline. There wasn't a cop in the squad who'd say a word about his shirt to his face.

'Jackson. Hutchinson. I want you over at St Vincent's. Davis is going with you. Davis has the case. I only want you there because there seems to be a tie-in with the case you're working.'

'Another bashing?' Jill asked.

'Davis'll fill you in on the way over,' he said, then bellowed, 'Robinson!' looking over Jill's shoulder, calling out to another detective. That was it then.

Charmaine Davis was one of the youngest cops in New

South Wales history to make detective. Her father was a barrister, her mother a GP. She'd chosen policing, while her siblings were academics or lawyers. She dealt predominantly with sex crimes, working closely with the victims to good effect; over the past year she'd helped successfully convict four serious offenders.

The three of them took a departmental Commodore to travel over to the hospital. Davis drove. She told them about the case as she manoeuvred through the light traffic.

'She's an eleven-year-old girl,' Davis began, and Jill felt her heart sink immediately. 'She was abducted from Bondi Junction shopping centre on Wednesday two weeks ago. She stopped in on her way home from school. CCTV caught the perp leading her away from the shop, almost carrying her. He'd drugged her Coke – slipped it into the can somehow. She was still holding it as he helped her walk. She showed up two days later, Newtown train station, asleep on a bench. No camera vision this time.'

'I heard about this one,' Scotty grunted.

Jill had too. She just listened.

'Anyway, she remembers pretty much nothing about the two days she was away. Bits and pieces. No names or places. She had different underwear on when she was found. She says she thinks she remembers the perp say he was taking her to a party. Rape kit was positive for semen in her vagina and anus. Physically she was otherwise okay . . . except her eyes.'

'Her eyes?' asked Jill.

'She was blinded. Some kind of chemical that fucked with her pupils. The doctors aren't sure what was used. She couldn't see more than light and dark when she first came in, but her vision improved over the next couple of days.'

Scotty swore under his breath. He shook his head, eyes dark. Jill's thoughts shouted in her head; she fought to keep her memories down.

'Anyway,' Davis continued, her eyes on the road, 'she's home now. She and her mum are coming in to the hospital today and I'm going to try to get some more from the girl, see if she's remembered anything else, but I doubt we're gonna get anything. These so-called date-rape drugs really fuck up the memory.'

'So they've got no real hope of getting him, then?' asked Scotty.

'Oh, we know who he is,' Davis answered, indicating right to turn their vehicle into an emergency-services bay at the front of the hospital.

Jill and Scotty stared at her.

'It's your perp from the beach. David Carter. Shopping centre cameras got a perfect shot of his face.'

32

DAVIS HAD ARRANGED TO meet the victim and her mother in an office in the outpatients' department of the hospital. She, Jill and Scotty were perched on classroom-style chairs in the sterile, windowless room. The space was small, and Scotty had had to search the department to scavenge another two chairs for Martha McKenzie and her daughter Madeline. Madeline, the eleven-year-old abduction victim, was having her eyes checked by a nurse in a room nearby.

To distract herself from the airlessness of the room and the fist of dread that had been groping at her stomach since she'd heard the details of this case, Jill focused on the features of her companions. She found that if she used all of her senses to absorb herself in her environment, she could stay out of the basement that was always waiting in her mind.

She started with Charmaine Davis. Mid-heeled black

leather ankle boots. Straight-leg navy pants, cut higher than was fashionable last year – a look her cousin Alyssa would say was 'so right now'. A thin black belt looped through her pants and contrasted with the tailored white shirt, casually open just below the neck. Her dark brown hair fell below her collarbone and feathered around her face. Her cheekbones were high; her make-up shiny and see-through. The distraction exercise, taught to her by Dr Merris, was supposed to move on to the other senses next, describing things she could hear, smell and feel in the room, but a cough from the doorway interrupted her.

Jill hadn't figured on Madeline being so very small. She felt a flare of anger towards a mother who could let a child so young go to a shopping centre alone; then she mentally chastised herself. People had criticised her parents for not being at the swimming carnival from which she had been abducted. The blame should only be directed at the offenders. The men who spent their lives devising methods to exploit any chink in the armour parents tried to build around their kids.

Martha McKenzie, petite and in her mid-thirties, wore a summer skirt, sandals and a well-cut blouse. She looked puffy-eyed and pale. Crying too much and no sleep, thought Jill, remembering her mum's eyes looking that way for a year after she got home. She stared at them in the small room and waited just beyond the doorway, clearly reluctant to enter. Only a sliver of the little girl was visible, as she stood close behind her mother in the entrance. Dark glasses protected Madeline's eyes.

'Hi, Martha. Hi, Maddie. Thanks so much for coming. Please come in.' Charmaine stood, a warm smile lighting up her face, her hands extended, palms up. She touched

Martha's shoulder in welcome, then stepped backwards to give the mother and daughter room, and to introduce Jill and Scotty to them. Jill stood, but Scotty, aware of his size in this room, remained seated. He edged his chair as far back against the wall as he could. He tucked his endless legs behind Jill's chair, and scrunched down in his own.

'How'd the eye check-up go, Martha?' Charmaine asked after she'd presented Scotty and Jill.

Martha took a seat, with Madeline perching on the edge of her chair like a little bird, closest to the door, head down, her foot touching her mother's.

Martha sniffed and Charmaine reached for a tissue box from a sideboard in the room, and placed it close by. 'God only knows,' Martha answered, her tone angry. 'It's hard to find one bloody doctor in here who speaks English.'

Charmaine looked troubled and offered, 'Would you like me to arrange for a nurse to come in and explain things better, Martha?'

'No, don't bother. Apparently her eyesight will be okay. The nurse said she doesn't really need the glasses now, but . . .' She looked down at her daughter, face still pointing at the floor. 'Anyway, maybe tomorrow we'll take them off.'

Madeline said nothing, a sheet of blonde hair hiding even her glasses. She was skinny and brown-limbed, baby hair still on her legs, pink socks, white sneakers. Jill shook her head to shut out the image of an adult male pawing at her drugged body.

'Maddie, have you been back to school yet?' Charmaine asked the little girl, who shook her head.

'The school's been bloody hopeless too,' answered her mother. 'I've asked for someone to drop around some of her work, but they won't do it. They reckon it's best for her to get back there as soon as she can.' She raised a trembling hand to her eyes. 'Don't they know how stressed out I am? They'll be lucky if I let her go back next year. I'm too scared to even leave the house. What if the perverts who took her are watching us?'

Madeline gave a tiny mew and raised her face to stare at her mother. Martha McKenzie groped around for her bag. 'Are we going to be much longer? I've got to have a smoke. My nerves are bloody shot to pieces.'

'I know you don't want to be here, Martha, but I've got one thing I have to ask Maddie to do today.' Charmaine leaned towards the little girl, her voice warm and reassuring. 'Maddie, I know I said we wouldn't have to talk for a while, so I've brought you a present for breaking our deal.'

The dark glasses peeked up. Charmaine held out a small gift bag.

Madeline looked towards her mum, who was still rummaging in her bag. She looked up briefly, 'Come on then, Maddie. What do you say?'

'Thank you.' A whisper.

Earlier, while waiting for Madeline and her mother, Charmaine had shown Jill and Scotty the Polly Pocket toy she had bought for the child. These were tiny little dolls with accessories that Maddie had previously told Charmaine she collected.

No wonder she's so great at getting important details from victims, thought Jill admiringly.

Madeline took a surreptitious look inside the bag. A tiny smile flashed white teeth for just a moment.

'We have a photo we want you to have a look at, honey. I

just want you to see if you know this person,' said Charmaine. 'That's the yucky thing I need you to do today, okay?'

Martha McKenzie's hand went to her throat at Charmaine's words. When the detective pulled an A4 envelope from her briefcase, the woman covered her mouth as if to stop herself screaming.

'Is that him?' Martha's hand shook. She reached out for the envelope, and then pulled back as if it might burn her.

'This is a photograph of a man, and we need to know whether Madeline recognises him from anywhere.' Charmaine's voice was still warm, but also firm.

A violent red flush had spread up Martha's throat and into her cheeks. She stared at the envelope as Charmaine withdrew a large glossy photograph.

Jill and Scotty had checked out the photo while waiting. It was of a fifty-year-old, balding white male, in a cheap suit and tie. He was standing on the steps of the Federal Court, a cigarette in his podgy hand. Police had taken the photo during his last court appearance.

Jill felt uncomfortable when she found herself thinking that she preferred the image of the only other time she'd seen this man, when his head was broken open like a ripe rockmelon on the sand at the beach.

Slowly, Madeline stood. Her face pale, her mouth a thin line, she moved hesitantly towards Charmaine. Her mother reached out towards her, then dropped her arms in her lap, her hands compulsively grasping one another as though to stop them grabbing Madeline and running with her from the room.

Madeline stood before the desk on which Charmaine had placed the photograph face down.

'Now, Maddie, I need to let you know something before

I turn this page over.' Charmaine was seated and her head was on the same level as the little girl's. 'The man in this photograph is now dead.' She paused at the sharp intake of breath that sounded like a sob from Mrs McKenzie. 'So if you recognise this person, you need to know that you will never, ever have to see him again, okay?'

A barely perceptible nod from Madeline.

The little girl reached up and removed the dark glasses. Blinking, she placed them carefully on the table. They made the softest of sounds in the tiny room.

'Good girl. I'm going to turn over the photo now,' said Charmaine.

Jill held her breath.

Charmaine turned the photograph over. Carter's face stared up from the table. For a moment the scene was frozen. When Madeline cried out and dived across the room into her mother's lap, Jill jumped to her feet. Martha enveloped her daughter and the two rocked together as one, as if they were alone in the room, distress emanating from their single silhouette.

33

SCOTTY AND JILL LEFT Madeline and her mother with Charmaine and their grief, and quietly exited the office. They walked silently through the corridors of the hospital. Jill mostly felt numb, but she was also aware of a vague sense of satisfaction that the man who'd caused that chaos was dead. One day that was going to help Madeline recover. She remembered the fear that had chased her everywhere after the police brought her home. She'd believed the men who'd taken her could find her again any time they wanted to. After leaving her naked and still blindfolded on a school oval two suburbs from her house, there'd been no sign of them. If she'd had proof they could never hurt her again, that they were dead, she knew that would have helped.

When the glass doors of the hospital slid open to let them out, Jill blinked in the sunlight. She rubbed at her arms with her hands, chilled by the refrigeration of the hospital, and wrinkled her nose at the cigarette smoke that hung in a cloud around the entryway. Patients in pyjamas and gowns, leading their drips and monitoring machines like pet dogs, sucked in lungfuls of smoke while they chatted to each other and their visitors.

Scotty strode towards the road in front of the hospital. Jill had to jog to keep up.

'We're going to see Sebastian.' Scotty's face was closed. He stared into the distance. 'If there is some sort of club for these arseholes, we're taking it down.'

Jill sighed. She'd seen her partner in this mood before. If she didn't work with him, he'd charge in there on his own.

'We'll need a plan,' Jill said. 'They're not just going to admit they all hang out together.' They crossed the road and began walking through the park opposite. Jill negotiated around a homeless man lying face up in the 11 a.m. heat, his bottle already empty beside him. She was going to stop to make sure he was alive, when he grunted and opened his eyes. He mumbled something about the ozone layer, staggered to his feet and began to shuffle over to the shade of a tree.

'Surveillance, then. Let's at least go have a look at where this prick lives. Check this club out. And I want to talk to him. Shake him up a bit.' Scotty was in full stride, his features set.

Jill assumed they were heading for the bus stop at Taylor Square. They'd left the car with Charmaine Davis and would need to use public transport to get back to Maroubra.

'All right, we'll check out his place, Scott,' said Jill. She hoped to stall before they actually spoke to Sebastian. He'd just shut up shop if they were too inquisitive.

Jill took two steps for every one of Scotty's. The sun felt good on her shoulders after the chill of the hospital. They were approaching The Wall, a sandstone barricade that was formerly the outside wall of an old gaol.

The Wall ran along Darlinghurst Road, and was a well-known strip for child prostitutes. Jill remembered a time when up to twenty young boys would hang here, blatantly soliciting, waiting for one of the steady stream of vehicles to slow down and pick them up. There was often a raucous atmosphere – sometimes there'd be a brawl that spilled into the traffic, over a client, a patch of turf. It only helped to draw the crowds; many, visitors from the suburbs with their car doors locked and windows up, were just out for a look at the seamy side of life. There was always at least one boy leaning into the driver's window of a car with dark windows. Nowadays the show was over, police routinely busting the kids, and sometimes the men who preyed on them. Most times of the day and night, however, if you waited long enough, you'd see a boy dart out from the park and hop into a car, or notice that there was a disproportionate amount of youth hanging around the mobile needle exchange or food van that was often stationed at The Wall.

A van stood there now, distributing sandwiches and cups of tea and water to the homeless and poor that lived in this area. Jill followed Scotty as he walked straight up to the van.

'Detective Scott Hutchinson,' said Scotty to the middle-aged man and woman in white T-shirts handing out the food and drink. 'We're investigating a paedophile network, and we're wondering whether you see many people around here taking young boys into their cars.'

'You're kidding, right?' the woman said flatly, continuing

to distribute her styrofoam cups. 'You know this is The Wall, don't ya?'

'There's no need to be sarcastic, Beryl,' the man next to her said, stopping his work for a moment and staring down from the van. 'Yes, son, unfortunately there are still many cars stopping regularly for the kids around here.'

'Same cars all the time. We take the plates and call you guys, but we see 'em here again the next week. Bloody perverts.'

'We don't know about a network, but there does seem to be a regular group that comes around . . .'

'There ya go. Do some good right now if ya want.' The woman interrupted her partner. 'That bastard's here all the time.' Beryl was pointing at a dark, late-model Range Rover that had pulled over about a hundred metres from where they stood.

Scotty was in full flight before Jill had even turned. She had started to run after him when the big car screeched away from the gutter, leaving Scotty standing in the street staring after it. He was writing in his notebook as she reached him.

'Well, I know what I'm doing this afternoon. Gonna hunt down that squirrel and then do some work looking into who this Sebastian is, where he lives and what he eats for fucking breakfast.'

'I'll go and see Honey again, then.' Jill could see Scotty was on a mission and wouldn't need passengers.

Ninety minutes later, Jill sat in a coffee shop in Surry Hills waiting for Honey. She'd ordered a coffee, but it had grown cold in front of her. Her head already buzzed, and she didn't need any more of a rush.

To try to block out thoughts of little Madeline and her mum, she paid attention to the patrons with whom she shared the café. Although it was now 2 p.m., she knew that many of these people were eating breakfast. This suburb caught up an eclectic mix of university students, artists and clothes designers, young professionals, and the unemployed from the numerous housing commission high-rises. A scowling gay couple periodically spat a few words across the table at each other and then studiously ignored one another; a dreadlocked girl in a multi-coloured caftan yawned over a herbal tea, while her multi-pierced companion munched muesli. A woman in a serious suit and heels clattered away on a laptop; while at the next table a scrawny blond man was on the heroin-nod over bacon and eggs. The disgruntled waitress nudged him awake with her hip as she walked past carrying empty coffee cups.

The waitress had fixed Jill with a stare a couple of times before Honey finally breezed in. Wearing pelvis-skimming denim shorts, midriff-baring white halter top, over-sized white-framed sunglasses and gold gladiator sandals laced halfway up her calves, she woke everybody up. Used to making an entrance everywhere she went, Honey gave Jill affected air kisses, bending forward and giving half the café a view to remember. Jill heard the gay couple, united at last in whispered theatrical mortification.

'Hi, Honey.' Jill was pleased to see her, happy to be distracted.

'What are we eating, sweetie? I'm starving.'

'Order whatever you like.' Jill knew by now that Honey enjoyed being spoiled, and today she felt content to indulge her. Honey ordered eggs Benedict with toast, mushrooms, coffee and a blended fruit juice. Jill ordered bottled water and a smoked salmon and avocado sandwich on wholegrain bread. No butter.

When the waitress bustled away, leaving their table covered in food and drink, Jill pulled a cloth carry bag from under the table.

'Your clothes,' she said. 'Thanks for lending them to me.'

'Oh, no problem, sweetie, any time. You should wear stuff like this more often. You were hot!' Honey put the bag down beside her. 'What happened to you when the alarm went off, anyway?'

'Just called it a night,' said Jill. 'I couldn't see you, but I figured you weren't ready to go home.'

'Are you kidding? I didn't get home until Thursday night.'

Jill gave a short laugh, and then got down to business.

'So, Honey, remember you said that Sebastian had a youth drop-in centre in the Cross? You said he used it for recruits.' This time she wanted to make sure she and Honey were talking about exactly the same thing before they went anywhere.

'Yeah, so?' Honey's sunglasses perched on top of her head, holding her long black hair off her face. She was making short work of her breakfast, seemingly oblivious to the stares of every male that walked past. The front wall of the café folded back while trading to allow it to be part of the street.

'Well, I want you to take me there.'

'He's hardly ever there, but whatever. It's not like it's some secret place. It's been there since I was a kid. Charities even use it to try to get the kids off the streets.'

'So it's like an amusement centre?'

'Yeah, you know, some pool tables, a few computer games. There's a half basketball court, a room to do art and craft and shit.'

'And Sebastian set this up?'

'There's always plenty of kids there. It was a great place to go. And close to everything.'

'Well it's in Kings Cross, so it's not really close to anything a kid should be close to,' Jill commented.

'But the kids who go there are going to be around the streets anyway, so it's a safe place to hang out.'

Jill stared at her. 'Honey, there's something I don't under-stand about you.' Jill kept her voice quiet and careful, but she felt exasperated. 'You told me that Sebastian runs this place to recruit children. I assume you mean recruit them for sex. You told me that man started you in child prostitution and got you addicted to heroin. And you just called a place that this man runs *safe*.'

Honey glared at her for a moment, then slipped her glasses back down over her eyes.

'You wouldn't understand,' she said. 'When you're on the streets, a place with a roof is usually a safe place. At the centre you don't even have to give a blow job to stay warm.' She stabbed at her eggs. 'You just don't get it. Sebastian is an arsehole, but he gives those kids stuff as well. Not everyone who goes there gets molested, you know.' She pushed her plate away, folded her arms. 'I'm done here. To be honest, I've got other things to do today.' She looked out to the street.

Jill reached across the table, and then pulled her hands back, remembering Honey didn't like to be touched. 'Come on, Honey. I'm just frustrated, that's all. Don't shut down on me. I'll get you an ice-cream at the Cross.'

Honey was silent for a few moments, then she spoke, still looking at her plate.

'Yeah, well, whatever. I guess I can come.'

She grabbed her juice and stood, and Jill went to pay. The male couple now held hands across the table.

Jill parked her car out the front of a prestige car dealership; she and Honey passed the front of the sleek showroom selling fat Mercedes and walked straight into hell. The drop-in centre was a block from the Matthew Talbot Hostel, a refuge for homeless male alcoholics, and today the afternoon sun bore down pitilessly on close to fifty men lying in the street that led up to the hostel.

'We don't have to go up that street, do we?' Jill asked Honey.

'Nah, it's the next one up.'

They walked past a man in a singlet and shorts who was asleep in the gutter. The cheek exposed to the sun was the colour of a cooked, wet lobster.

The drop-in centre was not what Jill had expected. A two-storey terrace house in a mostly residential street, there was no sign out the front indicating the function of the building. Honey walked up the two front steps and went straight in, Jill following close behind. The front room was dark compared to the white heat bouncing off the pavement outside. Jill blinked as her eyes adjusted.

Three Aboriginal children scribbled with textas on a large canvas. A rack containing pamphlets stood in the corner; the only other furniture a couple of lounge chairs and a desk. There were no adults in sight. The kids did no more than glance at them before going back to their colouring. Jill and

Honey walked through to the next room. A kitchen. Large jars of coffee and sugar, a big refrigerator, a bowl of apples. No-one in there.

In a small courtyard off the kitchen, two teenage boys smoked cigarettes. They blew out insolence with their smoke. Jill thought she'd at least try to talk to them.

'You guys know Mr Sebastian?'

The oldest boy looked her up and down and whispered something to his mate. They both laughed.

'I asked you a question.' Jill felt hot and tired.

The boys sniggered again, and she had a sudden image of herself slapping the spotty face of the closest boy. She walked back into the kitchen. Honey had the fridge open and was poking around inside. Jill saw loaves of bread, margarine, a catering-sized jar of Vegemite.

'I'm going upstairs,' Jill said, walking from the kitchen.

The muted music of a computer game led her up the stairs. She walked into one of three rooms off the first-floor landing, following the sound. A dark-haired boy who looked about twelve sat on a dirty, pink fabric-covered couch. His eyes were locked on a TV screen, his hands on a game control panel. She sat next to him, watched the game.

'These guys are the worst.'

Jill was surprised to hear him speak.

'They come at you so fast.'

'Shit! Look out for that one,' she warned him.

The muscleman controlled by the boy blasted the flesh-eating zombie just in time. Green brains splattered from its skull; grey limbs flew into the air. Moments later, another zombie shot the muscleman in the head and the boy turned to face her.

'I'm Jill,' she told him.

'Jack.'

'Ha. Jack and Jill.'

A white smile split his brown face, and the sun came out in the small room.

'Jack, I'm a police officer.' She decided to be honest. These kids all knew anyway. They always said it was the shoes cops wore, but Jill felt street kids developed senses others didn't, survival skills, honed living in the urban jungle.

'Got a gun?' They always wanted to know.

She lifted the short jacket she wore over her T-shirt, showed him her revolver.

'Cool. Can I touch it?'

That was always the next question; either that or, 'Have you ever shot anyone?' His brown eyes were young and old.

'Not today.' The answer would do for both questions.

'You lookin' for Jamaal?'

The air was very still in the room; dust motes danced in a sunbeam near the window. A pulse beat in her neck.

'Why would you think that, Jack?'

''Cause you should be.' He put his chin on his chest, fiddled with the joystick.

'You know what? I am looking for Jamaal. Does he come around here much?'

Jack shrugged.

'How do you know him?'

'He told me about this place.'

'Has Jamaal ever hurt you, Jack?'

Eyes down. Nothing.

'Why should we be looking for him?'

'You should know why.'

199

'Could you come to where I work and tell me more about him?'

'You're crazy.'

She looked up when the light altered in the doorway.

'Hello. May I help you?' came a sharp female voice.

Jill stood. The woman looked about thirty-five maybe, hippie clothing, closed face, no smile.

'Sergeant Jillian Jackson.' Jill held out her hand.

'Do you have an appointment with someone here?' The woman ignored her hand, didn't offer her name.

'Do I need one?'

'Well, adults are not encouraged to drop by unannounced,' said the woman. 'Are you all right, Jack?'

The boy said nothing. Jill asked, 'What about Jamaal Mahmoud? Alejandro Sebastian? Do they drop by unannounced?'

The woman paused a few beats. Looked at a point over Jill's shoulder, then fixed her eyes back on her face.

'I'm afraid I'm the wrong person for you to speak to. If you'll come to the office next door I'll give you my supervisor's card.'

'Simple question, though, really – do those men drop by? What role do they have here at the centre?'

Jack stared at the woman, also waiting for her answer.

'Yes, as I said, Ms Jackson, my supervisor's best placed to answer any questions about the centre. If you'll just follow me?'

'It's *Sergeant* Jackson, actually, and yes I will take that name.'

The woman turned and lead the way out of the room. Jill lingered behind and slipped her work card into Jack's hand.

'Call me any time, about anything. If I'm not there, leave a message and I'll call you the next day. I promise. I'll be back here, Jack, but if you need help, call me.'

When the woman made an officious noise in the hallway outside the door, Jill left the room and followed the wide, bright-orange skirt in front of her.

34

SOMEHOW, MERCY SEEMED to have cut almost everything else from her life. She'd arrive home from the hospital and ignore the flashing light on her answerphone. The birds on her balcony would call for her attention, but now there were fewer than there used to be; she hadn't bothered to fill their water and feeder for weeks. They'd covered the deck with shit in protest. She'd go straight to the fridge and eat standing there, whatever was in front of her. Cold. Sometimes she'd make her way into the lounge room and take off her shoes, head for the bar, but, more often than not, she'd instead just grab her keys again and head out.

She knew it was a compulsion now. She couldn't rest at night unless she'd been to one of their houses. The feeling of impotence that had been growing like a parasite inside her for years was diminishing. She could reach out and hurt them any time she wanted. The hunters became the hunted.

When she'd left work she hadn't even bothered to go home. She'd brought everything she would need when she left the house that morning.

She pulled into a big all-hours convenience store and bought a jumbo bag of cheese Twisties, some chocolate and Coke. Sometimes she had to wait a few hours before they got home. A queue had formed in the service station. A sign pronounced a record lottery draw this week; the people ahead of her were all stocking up on tickets. Their motivation seemed alien to her.

Looking at two women about her age in the queue ahead of her, she wondered suddenly how the hell it had come to this. How had she ever become so lost? She thought again about going to the police, but images of what had happened to kids, to her, what was happening to someone right now, interrupted her thoughts again. Asleep or awake, her mind was filled with little else.

Last time she'd tried to have dinner with friends it had been a disaster. As soon as their kids were in bed, she'd started in on her second bottle of red and her stories of horror. Trying to tell her friends, to convince them, that their children weren't safe, to teach them what to watch out for, how often to check their kids' rooms for evidence that someone was grooming them for abuse: she wanted to keep them vigilant. When they'd tried to change the subject, she'd become belligerent, loud, unconcerned if the children awoke – they should be hearing this too. When she broke down in mortified but unstoppable sobs, they'd driven her home, and had not called since. Not that she blamed them, and not that she cared, frankly. People didn't understand, and there were other things she needed to do.

Throwing a bulging bag into her passenger seat, Mercy got back into her car, lit a cigarette and drove with purpose into the deepening evening.

35

THE BITE IN THE pre-dawn breeze stung Jill's ears and woke her fully. The chill told her that summer was nearing its end. Dressed in white shorts and a singlet, her bikini underneath, she realised she'd need a tracksuit for her morning runs soon.

The change from summer to autumn always filled Jill with melancholy. For her, spring and summer represented youth, childhood. Autumn was about endings, the loss of innocence. And, of course, it was the precursor to winter; it was the beginning of winter when she'd been kidnapped. Those three months were the longest of the year, every year, for Jill.

She jogged down the steps of her apartment block and out into the quiet, dark streets of Maroubra. She had been restless last night, thinking about little Jack at the drop-in centre. She hoped he'd call.

She shivered as she crossed the street and lifted her pace, trying to warm up. But the coldness was inside; her mood matched the gunmetal-grey ocean, the surf roiling and messy this morning.

The beach was deserted. Even the gulls weren't playing. There were no surfers; she was alone. Familiar feelings of despair and apprehension rose up inside her with the isolation, and she caught them in her throat before they forced out a sob. She dropped her towel on the sand in her regular spot, put her head down, and ran.

For the first time in a long time, she thought about Joel. Maybe she should get in touch. She smiled wryly, realising she'd just slipped into the same pattern she did every year – when the weather got colder, she got lonely, and for two years in a row she'd spent winters casually dating Joel, only to feel stifled and resentful by summer. It's not fair to do that to him again, she thought.

Each footfall on the hard sand sent some pain through the area around her healing ribs. She tuned it out. Gotta get back to it sometime, she thought; I'll go mad without running. She reached the end of the lap and turned to make her way back to the other end of the beach. Spray from the turbulent surf blew into her eyes, and she wiped her face with her hands. As her vision cleared, she thought she saw someone else on the beach. There. She didn't break stride, continued running back the way she'd come. The hooded figure ran back from the edge of the ocean towards the street. That's weird, she thought, he can't have been down here more than five minutes. Must be too cold for him.

As she approached the place where she'd left her towel, Jill realised that this person, the only other person on the beach this morning, had also picked this very spot to stop. From three long strides away, she could see her towel was disturbed. She always left it folded tightly. She looked up towards the road to try to spot the runner, but it was still grey and misty and she couldn't see anyone. She thought about stopping, but figured that it had probably been a vagrant hoping she'd left her wallet under her towel.

'Been living at the beach too long to do that, dickhead,' she muttered under her breath and kept running.

Jill ran laps until the sun grudgingly rose in the east over the ocean, but the day stayed dull, and there were still few people on the sand when she finally stood dripping over her towel.

'What the fuck?' she said aloud, looking down at the edges of a manila folder protruding from underneath her towel. She stood there a few moments longer, just staring at the folder, and then looked up and down the beach.

A chubby female newsreader who lived a few blocks up from Jill was sparring with a personal trainer, throwing half-arsed punches at his gloves. There were a couple of board riders out beyond the chop, just sitting there, hoping. A middle-aged couple drank takeaway coffee silently, looking out to sea. A dog barked like a mad thing, chasing pigeons and waves, while his owner stood watching, lead in hand. That was about it this morning.

No-one was anywhere near her towel.

She bent and picked the towel up, leaving the envelope there. She hugged the towel to her body, drying her face, starting to shiver. What the hell was in there?

She wanted to delay the moment when she looked inside. She absolutely hated surprises. She scooped up the folder, flicking it to remove the sand that had settled on top. She walked back towards her unit.

The folder had broken her routine. She didn't stop for the paper, and as she ran up the stairs her nerves jagged. She pulled her key from the small pocket in her shorts, and let herself into her apartment.

She threw the folder onto her breakfast bar and stared at it balefully. She wanted to open it now, but felt she needed her routines more than ever at the moment. It was a shower first, coffee, the newspaper on the balcony. The folder would be her paper this morning. She stripped, and walked naked into her black granite bathroom.

Twenty minutes later, coffee in hand, and dressed in black combat pants and a fitted navy shirt, her blonde hair pulled into a tight ponytail, Jill was ready to check out the folder, and she carried it out to the balcony. Suddenly in a hurry, she didn't bother to sit. She dropped the folder onto her outdoor table and flipped open the cover. A photograph, blown up to A4 size, lay before her, but it took a while to understand what it depicted, her brain not at first recognising the tangle of colours and shapes.

When she realised what she was looking at, Jill's coffee cup slipped from her fingers and crashed to the terracotta tiles of her balcony.

The photo showed, close-up, a face so pulverised that its features were almost unrecognisable. One half of the head was caved in completely, so that most of the mouth was lost in a black, red and white gaping hole. One of the eyes was missing; the other was just visible through the blood. It looked like there was a tooth or bone fragment stuck in the blood above the eye. The blood looked wet. Whoever had taken this photo had been there when this violence was inflicted. Jill knew it.

She dropped into a chair and put her head between her knees. The action caused her to notice the spilled coffee seeping into the porous terracotta, and this revived her a little. She went inside to her kitchen and grabbed a sponge and cold water, and came back outside to clean up the mess.

The photo image had seared into her retinas, though, and as she cleaned, she scanned it mentally. Even with that much damage, she knew it was a male. She wondered when it had been taken. And why it was given to her? Was this a warning or a clue? Was it a sick joke? She thought of the crude penis inked onto her locker and knew it could be a prank by another cop – a photo of an accident victim maybe. It could be Elvis-style humour.

Regardless, she had things to do today. She couldn't let this rattle her. She closed the cover of the folder and walked back inside her unit, sliding shut both glass doors as she did so. The sun struggled through the mist outside now, and light washed into the orderliness of her living space, which was in sharp contrast to the mess that still floated in her field of vision. She blinked it away and clicked her TV on, listening to the morning news program as she made herself some toast and Vegemite. She fixed a fresh cup of coffee and took it, black, into her living room, curling up on one of her sofas to eat her breakfast.

The giggling of the announcers on the morning program always annoyed her. She didn't mind the human interest stories and sports reviews that filled the spaces between the half-hourly news broadcasts, but she had no patience for the self-indulgent prattle of the presenters, giving their opinion on every topic. She was relieved to see the 7 a.m. broadcast was about to start.

'Police are today considering the establishment of a special taskforce to investigate a series of brutal deaths that have taken place in Sydney, following the discovery of the fatal stabbing of a man in Leichhardt. The victim has been identified as Wayne Crabbe, a 43-year-old single man, whose body was discovered by neighbours late yesterday afternoon. Mr Horace Green and his wife, Ida, made the gruesome discovery when they went to investigate a terrible smell in the unit next door.'

Jill watched, transfixed, as an elderly man spoke directly at the camera, his arm around his pale and teary wife.

'Haven't seen anything like that since Vietnam. This country is going to hell. If it's not the Triads, it's the Middle Eastern gangs. We're not safe here any more, I tell you. My wife and I have lived on this road for thirty-seven years, but we won't be staying. Australians are going to have to bear arms in their own houses if police don't take back the streets.'

The attractive female broadcaster, serious now, nodding her head to punctuate her remarks, went on to say that the victim's face was so badly beaten that he was unrecognisable and he had been identified by his fingerprints.

For once Jill didn't heed the toast crumbs falling from her shirt when she stood. Another victim, bashed beyond recognition, most likely with a criminal sheet, given that he'd been identified by fingerprint analysis. Jill was ready to bet she knew what this man had been arrested for in the past, and she figured she also knew what had so shaken the elderly couple who'd discovered him.

She grabbed her keys, bag and the folder, and headed out the door.

36

'SO WHAT'D YOU GET?'

Jill and Scotty sat at their desks, murder book out. Scotty wiped egg from a breakfast McMuffin from the side of his mouth.

'You first,' Jill replied.

'The Range Rover at The Wall belongs to Graham Rivers, a fifty-eight-year-old architect from Lane Cove. Divorced. Lives alone. Was picked up at The Wall a year ago by the guys at the Cross. He had a boy in the car, but they both claimed he was getting directions. They charged him anyway, but his barrister got it thrown out of court. No conviction recorded. I'm going to his workplace after lunch to ruin his day. He works at Milsons Point, on the harbour. It's nice out; wanna come?'

'Pass. What'd you get on Sebastian?'

'Well, he inherited his wealth. His father grew a huge transport firm from nothing, and his mother's parents made millions in retail. He lives in a penthouse in the Rocks, but he's got residential property in Auburn, Parramatta and West-mead. The family mansion overlooks the harbour in Hunters Hill, and he owns eight shopping centres in the Western Suburbs and Queensland. Far as I can tell, he has someone manage his transport company, although he's scaled it down a lot since his father died in the early nineties. His mother's in a nursing home on the North Shore. He's never married, no kids that we know about.'

'Thank God.'

'Mmm. Hasn't stopped him helping himself to other people's, though, has it?'

'Has he got a sheet?'

'Juvenile only. Must've been a real blessing to his parents. Their only child. At age twelve, he got done for cruelty to animals. Tortured six swans to death in Centennial Park. There was evidence they'd been sexually assaulted. Sick fuck. It was in the papers for a week. Locals wanted the offender gaoled, but his parents got it all covered up and sent him to a boarding school in Bowral. After that, there were other charges, but his parents stopped every conviction. Unlimited money for lawyers. They couldn't keep him in schools though. The parents of the other kids united to have him kicked out of three schools. There was a big lawsuit settled following the sexual torture of two juniors at a school in Bathurst.'

'That kind of violence from someone so young . . . No adult relationships . . . A paedophile . . .' Jill stared down at Scotty's notes. 'We've gotta take this guy off the streets, Scott.

His pattern fits that of a true psychopath. Not the impulsive, antisocial dickheads we deal with every day in here, but a calculating sadist. He's got to be regularly finding a way to meet the urges he's had since he was a kid.'

'Well, put me in, coach. You know I'm ready to go see this guy whenever you are.'

'I know, Scott, but first it's my turn to tell you what I've been doing.' Jill rubbed at the aching muscles in her neck. 'I've been out to the drop-in centre in Wooloomooloo. Don't worry, he wasn't there,' she said when she noticed the look on Scotty's face. 'I knew he wouldn't be. Just wanted to check it out. Turns out Jamaal Mahmoud's been a visitor.'

'He's linked to Sebastian a lot, huh? We should find him this afternoon.'

'But you've got to see this too.' She reached down into her bag and pulled out the manila folder she'd found under her towel.

'Shit, Jackson, do you know what this is?' Scotty stared down at the mess in the photo.

'Yep. Been into Andreessen's office already. I haven't shown him the photo yet though. I just wanted to see if this was the same guy they found in Leichhardt yesterday.'

'Well it is, and they're talking about setting up a taskforce, Jill. We gotta go in with what we know about these deaths. Harris and Jardine look like they're going to head up a squad to investigate all three murders.'

'Four. And Andreessen told me this morning. I was just waiting till you got in before we went in there and told him together.'

'Chickenshit,' said Scotty, but Jill knew he'd have been pissed if she'd made the move without him.

They gathered up their paperwork and walked over to their boss's office. His door was open and he was sitting down with someone.

Great, thought Jill, peering in around Scotty. Elvis.

Scotty turned to talk to her, intending to wait until Andreessen was free, but the inspector saw them waiting and motioned them in.

'Hutchinson, Jackson. You're needed at a sit-down at Central at 1 p.m. Your case – Carter – is being wrapped up in a taskforce with some other cases. The civilians are shitting about these recent bashings.'

'Yeah, well, we wanted to see you about that, sir,' Jill said, looking pointedly at Elvis and then back at Andreessen.

'Well, fire away. Calabrese here is going with you to the lunch meeting. Looks like he'll being taking the Carter case off your hands and working on it with two boys from Central.'

Jill moaned, barely audibly. Scotty shot her a warning look.

'The thing is, boss,' he began, 'we've been working on a suspected connection between the three deaths for a few days now.'

'And we've evidence in the death of the fourth man, the one found yesterday,' said Jill.

'And you were going to tell me about this when?' A blotchy red flush suffused Andreessen's neck. Jill flinched.

'It's really only just come together this morning, boss. That's what we're doing here,' said Scotty.

'Well get your arses to Central at lunchtime. I'll talk to Beaumont over there and get you on this taskforce.'

'Great,' said Scotty, not even trying to sound like he meant it. He and Jill left the room.

*

I wonder if they actually tried to make this place look depressing, thought Jill as she looked around the private conference room at Central police station. She tried to get comfortable in the fabric-covered chair, but when she touched the seat, her hand came up slightly wet and sticky.

She and Scotty were on one side of a pockmarked board-room table. Elvis, Richard Harris and John Jardine were on the other. A couple of soggy sandwiches slowly curled in the centre of the table. Only Scotty was eating, but he still managed to scowl at the men they would have to work with for at least the next few weeks.

Inspector Beaumont had just left the room, leaving them now the official team investigating these cases. He'd told them they had access to uniformeds when they needed them, and he was also arranging to hook them up with some detectives from Adelaide who had experience in mass homicide.

Jardine got up and went to the electronic whiteboard that had been wheeled into the room when they arrived. He wrote the names of the deceased across the top of the board.

'Might as well get on with this, then,' he said, turning back to the group. 'Jackson, Hutchinson, could you tell us what you've got on each of these guys? I know you gave us a run-down on your connection theory last time you came out to see us, but we should hear everything you've got and collate it.'

'Why don't you tell us what you've found out about Rocla and Manzi first,' Scotty suggested. 'That way, Jill and I will have a complete picture and can tell you more about all of them.'

'Because he's the taskforce leader, fuck-stick,' interrupted Elvis, smiling coldly.

'How did you get your fat arse onto this case anyway, Calabrese?' Scotty's fists clenched under the table. 'There're no drugs to rip off. What do you want to work it for?'

'You think I want you on this squad, Hutchinson? At least I didn't have to suck the boss's dick to get myself over here.'

Jill could see Scotty poised to launch himself across the table. She spoke loudly.

'We're ready to go with what we've got, Jardine, if you want to start writing. I know none of us wants a pissing contest keeping us here any longer than we have to be.'

Over the next couple of hours, the small group put together all the information they had about the cases. They started with the body found in Leichhardt. When Jill brought the photo out of the folder, she felt the tension in the room ratchet up a notch.

'Where'd you get this, Jackson?' asked Harris.

She explained her run on the beach that morning – was it really only that morning? The group agreed that the photo was far fresher than the crime scene shots they had pinned to a murder wall next to the whiteboard, and Jardine asked whether Jill thought the killer had left her the photo, and if so, why.

'I've got no idea. None,' she said thoughtfully. 'It's not necessarily the killer who took the photo, though.' Jill didn't want to believe that the hooded figure on the beach with her had been responsible for the carnage in the photographs around her. 'We could have a witness out there.'

'If it was a witness, they must have shut the door and left Crabbe's body there to sweat, because he couldn't be seen from the street, and this photo wasn't taken through a window,' said Harris, looking with Scotty down at the mess in the photograph.

'One of the neighbours? Maybe the bloke who called it in?' Scotty took a bite of an egg-salad sandwich. The filling looked grey.

Jardine wrote this possibility up under Crabbe's name on the board.

'But why you, Jackson? How'd someone know to deliver this to you?' asked Jardine, turning around with the pen in his hand.

'Maybe it's someone we've talked to about Carter's case – maybe they know the deaths are connected, and wanted me to know too,' said Jill.

'So we should go through the people you've interviewed about Carter,' said Harris. 'Look at each one for possible links to the victims.'

Jardine listed this on the board.

'You can put Alejandro Sebastian up there as first port of call,' said Scotty.

'While we're on that, can you take us through everything you've got on him?' said Jardine.

Scotty filled the group in on what they knew, with Jill contributing a few key points. They outlined Sebastian's background, his demographics, and their belief that he ran a paedophile ring, with the hypothesis that each of the dead men was a former member.

'Why is he a suspect in the killings?' Harris asked. 'Why would this Sebastian want to kill his own group members?'

Jill frowned. She'd wondered the same thing. 'Could be that these guys weren't careful enough? Maybe they talked too much, were attracting too much attention? Maybe they owed him money?'

The group continued to pore through the evidence related

to each death and when Jardine's tightly written script had used all the space, he pressed the print button on the white-board, wiped it clean and started again. A PA would type the notes up properly later. As they collated the evidence, Jill learned that a men's size-eight footprint had been found at the homicide sites of both Carter and Crabbe. One salvage-able footprint was in the sand next to Carter's body, and in the blood just inside the doorway of Crabbe's house, a similar-sized footprint was clearly visible. There were no unidentified fingerprints at the first three murder sites. Smooth, uniform smears in the blood indicated that the killer had worn gloves, most likely disposable latex.

'There was a lot of blood at each crime scene,' said Jill. 'The killer had to clean that off themself somehow. We should get some uniformeds to go round to the servos and hotels in each area, see whether any of them found blood in their bath-rooms, or noticed anyone coming in covered in blood.'

'Worth a shot,' said Jardine, writing it up, as Elvis snorted.

Elvis next suggested that they stake out Crabbe's funeral.

'We'll need to get a photo of everyone that attends,' he said, 'Then meet with one of Crabbe's relatives, and try to identify the people who showed up. Could be our killer will come to say goodbye.'

'Good thinking,' Jill liked the idea, 'and some other mem-bers of Sebastian's paedophile ring might show up as well.'

'We're working a homicide case here, Jackson,' Elvis's voice was caustic.

'Yeah, I've caught up with that, thanks, Calabrese,' her voice just as hard.

'Really? Seems to me you've spent a lot more time looking

for this supposed rockspider group than you have on your own case. Maybe you'd have got somewhere by now if you weren't off trying to save the world again.'

'What's wrong, Elvis – you're not involved in this crime ring as well, are you?'

Jill knew she'd gone too far. Problem was, his words had cut deeply because she knew there was some truth to them – she hadn't been trying as hard as she could to catch Carter's killer. Calabrese rose to his feet on the other side of the table, and she quickly apologised.

'Look, I'm sorry. I didn't mean that,' she said.

Opposite him, Scotty stood as well; the men leaning forward, eyeballing one another. She stayed seated, ignoring the venom radiating from the man across the desk.

'Look, I said I'm sorry. It was a stupid remark. There's not a lot left to do here today, so if we could just keep our shit together for a bit longer.'

'Sit down, Hutchinson, Eddie.' Jardine's voice was authoritative. 'We're nearly done here.'

Harris watched the confrontation with a look of amusement. Elvis finally sat, face like a hatchet.

'We need to re-interview the man in the car with Manzi when he was killed,' Jardine continued. 'What was his name, Harris?'

'Jamaal Mahmoud,' Jill answered instead, all ears again.

'Yeah,' said Jardine, 'that's him. He told Harris that he didn't see who hit him. Said he was getting out of the car when he was hit from behind and reckons he must've fallen back in. Problem is, forensics say the blood pattern from the wound at the back of his head doesn't match his story.'

'We're wondering why he would lie,' said Harris.

Jill decided it was time to bring Honey into the picture.

'Mahmoud is a long-term associate of Sebastian. An employee, as far as we can determine. Their connection extends back at least a decade, probably longer.'

Jill then told the group Honey's story, adding that she'd also seen Sebastian visiting Jamaal in hospital after the attack.

'Don't you think you could have told us that earlier?' Harris said.

'Jamaal hadn't come up yet. I was going to.' Her tone was defensive. Truth was, she felt protective of Honey and did not want these men interrogating her.

The meeting wound down soon after, with Jardine setting a preliminary division of jobs for each member of the taskforce.

As she walked from the room with her partner, Jill could feel Elvis's eyes burning into her back.

Mercy willed her eyes to stay open, but her lids prickled and took longer to re-open following each blink. She gazed, dry-eyed and unfocused, at her 4 p.m. patient, Lynette Balaqua. Lynette cried quietly as she spoke again about the breakdown of her marriage.

'I really think you should be getting some more sleep, Dr Merris.' Her patient sounded offended. Mercy was shocked to find herself opening her eyes.

'I'm so sorry, Lyn. I haven't been well. I'm really very sorry. I've never done that before.'

Mercy saw her disgruntled patient from her room and sat back in her recliner. She looked around the office. This was all meaningless. She stood and made her way to her desk, gathered up her handbag and keys.

She turned at the sound of a polite rap on the door.

'Mercy, a word?'

Noah. She forced a smile to her lips.

'Actually, Noah, I find myself unwell, and have decided to leave for the day.'

'You haven't been well for a while, Mercy. It's being noticed around here, and I'm beginning to worry.'

'Well you needn't, Noah.' She dropped the smile, and made her way towards the door. 'I'm taking some time off. I won't be in again this month.'

'But what about our work, our sessions?'

'I'm stopping for a while. I said I'm sick.'

She tried to get past him to leave. He moved slightly, blocking more of the door.

'Have you told anyone?'

'I'll call Carole when I get home. Now please, Noah. I will be fine, but I really would like to go home now.'

'I'll drive you, you're not well.'

'Really, I will be fine with some more sleep. I insist you let me out of my room please.' Her voice carried now.

Dr Noah Griffen stood back, surprised, and watched his protégé walk down the hall.

He was still standing there five minutes later when a cleaning woman walked past.

'All right there, Dr Griffen?' she asked him, smiling.

'Yes, yes, Joan.' He smiled back. 'I hope so.'

37

THE TASKFORCE HAD agreed to split the murder sites between them, and Jill was pleased to be travelling out to Leichhardt alone. She could have waited until morning, of course – she knew the rest of the team would – but she didn't feel like going home right now. The onset of autumn was definitely getting to her.

The afternoon light was beautiful but the exquisite golden sunshine evoked more melancholy than pleasure for her. She wanted to be as far away from Elvis as possible when she felt this way. Vulnerable. Like the door to her heart had been blown open by the turn in the weather. She'd have to work harder to close it.

She drove into the street in which Crabbe had lived, and pulled in to the kerb in front of his house. A large townhouse, freestanding, Jill could see that it had been split into four apartments; the crime scene tape across the door on the left marked Crabbe's former residence. A wall had been built between the two front doors to stop the occupants having to greet one another every day unless they felt like it. Left of Crabbe's door, shrubbery shielded the house from a small park – a narrow strip of greenery with one bench and a small swing set.

As she was gathering together her notebook and camera, and an empty box in which to collect evidence, a couple in sweats and sneakers walked past, out doing their afternoon exercise. They threw an offended glance towards the homicide house. People in this neighbourhood were highly sensitive about anything that could affect property prices. If they'd recently bought into the area, they likely shouldered ridiculous levels of debt, and didn't want their neighbourhood associated with crime.

The forensics team was finished with the house, and had given her the okay to go through it. She'd picked up a key to the flat and a just-faxed copy of their report before leaving Central. The killer was right-handed. They'd confirmed that, as with the other sites, there were no fingerprints, just smooth gloved smudges. She let herself into the flat and snakes of blood screamed at her from the walls. She shuddered. It didn't surprise her that no-one had yet been around to clean up. Crabbe had no close family, and chances were that professional cleaners, paid for by the real estate agents, would get the job of washing away what was left of Wayne Crabbe's life.

Neighbourhood smells of jasmine and roast lamb couldn't mask the metallic odour of blood in the doorway. Jill imagined Crabbe here, fighting for his life two nights before.

Superimposed over the scene in front of her was the image from the photo this morning. Whoever took it must have been standing just about here, she thought.

The excessive violence betrayed the killer's emotion. Crabbe had died of stab wounds to the lungs, neck and stomach, and his face had then been smashed beyond recognition. The medical examiner was fairly certain that he'd been dead, or close to it, from the stab wounds when the bashing began. Jill tried to imagine someone standing right here, hammering down on the face of an unconscious or dead man at their feet. Blow after blow with some heavy, metal weapon, pulverising bone and flesh in a feverish bloodbath in an otherwise quiet suburban street.

Detectives from Leichhardt had interviewed the owners of the two upstairs units, and both had denied hearing anything that woke them from their sleep; the murder took place sometime between midnight and 2 a.m. The unit next door was currently for lease. Jill could see the proprietor having difficulty renting both of the bottom floor units for some time to come. By law in New South Wales, agents were compelled to advise people if the last occupant of a home had been murdered. People steered clear of the ghosts.

She put her equipment on the floor, avoiding the dried blood pools, and walked a little further into the house, her footsteps loud in the silence. She shivered; wrapped her arms around her ribs. A quiet click from the kitchen propelled her heart into her throat and her hand to the gun at her waist. Almost immediately, she recognised the sound as the refrigerator humming through a new cycle, and she forced herself to reduce her grip on the handle of her firearm. She didn't put it back in its holster.

The floorboards in the hallway were bare. A dilapidated sofa, the colour of vomit, was positioned in front of a no-name widescreen TV. Other furnishings were minimal, and the perfunctory curtains were open. There was a clear view of the swing set in the park next door. Jill would be willing to bet that this outlook had influenced Crabbe's decision to lease the unit.

Crabbe's kitchen held little food that could be considered fresh. Frozen goods, mostly white stuff made of flour – pies, pizzas, dim sims; packaged noodle meals in the cupboards, flavoured milk toppings, and bags and bags of salty snacks – potato and corn chips, Cheezels. A loaf of white bread, jam, and no-frills, plastic-wrapped cheese slices in the fridge, along with margarine, four litres of milk, and a can of whipped cream. Four litres. Sheesh. For one guy. Jill was willing to bet she'd find laxatives or suppositories in the bathroom cupboard. No way this guy's bowels were doing anything of their own accord.

She re-holstered her firearm and retrieved the box from the hallway. She knew what she'd find in the bedroom, but went in anyway. The rest of the taskforce would also be collecting anything incriminating left at their scenes, although most of their evidence had been collated already and was now over at Central. The Leichhardt detectives had found porno-graphy in the cupboard next to Crabbe's bed and on the PC he kept on a small desk in the bedroom. They'd taken most of this in and given Jill authority to clear the rest. A digital camera had been found, smashed, next to his body, but the techies had already managed to retrieve from it dozens of skin-crawling images of kids.

In the bedroom, Jill pulled on latex gloves and piled CDs,

magazines and videocassettes into the box, avoiding looking at any of the pictures. A huge, glossy-black cockroach scuttled across one of the pillows on the bed.

'Missing your master?' she said aloud to the insect, deriving some satisfaction from the fact that Crabbe's face had earlier been lying on that pillow.

She moved through to the bathroom; although relatively clean, the mould growing in the grout made her grimace. She stared at the fungus and thought about the man who had lived here. 'That's just what you were, Crabbe,' she said to the shower walls. 'Mould growing in wet cracks.' She turned to the small, mirrored cupboard on the wall. Anti-dandruff shampoo, condoms. The usual toiletries and medicines. Laxatives. She smiled deprecatingly and closed the cabinet. Her own face in the mirror startled her. Sometimes she couldn't recognise herself. She left the bathroom.

Jill picked up the box and left the house; she couldn't wait now to have a shower. Setting the box down, she took a few photos of the doorway, the shrubbery, the park behind it, the street. They'd have all these photos anyway, but she wanted to make sure she'd recorded what she saw. She put the box in the car boot and walked around to the driver's door, preparing to leave. A few porch lights were on at the neighbours', and the streetlights would come on soon. It was still a beautiful late afternoon. A sprawling frangipani in the park sat in a lake of sweet scented blossoms, the smell almost cloying on the warm breeze.

The swing set sat forlornly in the centre of the park. She walked over and sat on the swing, looked back at the house. This area would have been like a stage to Crabbe, on his lounge, leering through his window. She moved over to the graffiti-covered park bench and sat down. She realised that just as Crabbe could watch the park, someone sitting on this bench could watch him too. If his curtains remained open, anyone sitting here could see right through his house.

Her mobile pealed and she snapped it open.

'Hi, Ma,' she smiled into the phone. 'Working . . . Yeah, yeah, I'm going home now.' She talked for a few moments longer, agreeing to meet her mother in the city for shopping on the weekend, and then ended the call. As she was putting the phone back in her pocket, she looked at the ground at her feet. Next to a chocolate wrapper and a used condom was a small mound of crushed out cigarette butts. Gitanes, lipstick rimmed.

Mercy, what are you doing? she thought.

A dog barked a welcome to its returning owner, and a baby squalled. Jill got off the bench and headed back to her car for an evidence bag to collect the butts.

38

'IT'S POSSIBLE THAT you're describing a mission-oriented serial killer.'

As agreed in their first meeting, the taskforce had decided to consult a forensic psychiatrist. Jardine had arranged the appointment, and because the doctor was very busy and they were pressed for time, they'd agreed to meet on his turf, the university campus at which he taught part-time.

Jill shifted a little in the lecture-theatre chair and focused upon the doctor's words.

'You see, there are several types of multiple murderers,' the psychiatrist continued, instructing them as he might his forensic science and psychology students. 'Australia uses the American FBI system developed in the eighties to classify homicides by patterns and motives.

'Most mass murderers are sexually motivated, but I don't see a lot of evidence for this in these cases. Rather, your perp might consider they are ridding the world of evil – hence the "mission-oriented" label. The aim here is for power, control. Sometimes they see themselves as God. Of course, the motive could still be revenge, as you've speculated, but the killer may also see their acts as benefiting society in some way.'

Jill coughed quietly. No-one needed her opinion on that point right now.

'Given that the murders have been committed in such a short time period,' said the doctor, 'it could be the case that this is a spree killer, someone who is on a non-stop rampage, with little cool-down time between murders. Do you have any evidence that this person could have struck at any other time or place?'

'No,' answered Jardine. 'As far as we're aware, this is it, although we're in the process of checking past homicides across the country.'

'Although it's a rather arbitrary distinction,' the doctor continued, 'a serial killer differs from a spree killer in the amount of cooling down time they have between hits. The serial killer might wait weeks or months before killing again, and can function well between kills in an ordinary life. The spree killer, on the other hand, is in a frenzy, spending all of their waking hours planning and enacting the next death.'

'Does it really matter what we call this son-of-a-bitch?' Elvis was perched on the edge of a desk in the auditorium. Jill had spent a couple of moments wondering whether this was in order to be positioned at a greater height than the rest of them – a power play – or because his belly couldn't fit under the desks permanently attached to the chairs. Watching him move a little as he spoke, she suspected the latter.

'Well, you're right to some extent,' the psychiatrist responded. 'Labelling your chap as a serial or spree killer is not terribly important.' Jill saw Elvis smirk. 'However, finding the right motivation for these acts is essential, in my view, for hunting him down.

'As it's your task to catch this fellow, I'll run through a list of the motivations for multiple murders, and together we'll consider the appropriate taxonomy.'

The tall, slim, greying man moved to the whiteboard at the front of the room.

'Before you begin, Professor Mendelssohn' – Scotty was crammed into one of the little desks, and he'd actually raised his hand like a schoolboy – 'it's just that you keep saying "fellow" and "chap", and we're not positive it is a bloke doing this.'

Jill had so far only told Scotty about the distinctive cigarette butts she found in the park next to Crabbe's home, the type Mercy smoked. She wanted a chance to better understand what Mercy was up to before she sicked the dogs onto her. She didn't want to believe that Mercy could be responsible for the killing. It was more than that, though – how *could* she be responsible? The violence was so extreme, and Mercy just did not seem physically large enough.

'Quite right, young man,' said Professor Mendelssohn, 'we must keep an open mind. There have been female serial killers, although they are, of course, much rarer than their male counterparts. And so, keeping that in mind, we'll consider motivation.'

Up at the whiteboard, now in full lecturer mode, the psychiatrist listed the major motivations for multiple murder and gave an example of each. Jill noted them down on her lecture pad, watching Scotty and Harris do the same. Elvis gave a derisive snort in her direction when she started scribbling quickly. Her notes were always sought after in the academy; she tried to include the doctor's comments and his written words. She noted down:

Possible motivations:

Power: Killing to satisfy the need for control and dominance. Can include thrill killings and sexually motivated killing (the most common). Might be playing God, or obsessed with military might or justice. Includes the mission-oriented killer who kills for a cause, like ridding the world of evil, saving humanity. Although they might see themselves as altruistic, underneath they're serving their own purposes. E.g. taking back control over others because they have little in the rest of their lives; trying to deny a part of themselves that they identify with their victims (taking control over their own intolerable urges).

Revenge: The killer is trying to get even with people who've hurt him/her. Sometimes their victims may not have hurt them directly, but they've associated them with someone who has. They blame the victims for all the problems they've had in life.

Loyalty: Killing is seen as a necessity. E.g. cult members who kill when directed to by their leader; father killing his children after killing their mother so they don't have to suffer the pain of her death.

Profit: Killing for gain, sometimes for money, but most often to eliminate witnesses to crime.

Terror: A way of silencing others and creating terror amongst a group from which the victims are drawn.

'That's really helpful, Professor Mendelssohn,' said Jill

when he turned to face them again. She meant it. She'd been to lectures on this topic, of course, but to have these motivations spelled out while they were working through the case was opening her mind to fresh thinking.

'As you know,' she continued, 'we have evidence that all of the deceased were involved in paedophilia, and were possibly part of an organised network of pederasts. We have been thinking of this as probably a revenge thing: one of the child victims grown up and getting payback. It sounds like you think this could be more motivated by power than revenge?'

'Please understand that your hypothesis may still be correct. Profiling a killer is not an exact science,' said the professor. 'Indeed, the ferocity of the bashing of the face in the most recent killing displays a great deal of hate, and the killer might indeed have been a victim of these men in the past.' He paused and read his notes. 'The knife attack upon this last victim also represents some escalation from the previous murders, and stabbing could be considered a form of penetration. There may well be a sexual motive.

'However,' he continued, 'one might have expected to see some genital mutilation or possibly amputation if our killer had been sexually abused by these men. Sometimes, there's a deliberate attempt to take out the eyes, for what they have seen. Still,' he said, 'I would not discount either position, given the pattern at the present time.'

The professor began packing his briefcase.

'Right, well, we've lined up a couple of interviews with past victims,' Jardine told the group. Professor Mendelssohn was standing, obviously ready to go.

'I apologise for having to leave so soon. As I explained earlier, a lecture, you see,' he said.

'Thank you for your time, Professor. It's been invaluable.' Jardine shook the older man's hand. 'We will be in touch again soon.' The others were standing now too.

'Thank you, and good luck. I would be pleased to assist in any way I can as more information becomes available.'

When they left the lecture room, a mist of rain hung in the air. The taskforce agreed to meet back at Central, and they headed back to their vehicles. Jill watched a few young students slope across the quadrangle, shoulders hunched in the damp.

She jogged to her car.

39

IT WAS COFFEE ALL round when they got back to Central, with the exception of Elvis, who stirred what looked like a fizzing antacid drink.

'Okay, interviews this afternoon,' Harris began their meeting. 'Hutchinson and Jackson: we've got you guys in Room 1 with Travis O'Hare.' Jill saw Elvis smirking behind his cup. She recognised the name. O'Hare had briefly been one of Mercy's patients. She'd spoken to his older brother when she'd first begun investigating possible links between the dead men.

'He's twenty-three I believe,' Harris was looking at his notes. 'He made a statement against Manzi in 2001. Claims Manzi sexually assaulted him when he was ten. Happened in a caravan at the back of his mate's place. Says Manzi gave him some pot, then tied him up and raped him. Says here

Manzi later threatened him with a gun, said he'd kill him if he reported it. He didn't come forward until he was eighteen. Cops out at Castle Hill took a look at it, but the kid was pretty unreliable. Wouldn't show up for interviews, had a few assault charges just before and after he made the statements. Then cops got called out to his parents' home in Baulkham Hills. He'd threatened his brother with a knife and assaulted his father. They got out there and he was off his nut – claimed ASIO had implanted a computer chip in his brain and his brother was in on it all. He was scheduled to Cumberland for forty-eight hours.'

Scotty sighed. Harris continued.

'Since then, he's done six months in Junee for dealing ice, and six out at John Moroney in Windsor for assault. He's also made a couple more trips to Cumberland and Bungaribee House in Blacktown. Says here he's got paranoid schizophrenia.'

'What happened with the investigation?' Jill asked.

'Castle Hill cops talked to Manzi,' answered Harris, still looking down at the file. 'Said he never heard of the kid. When O'Hare started skitzing out, they had to move on. He could never have testified.'

'So Manzi just got away with it.' Jill was disgusted.

'Well, he did until someone caved his head in with a claw hammer,' said Harris.

'Because O'Hare's got a violent past, we thought we'd better bring him in.' Jardine spoke for the first time on the matter.

'Someone with schizophrenia is going to be too disorganised to commit all these crimes,' said Jill. 'It can't be him.'

'Yeah, well, he's medicated most of the time, so who

knows. Anyway, we've gotta cover all bases. And you're up,' said Jardine. 'Room 1. Take the file. He's not due in until two. His father's bringing him down.'

Jill and Scotty made their way to the interview room and started reading the file on O'Hare. The rape he had reported had been especially brutal and had extended over a couple of hours. According to the report, Manzi had inserted a bottle into O'Hare's anus.

At 1.15 a PA came in and told them that O'Hare was waiting for them, early and alone. They made their way out to the reception area and saw a huge young man in a suit coat and jeans, his body folded into one of the plastic chairs bolted to the floor. Jill and Scotty looked at one another. This guy's shoe size was going to be at least thirteen – nothing like the size eight prints found at the crime scenes.

'Mr O'Hare, thanks very much for coming in.' Jill made her way over to his seat. He stood, and Jill had to tilt her head right back.

'Sorry about the suit,' Travis O'Hare said, looking down at her. 'I've got court later on.'

'What's that for, Travis?' asked Scotty; even he had to look up a little.

'Um, assault. It's all bullshit though. My lawyer said there's no worries. Just another attempt to entrap me, but I've got all shields closed.'

'That's good then.' Jill led them into the interview room.

From the first question, Jill knew this interview would go nowhere. O'Hare's answers to even direct questions were confused and disjointed. His eyes glittered and stared through her. His hands were huge, and for such a big man, at times he made sudden, unexpected movements, quickly shifting position, at one time standing, causing Scotty to tense beside her.

Although she knew this was not the killer, Jill asked him anyway whether he'd seen Manzi recently. She later wished she hadn't.

'He'll never garden again.' O'Hare wasn't really looking at anyone.

'What do you mean, Travis?'

'Satan and his organised followers designed a time machine to take me there, but they didn't know I had recorded it all. The numbers took care of all that.'

'What are you talking about, Travis?' Scotty used an authoritative tone. The interview room seemed suddenly very small.

'Oh, I've made sure he'll never cut me up again. There's no chance of that now. It's all recorded. We can play it back anytime we want. It's beautiful. It's been designed with the gardens and the numbers.' O'Hare was smiling now, laughing and mumbling.

'Did you take your medication this morning, Travis?' asked Jill, moving her chair a little further from the huge man.

'That's all been cooked by Satan. They've tried too many times to poison me.'

Without warning, he was on his feet, and within one step had crossed the floor to reach Jill. She saw his huge fist coming towards her face, before Scotty crashed into him, knocking him off balance. It took both of them to even begin to restrain him, and the room was trashed by the time two other officers arrived to help.

In handcuffs and howling incoherently, Scotty and Jill led O'Hare through the squad room out to await an ambulance to take him to Cumberland. Jill heard Elvis's laughter even over O'Hare, roaring in restraints beside her.

'Let's get out of here, J,' said Scotty as they saw the ambulance off.

'We're supposed to be working with them all day.'

'Fuck them.'

'I'm with you. Wanna go find Jamaal?'

'Definitely.'

They both knew that they should let the rest of the taskforce know that they were going to re-interview the only person who had survived the serial killer, but neither mentioned doing so.

Jardine and Harris had last interviewed Mahmoud while he was still in hospital, but all of his details were on file. Jill always kept her copy of the file up to date.

'Let's go to Lakemba then.'

Jamaal, however, was in Hunters Hill, drinking Coca-Cola in the billiard room at the back of the mansion. As was the case from most rooms of this house, the view was incredible. Jamaal kept the hate from his features as he glanced at his boss's profile. Twenty grand he'd given him for the boy. Sebastian would make five times that. More. Jamaal knew he would never have a house like this if he wasn't allowed a more pivotal role in the business.

The pain in his head still bent him double at times. More than money, more than a mansion like this, or a life without his fat wife, though, Jamaal wanted to find the son-of-a-whore who had hit him with the hammer.

'Boss,' he began, interrupting Sebastian reading the paper.

'Yes, Jamaal.' Sebastian did not look up.

'Have you heard any more about who has been killing our friends?'

'Well yes, Jamaal. We are drawing quite close to finding this person.'

'You haven't told me anything about it.'

'I haven't.'

'Who is looking into this for you? How are you getting your information? If you tell me, I could help. Maybe I can find this person faster. You never know.'

'No. You never do.'

Jamaal's silent fury was palpable in the room.

'Jamaal. You know you are my right hand.' Sebastian finally put down his paper. 'We have been together for many years. You know I know you. You want this man very badly, as do I, but we cannot afford for there to be any mistakes. He knows us. What we do. He knows you, Jamaal. I am certain that he knows me.

'This man is more dangerous than you might imagine, Jamaal. It is not the risk to our members that concerns me most. We can always find more friends. It is that this man draws the police to us. Do you understand? They already have been asking questions about you and me. A female detective in particular is worrying me greatly. Just two days ago, Jamaal, she was at the youth centre. She asked for you, do you know?

'In short, my friend, I cannot allow any more attention to be drawn to us. Your temper at this time could be our undoing. We do have plans coming together to meet this person soon, but you must be patient.'

Jamaal stayed silent for a while. He would be patient a little longer.

'Who is the bitch that asks for me?'

'Now that, Jamaal, is perhaps something you *could* turn your attention to.' He paused. 'In addition, I will need your expert hand to prepare the welcoming party for our friend, Jerome.' He smiled. 'I do not think Tadpole can wait much longer to introduce him to our society.'

On the way out to Lakemba, Jill filled Scotty in on Jamaal Mahmoud's criminal history. She'd pulled his records after the hospital visit with Honey. While his boss, Sebastian, had managed to escape any criminal convictions, Mahmoud had had numerous charges laid against him.

'Assault mostly, both in gaol and outside. Drugs, goods in custody, two charges for kidnapping and extortion. The last two didn't stick.' Jill's feet were up on the dash again.

'Kidnapping a child?'

'Nope. Adult male. In the burns unit at Concord Hospital, the victim made a statement, claiming Mahmoud had abducted and tortured him. Kept him for two days. Cops were collecting his statement between his surgeries – he had a skin graft for one of the burns on his inner thigh; jaw wired; left eye socket and cheek reconstructed. They were getting ready to bring Jamaal in when the vic suddenly realised he'd made a mistake. Wasn't Jamaal at all that did this to him. In fact he was certain of it, and was sure he wouldn't be able to identify who did do it.'

'Of course.'

'Hmm.'

Scotty was silent a moment, then said, 'I've been wondering, Jill, if Manzi and Jamaal let the perp in their car, then Jamaal must know who hit him. Why do you reckon the killer's still out there alive?'

'I've wondered that too.'

'What if it was Mahmoud who did it? Could be the third person in the car was escaping him – hit Jamaal to get away.'

There was silence for a moment, until Scotty discounted his own supposition. 'Nah. Blood found on Jamaal was all his own, none of Manzi's. One thing's for sure though, J,' continued Scotty, 'we wouldn't be the only people out here hunting this bloke.'

'And we've got to get to him first. He's gonna give us Mahmoud and Sebastian, and whoever else is on his shit-list to do next.'

'His or her shit-list.'

Jill had her head in the street directory. 'It's left at the lights, Scotty. Then second right.'

Through the one-way mesh of a security screen door, and over the sound of a toddler crying, Mrs Mahmoud gave them nothing. No, her husband wasn't home. No, she didn't know where he was. No, she didn't have a mobile phone number for him. She shut the door while Jill was still saying goodbye.

'Friendly.'

'Real chatty.'

Jill and Scotty looked the outside of the house over, but nothing really distinguished it from the others in the street. Even the bars on every window were more common than not in this neighbourhood.

They stepped over a child's broken bike on the way back to their car.

40

'ABOUT THE CASE,' she said by way of greeting. 'We should tell the others about Mercy.'

The morning was clear and cool so Jill and Scotty had met for a bike ride, something they hadn't done since the murders began.

Scotty looked at her sideways.

'Like you said, the cigarette butts could be anyone's.'

Jill gave him back his sideways glance.

'So, do you figure she's capable of it?' Scotty's tone was sceptical.

'I dunno. What if she's just tailing these guys?' said Jill. 'What if she knows there's a paedophile ring and she's just watching them?'

'What for?'

Jill laced her shoes. Third time, prolonging the conversation. 'I keep asking myself that. But I think maybe she left me that photo.'

'You reckon she saw Crabbe get murdered?'

'Yeah. I think I do.'

'Just from the cigarettes?'

'And that she's worked with the victims of the first three dead men.'

'That we know of. We should check out Crabbe's vics.'

'And just that she is ... I don't know ... off.' Jill concluded.

'Well, we'll bring it up first thing tomorrow.' The task-force was to meet at nine.

'Meantime,' Scotty continued, straddling his bike and strapping on his helmet, 'let's get your ritual humiliation over with. It looks like it's going to rain again.' He took off on the bike.

Late that afternoon, her breath fogging the glass, Jill stood in her living room, staring out at the ocean, watching the surf creaming the rocks to the left of the beach, the playground of some diving gulls. The rain hung poised in corpulent thunder-clouds.

Immobile at the glass, she felt agitated. Her life mirrored the case at the moment, simultaneously hurtling forward, and stagnant, stuck. Thoughts and feelings boiled just beneath her awareness. She wanted to face them, but at the same time there was nothing in the world she wanted less. Her thoughts were a hundred swimmers drowning in her subconscious, raising hands above the surface for moments, before being swamped again by waves of repression.

The vodka in the freezer. There was always that.

A scream of frustration came out as a sigh, and Jill turned

from the glass doors. When she realised she was pacing the room, she walked to the front door and slipped her runners back on; she put the hood up on her sweatshirt, grabbed the keys and headed out.

The stairwell was always a little dank in autumn and winter, but Jill didn't notice as she flew down the stairs and out onto the road. For a weekday afternoon, Maroubra was quiet. Today was cool, and a storm was predicted.

The worries that had been buzzing around her head began to dissipate in the fresh air, and Jill jogged impatiently on the median strip in the middle of the road out the front of her unit block, waiting for a dawdling taxi to get out of the way.

She's got an arse like a boy, thought Jamaal Mahmoud, watching her from his white van in the carpark closest to the beach. I wonder what she'll sound like crying.

Jill turned right and ran up the incline towards Malabar; she needed a long run, a road run. The rain began to fall as she pounded the pavement. An Asian family ran back to their car to escape the fat drops, a squealing young girl holding her mother's hand. After she'd passed them, Jill stuck out her tongue and collected some rain. She felt a thrill of pleasure when the smell of newly wet soil and road hit the back of her throat with the raindrop. As usual, a rush of dread followed the pleasurable feeling. Her body's warning system had been switched on at age twelve, and had not shut off since. Feelings of relaxation registered threat, signalling her defences to snap on.

Her eyes narrowed through the rain and she scanned the environment for danger. The family had reached their station wagon; the young mother clipped on her daughter's seatbelt from outside of the car, her back in the rain. A few cars passed, wipers on, windscreens beginning to fog. There was no foot traffic anywhere near her. She got back to the rhythm of the run.

She could feel the damp on her shoulders now, as the rain made it through her thin windcheater, but the hood kept it off her face as it began to pour down steadily. A good rain; Sydney had been in drought all summer. She preferred the cool to the hot, scratchy feeling she'd had under her skin all day.

The clouds were pretty much sitting on the road, the sky connected to the earth by sheets of rain. She cut though it, her sneakers sending up small splashes with every step. Puddles and shadows formed quickly. She was only vaguely aware of the road traffic now.

Jamaal, cruising along the street a hundred metres behind her, was dry in his van. His image of her as an adolescent boy was working well for him – from the back view, there was no real difference – he had his erect penis in one hand, the other hand on the wheel. He was listening to love song dedications on the radio, looking very much forward to their meeting.

He hadn't planned on taking her today, but the weather was perfect. The rain was coming down so hard now he could hear it over the music. His wipers were on double speed. Crazy bitch. Running like this in the rain.

He let go of his member and popped open the glove box. The chloroformed cloth was there in a bag. Be prepared. He knew there was a big housing commission block coming up, with a park on the right. There was a vacant lot just before the housing project. He could take her there. All the windows would be closed in the units. Any screams would be lost in the rain.

Lightning rendered the clouds green for a moment and a huge thunderclap sounded. A sign, thought Jamaal. Braking a little, he reached into the glove box and removed the bag. He put it on the seat next to him, and struggled to put his penis back into his pants. He considered leaving it out while he took her, but she'd have plenty of time to see it later.

Jill came out of her reverie with the thunderclap. Shit. Close. She realised that her shoes were full of water and even her underclothes were soaked. Her visibility was poor, and a sudden shudder ran up her spine. To the next pole then, and then home, she told herself. She always had to have a goal to reach, couldn't just turn around. The pole was just before the housing projects up ahead. That would have to do.

Jamaal stopped his van just near the telegraph pole in front of the vacant block. He had enjoyed this feeling many times before. The quiet space before an attack. A building feeling. Adrenalin squirted from his sympathetic nervous system, triggering his heart to beat faster, engorging the muscles in his limbs with blood. His fingers opened and closed a little, grasping at nothing. His nostrils flared for more air, his pupils dilated to take in more light. The sweat glands on his hands activated to assist with grip. Jamaal was consciously aware of none of these physiological reactions, but he instinctively knew them well; he also knew his body would not fail him when he needed it.

Soon. All his thoughts focused upon the figure approaching. He knew that once he touched the handle of the door he would not stop until he had her in the van.

Jamaal stretched his left hand to the seat next to him and palmed the cloth with his right hand. He reached for the door handle.

Jill reached the telegraph pole, touched it, and turned for home. It was absolutely pissing down.

'*Sharmuta!*' Jamaal screamed in Arabic. He physically shook with the effort of staying in the car. His heart shuddered to slow down. He smashed his fist into the steering wheel. Once, twice. 'Fucking cunt!'

He threw the cloth onto the passenger seat and reached for a cigarette, his fingers trembling. The chloroform from the rag, the vapours still on his fingers, entered his nostrils and he swooned; he blinked back the blackness, still cursing, his anger, if anything, climbing.

His mobile rang four times before he answered, choking out a grunt.

Jamaal's wife was on the phone, wanting to know where he had been and where the money for food was. She wanted to know why the police had come to their home.

Jamaal's eyeballs felt like they were melting, and his head hurt so badly that he wondered whether somewhere in there his brain was bleeding.

41

'OKAY. TODAY'S THE day we round up our three best suspects. All of these people are linked to at least three of the dead men.'

Jardine stood at the whiteboard, addressing the assembled group; the taskforce had already met for an hour this morning, and Jill had told them about the cigarette butts at the park. The bosses had now come in for a run-down.

Jardine was average height, average build, with dark thinning hair. Wearing chain-store suit pants, white shirt and a blue tie, his vinyl shoes needed replacing and faint discolouration marked the neck of his shirt. Lunchroom gossip said he was in the process of a divorce and that his ex-wife had recently shown up at Central and accused one of the PAs of sleeping with him. Apparently, the females here considered him quite a catch. Jill couldn't figure it, but hell, how was she to know. Her gut instinct when she met most males was to walk the other way; half the time their smell alone made her want to run.

I'd do Jardine any day before him, though, she thought, as Elvis approached the board, pen in hand. The buttons of the shirt tucked into his low-slung jeans gaped, revealing a mound of hairy belly trying to push its way to freedom.

Probably thought you looked real good with your gut sucked in this morning, didn't you, Elvis, she asked him silently, giving him a cat-like grin.

Catching her sideways smile, Elvis seemed somewhat disconcerted for a moment, and then she watched him pull himself together. Suddenly Calabrese's smart-arse attitude was nowhere to be seen. The bosses were here now.

Oh my God, they've rehearsed this, she thought, as Elvis and Jardine took turns to run a presentation to the group. Inspector Andreessen and Inspector Beaumont sat together, both appearing tired and grey. A couple of uniformeds from Central also sat in on the meeting.

Elvis wrote the names of their three major suspects across the top of the board.

Dr Mercy Merris   Alejandro Sebastian   Jamaal Mahmoud

Huh. Me and Scotty gave 'em all of them, Jill thought resentfully. She tuned out as the song-and-dance-act out the front continued, but copied the contents of the whiteboard into her murder book in order to look busy. It was nothing she didn't know already. She copied:

Dr Mercy Merris
Therapist: treated victims of Manzi, Carter and Rocla.
To do: follow up any patients linked to Crabbe. Cigarette butts found at scene of Crabbe's murder.
To do: Forensics Did she supply police with a photograph of the Crabbe crime scene? No trace found on photo.
To do: Search car and home for camera and equipment.

Jamaal Mahmoud
Employed by Sebastian.
Injured in the car when Manzi was murdered. Claims he accidentally hit his head, but not supported by evidence.
Forensics does not implicate him in the death of Manzi, but ? involvement in company of a third person.
Suspected link to all victims in child pornography ring. Unconfirmed witnesses allege Mahmoud is part of the same ring.
To do: follow up witness reports (Honey Delaney).

Alejandro Sebastian
Suspected link to all victims in child pornography ring. Unconfirmed witnesses allege Sebastian is head of this group.
To do: follow up witness reports (Honey Delaney); investigate youth club in Kings X.

'Harris and I will take Sebastian,' said Jardine. 'His direct link to the men is least clear and we'll be tentative in the interview, keeping things general. We'll let him know that we've become aware that he knows the dead men, and that we're effectively just seeking his assistance. Apparently this guy knows his way around the legal system.

'Because Jackson has consulted Dr Merris on a professional basis,' Jardine continued, 'we're –'

'What did you say?' Jill was aware of the heat in her face and voice. All eyes were on her. She saw Elvis raise his hand to his face as though to push his hair back. His middle finger was extended; his eyes danced.

'No big deal, Jill,' Jardine played mildly surprised, placatory. 'You had some counselling with her a couple of years ago, didn't you? We just thought it'd be better for Eddie here to take her, given your history.'

Jill modulated her voice to match Jardine's. No way were these boys going to make her out to be some unhinged female.

'Just so we're all clear' – you arsehole – 'I attended a mandatory debrief following a discharge of firearm incident. Not sure whether you'd be aware or not, Jardine, but you get sent to these compulsory meetings when you have to use your gun.' She saw the uniformeds smile slightly. Most people knew she'd been promoted after she'd taken out a scumbag. 'It's an OH and S issue.

'Regardless,' she continued, everyone still watching her, most hoping for a car crash, 'Scott Hutchinson and I are happy to take Mahmoud. Scotty and I interviewed Merris once already when we first found the link between these suspects and the dead men. We've also already started on Mahmoud – we went out to his house in Lakemba on Wednesday. We were planning on following him up today.'

'Good work then.' Andreessen and Beaumont were standing; they'd addressed her. The meeting was over.

Jardine and Elvis stood stock still at the whiteboard.

'Eat shit,' she mouthed at them, smiling, while the bosses left the room.

An important detail was maddeningly close to Jill's awareness, but she couldn't quite grasp it. She was distracted as Scotty unlatched the low metal gate that led up to Jamaal Mahmoud's front door. A van in the driveway indicated that Mahmoud was almost certainly at home. Jill took a look through the driver's window as they passed the van. A partition blocked the front seats from the rear of the vehicle. There was nothing to see in the front, and blackened glass obscured the contents of the rear.

Scotty's loud knock on the screen door raised muffled sounds from within the fibro home, but they waited for some time before anyone responded. The street was relatively quiet. The engine of a delivery van resembling the one in the driveway coughed to life a couple of houses down. A woman wearing a hijab crossed the street nearby after leaving a halal butcher shop on the corner. She used her remote to pop open the boot of her car, and put two heavy-looking plastic bags inside.

Scotty looked at Jill and had raised his fist to knock again when the interior door suddenly opened; Jill sensed a male presence behind the one-way mesh of the security screen.

'Good afternoon,' boomed Scotty, smiling broadly, 'Sergeants Hutchinson and Jackson. We dropped by the other day. Here to speak to Mr Jamaal Mahmoud.'

A malevolent silence followed. Finally, a dark-skinned man with hooded eyes and a coathanger of a nose opened the screen door.

'Ah, Mr Mahmoud, is it? Hope we aren't interrupting anything?'

The man wore a tracksuit and slippers. He stared flatly past them into the yard.

'Mr Mahmoud,' said Jill, 'I met you when you were hospitalised at Prince of Wales. You might remember? I believe your friend Mr Sebastian was visiting you at the time?'

Mahmoud hawked phlegm in the back of his throat.

A pigtailed girl aged around five poked her head around her father's legs and stared up at Scotty, eyes wide. Too late, she grabbed for a ginger cat that darted out through the gap in the door. Mahmoud uttered a curse under his breath, aiming a kick at the cat that would have sent it flying had it not launched itself from the step before the foot could connect. The cat sat in the sun near the white van and looked back at them, seemingly nonchalant, cleaning a paw, its tail sweeping the path. The girl was gone.

'What do you want here?' Jamaal addressed Scotty.

'Well, we need your help, Mr Mahmoud. We have some more questions to ask you about the night you were assaulted and George Manzi was killed. It would be easiest if you came back to the station with us so we can record your statement.'

'I have already given my statement. There is nothing more I can say. I can remember nothing about the night.'

Scotty was still smiling, enthusiastic. 'Yes, we've read your statement, Mr Mahmoud, but I'm afraid we need more information.'

A woman's voice speaking Arabic cut off Mahmoud's reply. The woman who had answered the door on Wednesday now filled the space behind her husband. She continued to speak, and the man's eyes narrowed in anger. He snapped back a response, also in Arabic, and stepped forward away from her, his fists clenched.

'We will go.' He kicked off the slippers and stepped into some shoes lined up next to others at the door.

Jill prepared the interview room while Scotty found a place in the police carpark for Mahmoud to park his van. A female probationary constable helped her become familiar with the recording equipment. The two sound-activated audio recorders and a digital video recorder were newer than those at Maroubra.

'Do you need both audios?' The girl looked to be about nineteen, perfect skin, clean brown hair tucked behind unpierced ears.

Was I ever that young? Jill smiled, thinking of her mother's saying, 'You know you're getting old when the police look like kids.'

'Yeah, thanks, Audrey. Don't want to miss anything this guy says. Are you sitting in?'

'That okay? Beaumont assigned me to you guys today.'

'Yeah, of course.'

Jill checked her notes and scribbled down a few more questions. She kept her head down when Scotty bounded in, chatting away to the taciturn man next to him. Mahmoud dropped into the seat to which Audrey Galea, the young constable, directed him. Galea fussed around the video camera, ensuring she had the equipment working smoothly. Scotty took his seat and looked up at Jill, ready to begin the interview.

Jill stated the time and date, and identified those present

in the room. 'Mr Mahmoud,' she continued, 'would you please state your name and date of birth?'

'Jamaal Mahmoud. Fifth of July, 1967.'

'And your address?'

'Forty-one George Street, Lakemba.'

Jill recited the verbal preamble that preceded each police statement, and asked Mahmoud to agree that he would tell the truth.

Jamaal found that he could keep his anger from his voice by speaking to the bitch's tits. While he gave them the same bullshit about the night George was killed, he fantasised about putting this whore to work. A week on Canterbury Road servicing the Australians on their way home would show this one her real place in life. He ground his teeth when she fired another question at him, demanding he answer to her.

He felt some satisfaction when he heard all the questions about Sebastian. He knew he should be worried that the police had an interest in his boss, but why should he be the only one they question? He was no-one's dog. He imagined Sebastian on the inside, having to suck cock to make enough friends to stay alive in gaol. He almost laughed aloud, but was drawn back to the interview by a question asked by the big Australian.

No, of course he did not know anything about the child pornography found in the front of the car with Manzi, he told them. Jamaal wondered what sort of a man could take orders from a bitch. Even one this big would drop like a bag of shit when hit from behind. Jamaal hoped one day to make that happen.

Caring little for the answers he gave, Jill concentrated on questions that she hoped might rattle Jamaal. She knew better than to hope he might respond with the truth, but his answers now could trip him up in a lie in the future. She also wanted him to believe that they'd connected him and Sebastian to Carter, Crabbe and Rocla. She asked him whether he knew each of them, intimating that Bobby Anglia had told them more than he actually had. She registered a tick of satisfaction when Jamaal lost his temper momentarily.

'How do I know if I know this man? Do you know the names of every bastard you have ever met? Maybe I did see him somewhere. I don't know.'

She also made sure to mention Alejandro Sebastian whenever she could. It was too late to prevent Sebastian knowing they were watching him. Harris and Jardine were approaching him right now. If they were going to come down, she wanted it heavy. She disagreed with Jardine that they should play it safe with Sebastian – if they caught him by surprise, he could make a mistake. Of course, it was possible, although unlikely, that he could panic and maybe take out another member of his special club, a witness perhaps. What a shame if it was this man, she thought, wanting to slap Mahmoud's eyes away from her chest. She was relieved when the interview ended; she felt like she needed a bath.

Out in the carpark, Jamal's eyes felt too hot to close, like the lids would stick to his eyeballs if he did not stare straight ahead. A molar silently fractured as he bit down on the anger at the back of his throat.

He started his van and pulled away from the Central police station.

42

NATHAN SANDERS PUSHED his mouth further into his pillow, trying to suffocate his sobs. He couldn't bear his mother coming to comfort him, only to end up trying to calm her again when she crumpled to his bedroom floor. Jerome had been missing for six days, and Nathan wished that he could be as staunch as his father, driving the streets relentlessly looking for his son, returning only for food and brief naps in his chair before heading out again.

Nathan replayed for the hundredth time the words he'd said to Jerome on the last night he saw him. He whispered a prayer, and told God that he could never forgive himself or his father if his brother did not come home alive.

Into his wet pillow, he offered God more promises and threats.

*

No-one else at his school had these sneakers yet. Vans, skaters' shoes; his dad got them from America at Christmas. Not even Scott Emery in Year 8 had 'em, and he always got everything first. Jerome found that focusing hard on his clothes, stuff from home, helped him to not cry so much. His throat hurt from crying and he needed to stop.

But they'd all been pretty nice to him, actually. Well, except for *kidnapping* him. Jerome gave himself a mental head slap.

When he realised the big man was not going to call his mum, and they were going to keep him, Jerome's mind had filled with every horror he'd heard about in his twelve years. And that was a lot. Like the time he'd had nightmares for a week after the party at Logan's house. Assam Ravinder, whose dad was a cop, had snuck over this police magazine. There was a picture of this guy in there who'd tied a rope to the trunk of a tree, got in his car, tied the rope around his neck, and driven forward. They showed the head next to the body, really close up. Braydon had been sick in his sleeping bag and had to go home.

But, except for that guy who said his name was Tadpole putting his hand on Jerome's back and leg a couple of times, no-one here had touched him. And they'd even been pretty nice to him. He could help himself to anything in the fridge, they'd told him, and he'd had a few of cans of Coke, some cake and sandwiches, but mostly he didn't like to move. Tadpole had brought pizza down a couple of times, but it had those anchovy things on it, and he hadn't been able to make himself eat much. He had no idea how long he'd been here, but he thought it had to be more than four nights. He could hear nothing from the outside. When the white van had left, the big room seemed more like a lounge room than a garage; there was a big TV on one wall, some chairs and stuff, a kitchen and a bathroom. Feeling like he was going to have a heart attack, he'd tried once to open a door at the end of the room, but he couldn't make it move. It was the same story with the door they drove the van through.

Sometimes he'd forget anything was wrong. He even fell asleep a few times. Mostly, though, there was this bad feeling, like when Nathan would jump out from the hallway in the dark, except the feeling just went on and on.

At least Big Nose hadn't been back. They called him Jamaal. Jerome had seen him opening and closing his hands like he wanted to choke something. He did it mostly when the big one was talking. Once when he saw Jerome watching him, Jamaal had smiled and Jerome had nearly gone to the toilet in his pants.

Until today, he hadn't left the underground room, but maybe half an hour earlier, after Tadpole had found him crying again, he'd told Jerome he'd take him to see the ocean if he promised not to say a word. With a tea towel wrapped around his eyes, he'd climbed some stairs with Tadpole behind him. He'd smelled the outside air, but then Jamaal's voice made him freeze. Tadpole had shoved and sort of carried him back down the stairs, back to the big room. Tadpole had been giggling, with his hands over his mouth, but Jerome didn't think it was funny. He wanted to be at home, but down here was much better than up there with Jamaal.

He wondered what time it was. What his mum and dad were doing. He hoped they were still looking for him. Maybe Assam Ravinder's father would be trying to find him too.

How long do people keep looking for you when you've been kidnapped? Is there a time when they decide you're not coming back and they stop looking?

Jerome rubbed his eyes, and focused hard on his sneakers.

43

ALTHOUGH SHE WAS fully alert before she picked up the phone that woke her, Jill still couldn't make out the identity of the caller. She sat upright in her bed, telephone receiver in hand; it sounded as though the speaker was trying to disguise their voice. She flicked the switch on her bedside lamp and wondered how this person had got her number.

'I'm there right now,' the voice sounded muffled. Jill struggled to determine whether it was male or female. 'I can't make it all stop, but tonight I'm going to try.'

'Would you please tell me who this is?' Jill's eyes were grainy; her body urged her back to her pillow, the warm quilt. The red numbers on the clock next to her registered 12.18 a.m.

'I'm on Kensington Drive, Hunters Hill. I'm in my car out the front of Sebastian's house. I know you know who he is. The Owner.'

'How did you get this number?'

'Is that really all you've got to say? I thought you, if no-one else, would want to put a stop to what these men are doing.'

'What are they doing?'

'Why, they fuck children, Jill. But you already know that, don't you?'

The voice sounded like the person was speaking through cloth.

Jill got up and walked with the phone now, pacing through her living room.

'Jill, they have a child there tonight.' Jill gripped the phone in her hand. 'I think it's a boy called Jerome Sanders; he was snatched last week. There's a party going on right now. Some Japanese high rollers have come here to celebrate, and Jerome is the party favour.'

Jill stood very still. 'How do you know all this?' she asked.

'I've been watching. I know you got my photo.'

'What is that address again?' Jill scribbled it down on a notepad in the kitchen; she tasted acid at the back of her throat. 'I'll be there within half an hour. Whoever you are, do not enter that house. If there is a child in there you cannot risk him being hurt.'

'Jill, there is a child in there. I told you. And it's probably a little too late to hope that there's just a risk of him being hurt. You know what kind of men these are.'

Jill unlocked her door; a jacket over her tracksuit would have to do. She slipped her firearm into the pocket of her windcheater. She'd telephone Scotty from her mobile, in transit.

Scotty confirmed what she already knew. The kidnapping of Jerome Sanders had been in the news and on their bulletin boards for a week. Scotty promised he'd meet her at Hunters Hill within half an hour.

'Jill, you don't know what this is. Do not get out of the car until I get there. Are we clear?'

'Yep. Just get there fast, and bring the cavalry.'

She knew neither of them could get there in less than forty minutes, and because Scotty would need to find Andreessen and arrange for back-up, he'd probably be considerably longer.

Jill stayed not more than twenty over the speed limit, overriding the instincts that were urging her to floor it. Jerome Sanders was with them right now. She blinked her eyes rapidly to stop images forming of what could be happening to him, what had happened to her.

She did not have to look to know that the girl with the white eyes sat in the passenger seat next to her, staring fixedly ahead, on her way to help Jerome. Somewhere Jill was faintly disturbed that this girl from the basement, who since then had lived only in her nightmares, was taking this ride with her.

She tried to ignore the girl's burning presence as she drove into the night.

Jill had rarely used the portable navigation system her father had bought her for Christmas a few years ago. Being told where to go by the British nanny voice irritated her. Tonight, however, she obeyed the voice, and at 12.50 a.m. she pulled into the sleeping wealth of Kensington Drive, Hunters Hill. Crawling forward with her headlights off, she saw Mercy

Merris's red Mercedes parked with a group of its newer, more expensive cousins. She felt no surprise. She rolled past the car, lights still off, and glanced inside. Empty.

She drove to the next street and turned left, parked a few houses down. Hands in her pockets, one cradling her gun, Jill jogged back towards the Mercedes, sticking to pools of darkness. She could see no-one. The homes in this street were set well back from the road. The night was still, the air cool on her face.

She reached Mercy's car, parked close to the house with the street number she'd been given. She assumed the caller had been Mercy. So Mercy had sent the photo. What was she doing?

Next to the Mercedes, a long sandstone wall protected a high, perfectly maintained hedge; the hedge protected a million-dollar view from those too poor to see it from their own homes. There was still no movement on the street.

Jill felt the girl with the white eyes jump over the wall before her. Shit. She waited a beat and followed her over, then she pushed her way through the hedge, the fragrant twigs pulling at her hair, clawing her clothing, trying to trap her within. When she finally broke through, the white-eyed girl was running down a hill towards the house. 'Wait for Scotty,' she wanted to yell after herself. Instead, she moved cautiously down velvety lawns towards the dark house.

She was halfway to the back of the huge home when the floodlights flared, turning night to day. Jill threw herself into a bush at the side of the gravel drive and lay there, her heart in her mouth, watching. The girl with the white eyes lay next to her, breathing evenly, waiting for Jill to get up and do something.

I should wait for Scotty, she told herself, even as she moved from her stomach to a crouch, readying to move. The lights had not brought anybody to the yard, and there was no noticeable movement in the house. Jill could see all of the grounds now, a wave of dark green flowing down to the inky harbour fifty metres away. The owners were perhaps used to large water birds triggering the sensor lights. In any event, they had not bothered to come and check why they'd been activated.

Jill made her way along the edge of the driveway, creeping through the shrubbery to avoid the crunch of the gravel on one side and the well-lit lawn on the other. When she drew parallel with the back of the house, she saw huge windows filled with light, and movement inside. She froze again. Should she try to get closer to the house? Scotty would be on the way, but she knew it would have taken him some time to wake the inspector, explain the situation and coordinate a plan of approach. The boss would probably want a search warrant before anyone came near the place. He'd have started out, but she knew he'd be a while yet.

Swaying slightly on her feet from the mental tug-of-war, Jill suddenly swore under her breath. The white-eyed girl was running down the lawn towards the ocean. Jill noticed a boatshed at the bottom of the grounds. It was a better place to wait than here, exposed. She followed her down to the water's edge.

It wasn't until Mr Sebastian told Jerome that he wouldn't be able to stop Jamaal from hurting him that Jerome managed to stop himself crying.

'He doesn't have a lot of patience, I'm afraid, Jerome,' said the big man, smiling down at him kindly. 'He particularly dislikes crying, you see. He once told me that his father would punish him when he used to cry, and now it seems that the sound of it triggers something quite ferocious in him.'

Jerome swallowed hard. Jamaal was looking at him as though he were food.

Jerome thought it was maybe an hour since the big man, Tadpole and Jamaal had entered through a heavy door into the garage. The big man had spoken first.

'Jerome, I realised only this afternoon that I have not properly introduced myself to you. My name is Mr Sebastian, and I hope that we can be firm friends.' His eyes crinkled in a friendly fashion. 'I know you've met Tadpole here' – Tadpole positively beamed – 'and this is Jamaal, who brought you to us, of course.'

Although he was ashamed of it, Jerome could not stop some hot tears falling.

'I–I want to go home.'

'Of course you do, but not before the party, young man!' Mr Sebastian continued. 'Jamaal has some clothes for you to wear, and I'm afraid you'll have to have a shower now.' He leaned forward and stage-whispered conspiratorially, 'You're starting to smell!'

Tadpole giggled.

'I ... d–don't want to go to a party,' Jerome cried in earnest now. He felt like someone had punched him in the throat.

'Oh, but of course you do. There will be balloons and cake, lollies and chips, and you're the guest of honour, young man. Some very important men have come here to meet you. We've told them all about you. You wouldn't want them to be sad, would you?'

'N–no.'

'Of course not.'

'And then can I go home?'

'Well, that will be then, and this is now, is it not? And you've a shower to take, and a party to attend.'

It was around then that Mr Sebastian had told Jerome about Jamaal's aversion to crying.

The floodlights didn't reach the water's edge, and Jill approached the boatshed by padding quietly across the thick lawn. Boats clanked gently, rocking in the calm water where the property ended. The harbour smelt like life and death.

The white-eyed girl stood on her toes at the boatshed, peering into a rind of light around a window. Jill crept up to join her, the grass giving way to sand beneath her sneakers. The boatshed sat at the very edge of the water, a single-room wooden structure that could have been sold for twice what Jill's flat was worth. Silent, she stepped up on a rock upon which the shed was built, and peered in through a crack in some sort of window covering.

A small gasp of surprise from the white-eyed girl made Jill want to scream. Dr Mercy Merris lay on the floor of the boatshed staring unseeingly at the window through which Jill peered. Blood pooled on a white concrete floor lit by a single overhead bulb. Probably she's been knocked out, probably she's going to be okay, she tried to reassure the white-eyed girl.

Jill determinedly ignored the cabbage-sized hole of an exit wound in the middle of Mercy's chest.

There's definitely going to be a problem with her brother, thought Jamaal. The father he could talk around – Allah knew the father could manage his own women – but his wife's brother was going to be difficult. The last time his wife had got out of control, her brother had promised Jamaal he would kill him if he ever saw her bruised that way again. This time she was in Westmead Hospital with a fractured jaw. And his brother-in-law was no softcock. He'd done infantry training in Lebanon, he'd been shot twice in Sydney, and he had a lot of friends, inside and out of gaol. The brother was going to be a problem.

Jamaal knew where the blame lay, and he intended to make the bitch pay. His wife's questioning about why the cops had come to his home had been too much to bear after the interrogation that morning. He had a hard-on for Sergeant Jillian Jackson that would not go away until she was bleeding.

Now in the basement, Jamaal chewed on an antacid tablet and stared at Jerome. Just give me a fuckin' reason, his eyes told the boy. The kid didn't, showering and dressing in the small bathroom off the garage without saying another word.

Tadpole danced through the basement room, whipping himself up for the special party. He stopped mid-pirouette in the kitchen when he caught the look in Jamaal's eye.

'Coffee, Jamaal?' asked Tadpole uneasily.

Jamaal just chewed the tablet; the burning in his diaphragm remained.

'Mr Japan is going to love our little friend in there,' Tadpole continued. 'Let's just hope he doesn't love him too long 'cause Sebastian's promised me seconds.' There was a pause. 'Unless, of course, you wanted to play first, Jamaal? You found him, after all. Fair's fair.' He smiled ingratiatingly.

His face full of the acid in his gut, Jamaal left the room. I'll cut that fuckin' poofter's throat if I have to listen to any more, he thought. He'd take what he wanted when he was ready. Using the hidden stairwell, he made his way up to the house.

When the foundations had been laid for the harbourside mansion, the basement garage had been cut deep into the hill upon which it sat. There were no windows in the huge room, and it was undetectable from the outside of the property. The two entrances to the basement were also concealed, and neither was accessible unless one knew where to look. Sebastian had told him years ago that his father had bought the house in the sixties from some paranoid Jew. Along the back of the regular, above-ground, triple garage was a motorised fibro wall that slid sideways to reveal a truck-sized entry dropping to a short, sharply angled concrete tunnel. Jamaal had driven his van, with the kid in the back, down through this tunnel to the basement. A couple of other kids had made the same journey with him in the past. Enough room existed in the underground bunker to drive the van full-circle and exit back up the same way. Not many had made this journey back with him.

Tonight, however, Jamaal left the room through the second access door. He knew Sebastian did not like the door used when there were guests in the house, but it was after midnight and it was unlikely that anyone was still in the entry foyer. They'd bring the kid up to the main house this way soon. He climbed the steep wooden staircase in darkness, and pushed open the trapdoor that lay in the floor of the large coat cupboard in the lobby of the stately house. He leaned the trapdoor against the wall of the interior of the cupboard, careful to be silent, and climbed out of the hole in the floor. He stood upright and listened. He could hear nothing outside the cupboard. He cracked the door and, seeing no-one in the marble foyer, Jamaal slipped out and headed for the rear of the home.

Ten years ago, Jamaal had at first found it diverting to attempt to find the barely discernible handle in the cupboard that gave access to the basement room, but when the moments had ticked away, and Sebastian had laughed once too often, he'd lost patience. He would watch in admiration as Sebastian would instantly locate the recessed lever that lifted the trapdoor. Even after seeing it done several times, Jamaal would usually wait for Sebastian to open the door ahead of him.

As he made his way through the opulence of the house towards the lights and music in the ballroom, he looked down at his black jeans and jumper with satisfaction. Sebastian would be pissed that he was not wearing a suit. Sebastian's other minder, that cement-head wog, would be all decked out. Arse kisser. Jamaal's wife's 'accident' would serve as an excuse for not dressing properly. He enjoyed such small moments of power over his boss.

An air of expectancy filled the ballroom. Those invited knew they were a highly select group, and the ridiculous price they had paid as their entrance fee ramped up their expectations. Sebastian had promised them all a double delight. A live boy under fourteen. And a virgin. Jamaal could see the admiration in their faces as they drank and chatted in small groups – you have to hand it to Sebastian, he could imagine them saying; how does he do it?

It's *me*, he wanted to scream at them all; I got the kid. You should all be kissing my feet, you cocksuckers.

Near the fireplace, where tonight a low fire provided cosy effect rather than real warmth, Sebastian stood looking particularly pleased. He leaned against the mantelpiece, immaculately groomed in a dark suit, speaking to his Japanese guests, a middle-aged millionaire and his elderly father, both predisposed to the same pleasures. He looked up when he saw Jamaal. The light left his eyes for just a moment when he took in Jamaal's clothes. Jamaal suppressed a smile as Sebastian beckoned him over.

'My very dear friend Jamaal. May I introduce you to Mr Smith and Mr Roberts?'

The Japanese men gave a slightly drunken giggle at their Anglo pseudonyms. They were looking forward to using these names with one another in the future when they wanted to recall the particular delights of this special evening.

Jamaal nodded and smiled at the men. Another tiny frown from Sebastian. Good. Jamaal knew he was supposed to bow to these guests, but he bowed to no-one.

'Mr Roberts, Mr Smith, please excuse me for a moment,' Sebastian said, bowing, giving Jamaal a sideways glance to emphasise that this was how to greet and leave these men. 'Jamaal and I must go and attend to the entertainment for the evening. Please make yourselves very comfortable. My home is your own. We will return shortly.'

Sebastian placed a big arm around Jamaal's shoulders,

and, smiling affably, guided him from the room. They entered Sebastian's study, a luxurious, masculine room that overlooked the gardens on the left side of the property.

Sebastian dropped himself into one of his corpulent leather armchairs, and reached for a long cigar from a side table. Jamaal waited for the lecture. Sebastian just kept smiling, sending jets of blue smoke into the air.

'What?' Jamaal finally had to know.

'My friend, today has been a very good day.'

Jamaal could not have agreed less. He looked forward to telling this smiling bastard about the cops' questioning early today. Why should he be the only one with a burning gut?

'You want to go first, or should I?' Jamaal asked.

'I believe I will. I think that after I have spoken, you will be less dismayed about your ordeal with the police this morning.'

'You know about that.'

'Yes, Jamaal, but we've no need to worry about them any longer.' He paused for effect, and sucked again on the cigar. 'I told you I would take care of it, and I have. You see, the person who had been drawing the police ever closer to our world is now lying dead in the shed at the bottom of the garden.'

Jamaal started to the window, but he could not see the boatshed from this room. He turned back to Sebastian, stunned.

'I know!' Sebastian beamed at the look on Jamaal's face. 'I shot her myself. This evening. Just half an hour ago, in fact. I've had time for a lovely bath and to greet my guests, and all in all, I'm greatly looking forward to tonight.'

'Her? A woman?'

'Yes, yes. A female psychotherapist. She was very good, I believe. At one time, half of the Mosman tennis club was delving into their mummy-issues with her. She's been watching our activities for some time, and could really have hurt us very much. Fortunately, Jamaal,' he blew more smoke, 'I've taken care of that problem.'

Jamaal just stared at his boss. How did this guy get away with everything? Still, he thought, this was good news for both of them. He realised that his stomach didn't hurt so much any more. And there was more to come.

'Tonight, my friend, will be a celebration in more ways than one,' Sebastian continued. 'Although this bitch is dead, she has attracted more attention to us than is desirable. I've decided to sell this house and change the way we conduct our business. I'd like to be more . . . virtual about the way we do things from now on. I've determined that we shall expand our internet interests, and disband our little club. We can conduct such a business from anywhere on the planet, Jamaal, and frankly, I'm growing tired of Sydney at the present time. In short, my friend, what say you to a bit of a holiday, an extended overseas vacation?'

Jamaal just smiled. Praise Allah. Fuck my brother-in-law and my fat, lazy wife. He knew he was smart for staying loyal to Sebastian. Rewards come to those who wait, he reminded himself.

'That is good news, boss,' Jamaal said. 'I would like that very much. For now, though, I should go down to the shed. Make sure everything's tidy down there.' He wanted a look. They both knew it, and each understood the compulsion well.

'Thank you, Jamaal. I'd appreciate it very much, you know. Don't be too long, though. When you get back here we'll see the evening off with a bang.' He cleared his throat and smiled jovially. 'So to speak.'

Jill crouched behind the rocky outcrop upon which she'd stood to peer into the boatshed, her back to the water, her face to the house. She'd sent the white-eyed girl packing with a sharp mental shake. This is no time for nightmares, she told herself.

A glance at her watch told her that Scotty should be arriving soon. He and the others would approach the house from the street; go in through the front doors with the warrant. For the fortieth time she wished she'd had the good sense to bring her radio or phone from the car. She knew what she'd rather have, however; and she adjusted the heavy weight of her gun in her pocket.

She figured she'd wait down here until she saw the cops' lights, and then make her way back up towards the house. She hoped Sebastian or Jamaal would run down this way, trying to escape the police at the front door. She'd be ready.

Jill alternately stretched her thighs. While she waited for Scotty, she listened to Sydney Harbour breathing behind her back.

She pretended the white-eyed girl was not crouched on the sand beside her.

Jamaal left the house through the French doors in Sebastian's office in time to see the sensor lights at the opposite side of the building click off. He frowned. Who's out here? he wondered. The guests knew they weren't to go out the back of the building. Sebastian's nearest neighbours were Ethel and Beatrice Graham, a pair of spinster sisters who made it their mission in life to gossip about their neighbours with other neighbours. They would also call the police the moment a gathering became more audible than the gulls and the boats. The guests knew that within the house they were welcome to indulge in whatever took their fancy, but were not to venture outside unaccompanied. Even so, during past gatherings, Jamaal had several times had to usher the shy or the secretive out of the backyard and back into the ballroom.

He decided to go around the front of the house first, to ensure they had no uninvited guests. The front lawns stood darkly serene. The night slept quietly. He made his way around the other side of the house, avoiding the sensors for the spotlights he'd installed. Nothing around here. He inched to the rear of the home, moving through darkness, pressed against the walls. The light spilling from the ballroom windows splashed upon empty sandstone pavers and garden furniture. Anyone who might have been out here was not any longer.

From this vantage point, for at least a hundred years, the lights of Sydney Harbour had failed to bewitch very few. Jamaal didn't even notice them. Instead, he peered greedily at the boatshed, excitement mushrooming in his stomach and below it. He'd be alone with the body. Where did Sebastian shoot her? Did her face register surprise, the interfering fucking bitch? He moved from the shadows, needing to hurry now to the shed.

A light shone in the boatshed.

The shadow next to the shed did not belong. Jamaal fell back into the darkness.

Fuck.

His heart hammering against his ribs, Jamaal waited and thought quickly. Sebastian had said he had killed her in the boatshed. He knew his boss would never leave a body outside, not tonight. Someone else was there.

Cops? He thought about running, but figured that if it were the police, they'd have grabbed him already by now. They'd have staked out back and front.

Someone else must have discovered what was in the boatshed. Tonight Jamaal had been shown a chance at a new life, something he'd been working towards for a very long time. This intruder could not be allowed to leave the grounds.

He backtracked towards the front of the house, always in shadow. When he could no longer see the shed, he crept across the lawn and through the shrubbery that bordered the property. The Graham sisters next door were from an era when high fences were considered terribly gauche; fences prevented neighbours passing roses and teacakes across hedges to one another. Fences also ruined the parkland look of a neighbourhood, they argued. Jamaal had long tried to convince Sebastian to erect a high wall between them and the old bats, but he was now pleased to have lost this battle, as he stepped over a creeping gardenia bush and onto the Grahams' property.

He knew that Beatrice would have been in bed with a gin bottle hours ago, but Ethel was a light sleeper. It was his job to know such things. So he stole slowly down towards the water's edge, the thick carpet of lawn and leaves muffling his footfalls. He was now more aroused than anxious – he liked to hunt. Besides, tonight had turned to his favour. Even his serendipitous choice of clothing, black on black, was a sign that he was meant to be victorious.

When the grass gave way to soft sand, Jamaal slowed. To his left sat the boatshed. He could hear nothing but the soft harbour waves and the hulls of the luxury boats gently slapping the water. He knew his footsteps made less sound than these noises. He moved around the shed.

Jerome could not believe they would do this to him.

He was wearing slacks, for God's sake. And a belt! Shiny shoes. Oh my God, he thought, if Nathan ever saw me dressed like this . . . Nathan. Jerome sighed, and put his head in his hands. He sat on the edge of the bath in the bathroom off the basement. He felt really tired. And hungry.

The door opened and Tadpole walked in. Jerome cringed under his gaze.

'Oh, come on, Jerome. You don't look that bad!' Tadpole gave him a half-smile. 'I guess you've never worn anything like that before.'

A tear slid down Jerome's cheek.

'Look, I know you're hungry,' he said kindly. 'Mr Sebastian has just called down. It's time to go up to the party. You should see what they've got to eat up there. Chicken, chips, pies, everything. I could sneak you some beer. Let's go eat!'

'Couldn't you just bring me some food down here?'

'Jerome, everyone wants to meet you. It's time to go up.'

'I'm not going anywhere dressed like this. Let me put my other stuff back on.'

Tadpole sighed, and sat next to Jerome on the bath. A little too close. Jerome scrooched away a bit.

'Jerome, I'm gonna tell you like this. You get to go upstairs with me now, dressed like that, or Jamaal's going to come down here and make you come up.' He gave him a compassionate look. 'I'm not going to bullshit you, Jerome. Even I'm scared of Jamaal. I know you are, and you should be. I'm telling you as a friend – let's get out of here before he comes back.'

Jerome studiously avoided the mirror as he left the bathroom. At least there would be other people at a party. Maybe he could find a way to tell one of them he needed help. He'd already thought about writing a message on a paper napkin and passing it to an adult. He knew he had to be safer around a big group of adults than he was down here. Someone at the party would help him.

He followed Tadpole to the door.

You see, that's another sign.

Walking carefully through the sand, Jamaal had kicked against a rocky outcropping at the base of the boatshed. Of course! He needed a weapon – a rock would do nicely. He bent and felt around in the sand. There were several large pieces buried, but he could not dislodge them. He felt the next one give a little, and prised with his fingers until it came free suddenly. He nearly fell. He steadied himself, carrying the baseball-sized rock, and continued on his way along to the far edge of the back of the boatshed.

Jamaal's mother had tried to teach him religion, but he'd never really taken to it. Tonight, however, had taught him to believe. A tiny glance around the corner of the shed at who waited there showed him that God had brought her here as a gift. He took a very deep breath and raised his eyes towards heaven.

With one stride and a silent lunge, Jamaal crossed the sand between himself and Jill and smashed the rock down on her head.

44

A PAIR OF BLINDING headlights bore down upon Jill, filling her with a sense of urgency. Got to get out of here! The lights came closer, but she stood paralysed, pinned to the spot, frozen in the knowledge that she was about to be annihilated. The twin lights filled her vision; her brain burned with the heat of them. Any moment now they would smash her down, crush her completely. She moaned in pain, and the white-eyed girl woke her up.

The lights. Just her eyes – the white-eyed girl. Another nightmare was all. Jill tried to reassure herself, slow her breathing, open her own eyes.

What the fuck? thought Jill. It was pitch black. Eyes open or closed. Inside her head, the white-eyed girl nodded solemnly. You're blind too, she told Jill without speaking.

Jill sat up fast, shuffled backwards, trying to get away

from the little girl in her head, from wherever she was, from the knowledge, deep down, that she was once again captive somewhere and that she couldn't see. She whimpered when her head struck an object, pain sending a rolling wave of nausea through her stomach. Head between her knees, a hard surface beneath her, Jill tried to take stock. What had she last been doing? It all came back, still-shots in her mind of the last hours that she could remember. The phone call from Mercy; the drive to Hunters Hill; creeping down to the water's edge; Mercy, on the floor, her chest blown out. Then blackness. It was completely and utterly black.

She raised a hand to the back of her head, the movement bringing back the seasick feeling. Her hand came away wet. Did she slip and fall, hit her head? Maybe she was in hospital? Scotty found her injured and brought her here. That's it, she lied to herself, knowing that she was sitting on a hard, cold floor, probably concrete, not a bed; aware that nothing in here smelled or sounded like a hospital. Mentally, she pushed hard at the doors in her mind, holding back with all her might the horror of knowledge that bulged behind them.

She felt she was in a large room; it sounded echoey, kind of empty. It smelled earthy, like underground. Like a basement.

The white-eyed girl was back, nodding wisely. We've got to face it now.

Jill scrambled for something to think about, anything. Not in the basement. Not for real. Wake up! She reached up to her eyes, put her fingers on her eyeballs, pressed. A flare of orange inside her head, then nothing. Her eyes were wide open, and there was no light. It was not just the darkness of a room, she was sure of it. She could see nothing at all.

The little girl was right. She was alone, blind, and in the basement.

Jill ignored the silent admonishment of the white-eyed girl and, curled into a foetal ball, gave in to terrified sobs. The last two decades were an illusion. This was real. She'd never been safe. She had no control. Nothing could be worse than this.

And then she heard footsteps just outside the room.

Jerome had only seen houses like this on TV. When they got out of the cupboard, he stuck close to Tadpole, feeling minuscule under the cavernous space of the three-metre-high ceilings. Through huge windows, Jerome could see it was very dark outside. His footsteps echoed on the shiny floors.

Where was the party? Was this another trick? When his parents had people over, every chair was taken and there were people in each room, talking and laughing, ruffling his hair when he passed by. Kids running through hallways, slowing to a giggling walk when they passed a group of adults, whooping and running again when they turned a corner. He couldn't even hear anyone talking. He looked up at Tadpole, and the man smiled down at him, his eyes glittery and weird. Jerome looked back down at his shoes, wishing his dad would come get him.

They walked past several open archways, and he glimpsed gleaming surfaces and empty furniture. And then Jerome heard music. Quiet, tinkly music. By this time of night at a party in his neighbourhood, they'd be playing Cold Chisel or Midnight Oil, or something like that. He and his friends would be pissing themselves, watching the oldies jerk around like they thought they were dancing. It was the best bit, but you had to force yourself to stay awake long enough for them to have had enough to drink. Even though it was really embarrassing, he also kind of liked it when his mum and dad would start kissing in the middle of the dancing.

They walked through a hallway, approaching a corner on the left. He could hear people speaking in soft voices. He couldn't hear any other kids. Thank God, he thought, looking down at his shiny shoes, pulling at the belt. At least they wouldn't see him dressed like this. A belt, for godsakes.

When they rounded the corner, no-one really paid any attention at first. No-one dressed like this at any party he'd ever been to either. Jerome was pretty sure his dad didn't even own a suit. He looked around, and couldn't help but feel a little awed by the beautiful room, the fireplace, the long white table covered in platters of food that looked great, and the important-looking men, standing and sitting around. All men. He took another look around. Not one dress or skirt in here. These people were just freakin' weird.

Jerome stepped onto a thick, round rug he thought his mum would probably like. She was always trying to stop his dad to look at stuff like this as he marched through department stores ahead of her. Thinking of his mum and dad so much made his throat hurt again.

A man sitting in a chair to Jerome's left looked straight at him and gasped. The man stood up and several others near him looked up. Everyone started talking and then suddenly the whole room stared at him and Tadpole. He turned around to see if maybe someone else had come in behind them, but there was no-one else there. They all just gawped at him. This was absolutely the worst. The men had all stopped whatever they were doing and stood full-on staring. Jerome wished there was one of those trapdoors underneath him right now, and he could just bolt back down to the underground room. He knew he looked like a dork, but what the fuck were they all staring at, really?

And then they started to clap.

Jamaal knew that he was indispensable to Sebastian now. He had brought him the boy, and when he'd told him he had the cop bitch in the basement, he'd seen his boss was pleased. He told Sebastian that he'd dropped some of Carter's optometrist solution into her eyes, to keep her from seeing anything if she woke up before they got back down there.

'That was very quick thinking, Jamaal. And you're certain there was no-one else on the grounds?'

'She must have come alone. It's all quiet everywhere else. I looked carefully.'

'Oh, I'm quite certain that you did. Was the boy in there when you brought her in?'

'No. Tadpole had just taken him out. They'll be out there by now.' He indicated with his chin to the rooms outside the study.

'I see.' A wrinkle of annoyance creased Sebastian's forehead. 'Well, I really should be out there too, you know, Jamaal. We can't have people helping themselves before I've established the pecking order.' He stood to leave.

'Would you mind very much going back down there,' he continued, 'and checking to see that our new guest has everything she needs and that she is not getting herself into any trouble?'

Jamaal stared as the big man smoothed his suit and left the study. Our new guest. Why did he speak like that? In the dining room down the hall from this very room, Jamaal had once seen Sebastian pull out a chair for a whore, offer her a glass of wine, and drink with her, before reaching forwards and strangling her with his hands.

One sick motherfucker, he thought to himself as he left the room to go back downstairs.

I am not ready for whoever that is, thought Jill when she heard the movement outside the room. Then she remembered, and reached quickly into her pocket. Nothing. Her gun was gone.

Pretend you're still unconscious, then. The white-eyed girl could put the thoughts in Jill's mind without moving her mouth.

Jill moved forwards a little, quickly and silently, until she figured she was back in the spot where she had been lying when she'd regained consciousness. She lay down just before she heard a door open at the end of the room.

'You awake yet, bitch?'

The male voice, slightly accented, came from about ten metres away from her head. That's where the door is, she recorded for later. The room is big. She counted his footfalls, listened for the way he moved, began to picture objects he was manoeuvring around as he walked through the room. Good girl, the white-eyed girl whispered in her head. Jill lay still.

'Hey, Sergeant Jackson.' A singsong voice, close to her ear. He was leaning right down, his mouth close to her head.

Eyes closed, she could see him now, from where his voice had issued, from where she could feel and smell him breathing. She could swing, now, pivot her legs up from her hips, wrap his head in her thighs and snap his neck. She chose not to move, but she felt power seep back into her body with the knowledge that she could. She enforced stillness, body and mind.

'You know, you fucking whore, that I almost killed my wife because of you. You come to my house?' His voice sounded soft but outraged, hissing into her ear. 'Can you hear me? Does your head hurt, cunt? I'm going to make you hurt much more than that.'

She lay in the basement with Jamaal Mahmoud. She knew that now.

Because she heard him breathe in, and felt him move to take the shot, she knew the blow was coming and could block her reaction, but she couldn't block the pain. She let her head loll limply from the force of his open-handed slap to her face. The slap was nothing. It was the fist-sized mush of tenderness at the back of her head that made her want to vomit; the force from the blow caused it to roll on the hard floor beneath her. She focused her senses on the hand he had used to strike, his location now, mentally picturing his positioning. She thought of an alternate strategy to strike back if she had to, absorbing the energy of the pain to use later.

'Hmm,' she heard him say. And she waited. Waiting was important now, she felt. His movements were her eyes. She had to learn more about where she was in order to be able to get around in the dark; to find her way out. She felt him crouching there by her head, breathing with her, a bond between them, united by their hate for one another, and the desire to make the other one hurt; an intimacy in their silent understanding.

She heard him shift and undo his zipper. Oh no, no, no.

Be still, the white-eyed girl warned. Don't be silly now.

Jill smelled the sweet sweat of male genitalia that had never failed to flood her with distress and with images of being raped as a child. She retreated further into herself as she heard the man beside her stand; he took two steps from her head towards the middle of her body.

When she heard his derisive laughter and felt the warm stream of his urine splashing down onto her stomach and face, Jill knew that a feeling of relief was at odds with the situation. Anything but rape, she told herself. She stayed motionless, allowing nothing in her features to indicate that she was conscious.

Beside her, the white-eyed girl's mouth set in a hard, straight line.

Sebastian entered the ballroom at the tail end of the applause; it briefly swelled again when the men noticed his presence. He smiled warmly at his guests, but was worried about the wild-eyed look of the boy on the other side of the room. He needed to handle the situation quickly – the child looked ready to break down. While some present were quite partial to a bit of crying, others, particularly his overseas guests, considered it distasteful to be confronted by high emotionality.

He raised his hands slightly, palms down, indicating the men should calm themselves, be seated.

'Friends,' his voice reached all corners of the room, 'I hope you are comfortable. Tonight's games will be underway soon. For those of you who have had enough to eat and drink, a movie is showing in the room on the right behind me, and I believe these gentlemen to my left are engaged in a swap meet. You might wish to join them. I would like to ensure that our youngest guest has something to eat and drink. Please excuse me.'

He cut across the room, and was with Tadpole and Jerome in a few long strides.

'My boy, you must be starving,' he smiled down, speaking in a soothing tone. 'Please let me help you choose some nice things to eat.' He steered the dazed little boy to the food table, and fetched for him a heavy white dinner plate, some silver cutlery and a linen napkin. He put them on the table in front of Jerome.

'Feel free to use your hands, Jerome,' he stage-whispered, and then stood back, indicating that Tadpole should step back with him. They stood out of earshot of the boy.

'I'm surprised at you, Tadpole,' his voice was steely. 'Couldn't you have given Jerome a little something to take the edge off things?'

'I wasn't sure what you wanted, Mr Sebastian.' Tadpole gave a small sycophantic smile.

'No matter. Five milligrams of Valium will do nicely. See if you can get him to drink this.' Sebastian took a side step to the linen-covered drinks table and removed a bright blue bottle from one of several ice and bottle-filled silver buckets.

'Vodka-pop. Blueberry, I believe. Kids love them.' He removed the bottle top with a twist of his palm. His big body blocking the view of others, Sebastian took a syringe from his jacket pocket and squirted a small amount of clear liquid down into the bottle. He swirled it a little and handed it to Tadpole.

'He's had nothing to eat or drink down there has he?'

'No, Mr Sebastian. Not since this morning.'

'Good, he'll be thirsty. Give him this. In fifteen minutes, take him to the bedroom next to my study. I'll bring the Japanese in there in twenty.'

'Yes, Mr Sebastian.'

Tadpole smiled beatifically and made his way over to the food table.

Sebastian thought there was time to visit the basement before the fun began.

45

HE HAD NO IDEA why the Jew had made it that way, but Sebastian had found the soundproofing of the basement invaluable over the years. Although he'd tested its effectiveness in absorbing sound many times, he still felt uncomfortable leaving Jamaal alone with the policewoman while he had a house full of friends. He knew Mahmoud could make a mess at times.

He squeezed his big body through the trapdoor in the cupboard floor. Ordinarily, he avoided this small entry, preferring the big panel and tunnel in the garage, but he had little time tonight and this was the closer access point. When he'd traversed the last tight turn, he opened the door to the big room.

'Jamaal, it smells terrible in here.' He quickly took in the woman's body on the floor, Mahmoud standing over it. He hoped she was not dead yet. There was much she could tell them before she and the shrink went to the bottom of the harbour.

When he reached Jamaal, he saw she was still breathing and decided not to comment on the piss. Although it was distasteful, he understood Jamaal's urges. Perhaps he'd give her to him when he had what he needed. He knew it was important to keep his dog happy.

'She's still out, I see, my friend,' said Sebastian. 'I bet she didn't think she would be meeting you this way.'

'Fucking bitch,' Jamaal kicked Jill in the ribs.

'Yes, thank you, Jamaal. I do need her awake.'

Jill couldn't stifle the moan following the kick in her side. Her stalling for time was over. She opened her sightless eyes.

'Sergeant Jackson, welcome to my home.'

Jill heard his height, knew where he was standing in relation to Jamaal.

'What did you do to my eyes?'

She'd debated asking, knowing that it would betray her weakness. If her blindness had been caused by the blow to the back of her head, they would not know about it. Still, within moments of her rising, they would become aware that she could not see.

'Ah, yes. My apologies. Jamaal saw fit to limit your movements using medical means. I'm afraid you've been rather knocked around a bit, but you are not here by invitation tonight, are you? It really can't be considered our fault that you have not been welcomed.' He paused. 'Excuse me a moment.'

Jill shuddered in horror at the term 'medical means'. What had they done to her eyes? She forced herself to listen to the men next to her.

'Jamaal, I need you to go upstairs and assist Tadpole with our little friend. If he has not taken the drink I left for him, you must calm him down by other means. I will be joining you up there shortly.'

'What about her?'

'I'd like to speak to Sergeant Jackson for a few moments. I'll make sure she cannot leave us before we return.'

Jill heard Jamaal grunt an assent and walk out of the room. She wondered how many times, before and after Honey, that these two spiders had sedated their young prey.

'You are holding Jerome Sanders captive here, aren't you?' Jill needed to know that he was still alive, that it was not some other poor boy Sebastian had just been discussing.

'Yes, he's a guest at a party upstairs for some of my select club members.'

Jill had to keep him talking. She had no idea how long she'd been out, but surely it could not be much longer before Scotty got here.

'What are you going to do with him?'

'Why, Jill, you know that better than most.'

With those words, the doors in Jill's mind slammed open; full realisation flooded her consciousness. The white-eyed girl gave Jill a wise, sad smile, as she processed the knowledge of who this man really was. Her gut filled with terror, nearly forcing evacuation of her bowels. His tone, his size, his smell, the dark, this room.

'I was disappointed when we met in the hospital that night, Jill, that you did not recognise me.' Sebastian's voice barely registered over the howling in her mind. 'I had not imagined I could be so forgettable, especially for you. Your first. Still, we were both very young, were we not? I like to think I have gained in skill since we knew one another.'

The white-eyed girl's face was now blank, impassive. She quietly listened to Mr Sebastian while Jill screamed. Sebastian talked over the top of the noise.

'Certainly I have learned that it is easy to forget, so I do understand, Jill. That is why, since we had our relationship, I have learned to video-record my encounters. I regret that I have no record of our time together. My mentor at the time – you'll recall him I hope, we shared our time together – was an old-fashioned man, not taken with technology.'

The white-eyed girl watched the heavy man reach down to help Jill into a sitting position. She stayed silent, watching Jill keening on the floor.

'I'm sorry to have to tell you, Jill,' he continued kindly, settling onto a lounge chair close by, 'our mutual friend has passed on. He grew old and infirm, you see, and had taken to reminiscing out loud about former favoured pastimes, if you can imagine.' He gave a gruff laugh. 'I hope that a friend is one day kind enough to help me on my way as I did for him, should I become so indiscreet in my waning years.

'Jill, I don't have very long with you this visit,' he continued, 'and I was hoping that we could talk about you, your career. Do you think that you might be able to collect yourself enough for us to have less of a one-sided chat?'

He waited a beat, gently prodded at Jill with a toe.

'I suppose not. Perhaps later. I will be back to speak with you soon. I'll have to bring Jamaal, I'm afraid. He has an inordinate interest in you. Have you noticed, Jill, that the stupid are often terribly superstitious? He's quite taken by the idea of signs, you see, and he feels that finding you by the boatshed was his destiny. My apologies for the mess in the shed by the way. Your psychotherapist friend was entirely too interested in my club and its members. In fact, I believe she drew you to me.'

He paused, and began again reflectively, 'You know Jill, maybe there is something to this fate notion after all. Our relationship sent you to Dr Merris, I believe, and she, in turn, brought you back to me.' He shifted in the chair.

'Well, until our next meeting, then. But before I go for now, I must tell you, Jill, I have been proud watching you grow. Of course, I'm disappointed in your failure to pro-create. You don't seem to relate well to the opposite sex. I don't suppose you would know, would you, that my club members award special bonus points to those of us who can form a relationship with the second generation of our past friends. Not much chance of me getting to know one of your offspring now, though, is there Jill?'

The white-eyed girl blinked. Once, twice.

Sebastian used the arms of the chair to begin to lift his bulk from the low lounge. The little girl was standing, head slightly askew, white eyes watching Jill on the ground, now silent, with great interest.

'I'm off to make Jerome famous,' he said. 'I assure you he will be a superstar after tonight. A very tired little superstar.'

Although it happened instantaneously, and without her conscious awareness, somewhere inside Jill felt sad to see the white-eyed girl go. Suddenly, for the first time in twenty years, Jill felt whole. But none of that mattered right here, right now.

Her attention focused on Sebastian's breathing. She knew the placement of each of his feet, and where he would place them next; she heard the creak of his knees as he half-lifted himself from the chair. On the floor, legs folded beneath her, Jill found her centre of gravity; her mind completely clear. In one seamless move, she moved one arm away on the ground and stretched one leg straight. With the other leg, she swung with all her might, propelling herself around with a round-house kick that connected with Sebastian at the precise moment he was halfway between sitting and standing. The force of the impact smashed its way up through her entire body.

Had he been able to speak, Alejandro Sebastian would regardless have been unable to find words from his considerable vocabulary to describe the force of the blow that almost fractured his neck. As it was, his brain was still decelerating in a series of shuddering slides from one side of his skull to the other. Somewhere he was aware, however, that his bottom teeth now protruded through his top lip. This, along with the fact that he'd swallowed his tongue, led to considerable difficulty breathing.

Jill gave herself a few moments to collect herself, shake out the kinks a little, always aware of the wet, sucking gasps in the lounge chair near her. When she was ready, she again swung with her foot at the sound, and felt pleased when it stopped.

Jerome didn't feel too good. At Mitchell Claymore's tenth birthday party, the same thing had happened. At first, he thought he'd eaten too many chicken nuggets, but then half the kids at the party had started spewing and crying. Megan and Courtney had had to go to hospital overnight. He later overheard his mother saying that Mrs Claymore got really depressed because she'd poisoned half the party with the food, and for a while there he'd thought Mitchell's mum was some kind of mental murderer. He was scared of his friends' mums for a while after that. Hell, he was only nine.

He wondered whether this was food poisoning too. He felt really woozy and just wanted to lie down. He dropped a half-eaten chicken drumstick onto his plate, and looked for somewhere to sit. Tadpole stood at his side in a moment.

'Jerome, you look tired out. Want to go somewhere quieter to have a rest?'

Jerome managed to nod. He followed Tadpole through groups of whispering men; his heavy eyes watching his feet take one step at a time.

He now lay in the most comfortable bed he had ever been in, and those stupid shoes were off. The lights were soft and he felt much better. Probably his dad would be here in the morning . . . Was that Logan in the doorway? Too short to be Logan's dad . . .

Something scratchy stopped him sleeping. Like when you get bitten by sandflies really badly, and even when you're asleep, you're driven mad by the itching. But this was like itching in the mind – like something was wrong.

Someone kept rubbing his leg. Jerome opened his eyes, thinking maybe Nathan had left the TV on.

Mr Smith, the young Japanese dignitary, held a video camera, while his father, wearing only boxer shorts, sat on the side of the bed, his hand on Jerome's leg. The sheets were pulled back, and Jerome realised he was wearing only under-pants. His instinctive kick propelled the small, elderly man to the ground, where he landed on his hip. Mr Smith almost dropped the camera in his haste to help his father. He shouted in another language at Jerome, but Jerome jumped to his feet on the bed, his back wedged into the corner, yelling louder than both men combined.

Mr Smith helped his father to his feet and fussed solicitously around the older man, throwing spiteful looks Jerome's way. Jerome was just glad they seemed to be staying on their side of the room. He knew the yelling would bring help in a moment, and he was ready to kick again if the perverts came near him.

Thank God, he thought, hearing footsteps approaching. His eyes had not left the darkened corridor outside the doorway, willing help to come.

In moments of extreme threat, the human body will defend itself by instigating a series of preconscious neurochemical reactions that result in a fight or flight response. This response can be short circuited, however, if the magnitude of fear is overwhelming, resulting in the body 'freezing'. When Jamaal Mahmoud walked out of the semi-darkness into the light of the bedroom, Jerome Sanders' knees buckled, and he fell to the bed, paralysed.

Fortunately, the neurochemicals in Jill's brain were working to subdue pain messages that would ordinarily have seen her on her knees, retching. As it was, she had to keep swallowing hard to stop herself from throwing up the bile that squirted into the pit of her stomach every time she moved her head too fast. In spite of this, she felt relatively clear-headed, focused.

She worked her way to a wall, stumbling once only, remembering and avoiding several obstacles she had heard the two men manoeuvring around. She figured Jamaal had been gone about five minutes now. When Sebastian did not return upstairs soon, he would be back. Jill did not want to be here when that happened.

The spinning kick had disoriented her, and she was now unsure of the direction of the door through which the men had entered. Walking around the wall in the wrong direction would cost her valuable time, but she could think of no alternative. Keeping her back to the wall, Jill made her way around the room, the sounds of her footsteps and heartbeat accompanying her. She didn't let herself think about not finding the door before Jamaal returned.

Instead, she thought about the killer. Sebastian must have been behind all of the deaths. He'd admitted to killing his own mentor, the man with whom he had abducted and raped Jill twenty years ago. Another sensation of inner synchronicity settled over Jill with the sudden realisation that both of these men were now dead. She sighed deeply, and kept moving.

Sebastian had also killed Mercy, or had at least had her killed. Maybe he knew that Mercy had witnessed him murdering Wayne Crabbe, maybe he didn't. He knew that she was threatening his organisation, and he could never allow that to happen, even if that meant cannibalising his own members. He must have killed Crabbe, Rocla, Manzi and Carter because their crimes could somehow be traced back to his club. They'd all been charged, and all of their victims had seen Mercy. Mercy must have discovered a connection between the men and that led her to Sebastian, and to her death.

Jill wondered how far Jamaal was involved. Mercy had said he had kidnapped Jerome Sanders, and that fitted with all Honey had told her about the man. Had he staged the blow to his head and helped Sebastian kill Manzi in the car? Or had something maybe gone wrong, resulting in his injuries? Or did Jamaal not know that his boss had taken out four of their party pals, and he had perhaps been a failed fifth? Surely he would suspect it?

The wall felt hard and cold on her palms as she edged along. She sensed that the room lay buried under the earth, and she pushed away a brief image of herself entombed. Twice, she moved around heavy furniture of some type. She knew by now that she had gone away from the direction of the door, but it was too late to double back the other way. She gritted her teeth with the pressure of the passing moments. The low hum of a refrigerator escorted her through an open kitchen, and when she passed the second corner of the room, she knew she was on the home straight, heading back towards the exit.

Moving quickly now, Jill almost missed it when her hands ran over some sort of recessed panelling in the otherwise smooth concrete of the wall. This was not where the doorway should be, but, her hearing honed by years of training sessions in the dark, she could sense air moving behind the surface. She scrabbled at the area with her hands, trying to wedge her fingertips into the fine vertical fissure she felt running up the wall. Nothing. She couldn't make it move. She forced herself to slowly smooth her hands across each part of the surface, seeking a handle of some description. The moments ticked by, and her instincts urged her to move on. She forced herself to continue covering the area with her hands, but she could feel nothing marring the surface at all. Finally she reached another vertical crack in the wall and realised that this doorway was very large; it was probably a sliding door, and it might be operated by remote control, or by a button that could be anywhere in the room. With a squirm of frustration at the time she had wasted, she moved on, faster now, urgency bursting in her chest.

The third corner. She knew the other doorway had to be close to the last corner of the room. Almost there.

And then, from behind the wall, descending from a height, Jill heard someone clattering, running towards her.

She scrabbled at her eyes, in her terror thinking she had a blindfold on, as she had countless times when training. Her fear redoubled when she remembered that her eyes were wide open and staring, and she could see nothing at all. She wanted to howl in the dark. Instead, she did the only thing she could: tried to make herself as small a target as possible. She squatted on the ground and listened.

Pressed against the wall, Jill took several fast, very deep breaths to increase the oxygen in her blood, pumping herself up to attack. She crouched, poised, ready to spring as soon as the door opened. But the next sound shocked her so much that she almost lost her balance and rocked back on her haunches to the ground.

Instead, she stood, a sob in her throat, waiting for the child who was crying and running behind the door.

When the door opened and she heard his little body hurtle through, she called to him.

'Jerome? Jerome Sanders?'

He knocked her against the wall when he rushed at her, scrabbling, sobbing.

'Help! Can you help me? He's coming.'

'Jerome. We're going to get out of here. My name is Jill.

I'm a police officer. I'm going to help you, and you're going to help me.'

She reached for him, put her cool hands on his hot face, held his head still.

'Is Jamaal behind you, Jerome?' she asked him.

'The door in the floor was still open, but I slammed it when I got in. I could hear him behind me and I thought he'd follow me, but maybe it locked or something.'

Jill couldn't make sense of all this, but understood they had very little time.

'Jerome. There are three things I need to tell you. You've got to be brave okay?' She felt him nod. 'First thing is that there is another door in here, and you and I are going to find it and get out.'

'Yeah! He brought me in that way. Come on!' He tried to run from her.

'Jerome, I said three things. You have to wait, just a moment.' She held his shirt. 'I can't see anything, Jerome. They did something to my eyes. You're going to have to lead me.'

'Uh-huh.' He sounded small, scared, waiting for the third thing.

'The other thing, Jerome, is that there is a body down here. It's Mr Sebastian, the man who owns this house. I don't want you to freak out when you see him, all right? Best thing you can do is try hard not to look at him, take me to the door, and we'll get home to your mum and dad.' She paused. 'You ready?'

'Let's go. Now, please.'

Jill held Jerome's hand and they crossed the big room in about ten seconds. When she heard a sharp intake of breath, she squeezed his hand harder, knowing he'd just seen Sebastian.

When Jerome spoke, though, his voice sounded steady. 'I saw Tadpole press this thing. Hang on.' He let go of her hand. She heard him moving a chair, and then a deep mechanical rumbling. Fresh, salty air hit her face.

Next to her, Jerome suddenly screamed. She reached out, grabbed his arm and ran towards the air.

46

THE SOUNDS OF someone trying to move quietly woke Jill, but she felt so exhausted that she just listened for a while with her eyes closed. When she couldn't figure out what the *snick, snick* noise could be, Jill opened her eyes and saw the blurry shape of her mother's back standing near a sun-filled window. *Snick, snick.*

'What're you doing?' Her voice was gravelly.

'Good morning, darling!' Her mum bustled over to the bed. She held scissors in one hand, a couple of wilted flower heads in the other. 'How are you feeling?'

'Tired.' Jill looked around the hospital room, fingered a ribbon on the nightgown she was wearing. Pink. Definitely not one of her own.

'And, how does everything . . . look . . .' she trailed off.

'Blurry, but I can see. What did they do to my eyes?'

'I'll get the doctor, darling. He can explain. It's good to see you awake at last. They've kept you sleeping for twenty-four hours.' Her mum beamed, wiped her eyes, and left the room.

Jill stretched gingerly, registering surprise that she didn't feel too bad. She reached up and touched the back of her head, pressed her fingers against the bandage there. A bit harder. Didn't hurt too much. Her ribs ached a little, but she was getting used to that.

Sensing her body was going to be okay, Jill prodded a little at her feelings, memories. The knowledge that she had literally been back in the basement with Sebastian was there, but it didn't send her scurrying behind her mental doors. Nor did it drag forward image after image of what she'd endured when she was twelve. Huh.

She wondered how Scotty had handled the clean-up at the mansion in Hunters Hill. The waves of relief she had felt on hearing his voice when she and Jerome had run out of the underground room had dropped her to her knees.

When she'd come home from that basement the first time, when she was twelve, Jill had found herself waiting to feel safe again, to feel like it was really over, but the wait had stretched from days to years, and still the feeling had not come. Twenty years later, on her knees, sobbing in the grass, Jill finally felt like she had come home. She cried with relief. She cried for Jerome. She cried for what her mum, dad, brother and sister had endured. Most of all, Jill cried for the white-eyed girl who had watched it all, and was gone forever. The tears had not stopped until she was in the ambulance and felt the morphine take effect.

A voice outside her door interrupted Jill's thoughts; you

always heard Scotty before you saw him. She wiped her eyes before he entered the room.

'Loud bloody bastard,' she greeted him, as he strode through her door, laughing at someone outside on the ward. 'People are sleeping, you know.'

'Only lazy buggers who should be out working like the rest of us. When are you getting up, Jackson? There's shit-loads of paperwork.'

'Suffer. I'm blind, remember?'

'Bullshit. Doctor said your eyes are fine.' His voice softened a little. 'They used the same shit they put in little Madeline McKenzie's eyes. Turns out, one of the squirrels at the party was an optometrist; he'd handed round this stuff that makes you temporarily blind if you use enough. They had a vet too. They had a real-life e-Bay thing happening there. They were trading all sorts of shit with each other – horse tranquillisers, coke, some other sick shit.

'We've got ten of them locked up,' he continued. 'Six of them won't say a thing. Two don't speak English. But we got two in there who've spilled their guts about everything. One of them only wanted some McDonald's, and when he got that we couldn't shut him up.'

'Mahmoud?'

The clouds came over Scotty's face. 'We didn't get him. He hasn't been home either.' He blew off a sigh. 'He'll show up, J.'

'Yep. What about Mercy?'

Scotty's brow creased. 'Pretty sad all round, really,' he said. 'Her mother's dead, no siblings, and her father's a hard bastard. Didn't want to know. Wouldn't even come and ID her body. I thought maybe it was a shock reaction, so I went round to his house again a couple of hours later. He practically slammed the door in my face.'

Jill shook her head and stared at the sheets. Mercy's life had been dedicated to helping others, and in death she was on her own.

'We ended up having to get a bloke she worked with to come down to the coroner's,' Scotty continued. 'I don't know about you, Jackson, but I reckon some of those counsellors are more screwed up than their clients. What was his name – Noah Griffen – that's it.'

'What'd he do?'

'Nothing really. He pretty much didn't say a word. Didn't want to know a thing. Shocked I s'pose. I just thought shrinks were supposed to deal with stuff like that better.'

'That's what people think about us,' said Jill. 'Not exactly true in my case is it?'

'Yeah. You were a total stuff-up. Got the baddie, saved the kid, lived to tell the tale. You really dropped the bundle, Jackson.'

Jill hid a small smile with her hair. 'Jerome all right?' she asked, finally looking up.

The sun came back out when Scotty smiled. 'Him and his whole family got here at eight o'clock this morning. They wanted to come yesterday, but the doctors told them you'd be asleep all day and they'd be wasting their time. They got told to come back some time today. They walked in the doors as soon as visitors were allowed.'

'How do you know they were here that early?' Jill smiled.

Scotty looked sheepish. 'Someone told me. Anyway, Mrs Sanders and your mum haven't stopped talking all morning. You can't shut some people up.'

'What time is it?'

'Eleven.'

'What are you bludging around waiting for then? Let the poor people in.'

'You ready for them, Jackson?'

She nodded.

At twelve o'clock, with a box of tissues and Jerome Sanders eating chocolates on her bed, a nurse came in and told the Sanders, Jacksons and Scotty that it was time to go, that Jill had to rest.

Frances Sanders and Jerome were the last to leave. Jerome's mother bent as though to give Jill a final kiss. Instead, she just rested her forehead against Jill's own.

'Bless you,' she whispered, barely audible.

Jill swallowed.

'For God's sake, Mum! She's a cop. You don't have to go bawling all over her.' Jerome turned to Jill. 'Don't forget you said I could hold your gun some time.'

'I said you could see it.'

'Yeah, okay, then.' Jerome gave her a last big smile, stole another two of her chocolates when his mum wasn't looking, and they left the room together.

Jill leaned her head back against her pillows and was asleep by 12.05.

47

SCOTTY WAS RIGHT. There was shitloads of paperwork.

It had been a week since she'd been released from hospital and Jill sat opposite her partner, whose desk was also covered in files. Forensics were still sending in their reports, but the urgency had diminished given that Sebastian was dead and it looked like he'd done all the killing. Finding Mahmoud was certainly a priority. They had him for the kidnapping after Jerome had picked him from several photos, but whether they could implicate him in any of the murders remained to be seen. Regardless, the whole country was on alert for him now.

Jill was supposed to take another week off, but she knew Scotty needed her help and, despite her fatigue, she couldn't handle any more bed rest. Andreessen hadn't seemed to care either way when she'd shown up in her casual clothes that morning.

When they'd finished big-noting themselves about the bust at Hunters Hill, Harris, Jardine and Elvis had managed to get out of all the wrap-up work on the case. Jardine had taken compassionate leave: trying to get his marriage back together, they said. Harris caught another case back at Central and his boss could no longer spare him for the task-force. With them gone, it made sense to move the wind-up work back to Maroubra, but yesterday they'd been told that Elvis was on sick report – hurt on duty.

'What for?' Scotty had asked Inspector Andreessen.

'Back injury. Remember when he fell down those stairs chasing a druggie in Darlinghurst? It's playing up again.' The Inspector dismissed them.

Back at their desks, Scotty stared morosely at the reams of paper on his desk. 'Fat fuck. Hurt on duty, my arse. Gibson reckons he hurt his back after a pub crawl when he fell off the platform at Central station.'

Jill laughed. 'Hope it hurt.'

They worked quietly for a while, but Jill couldn't settle into it. 'Scotty,' she said.

'Mmm.'

'I'm gonna go out for a while.'

'Not you too, Jackson.'

'I want to go and pick up Mercy's files from the hospital. I want to have them all here to see whether she wrote any-thing in them about Mahmoud or Sebastian.'

'You right to drive?'

'Yeah.'

'You're on my shit list,' he growled. 'No really, that's cool. I'll see you tomorrow then.'

On the way out to Richmond, Jill wondered whether she

was holding off closing down this case because it would mean finally ending a huge chapter in her own life. That would mean changing the way she did a lot of things. Was she stalling? She'd had a couple of days in bed to think about her punishing food and exercise regime, her obsessive cleaning, her arm's-length relationships with others. None of her safeguards felt as relevant any more. She planned to change a lot of things in her life now.

She reasoned that she really did want to see what Dr Merris could tell her in death that she had been unable to share in life. She felt she owed Mercy something. It was really Mercy who had saved Jerome. It was Mercy's actions that had forced Jill to finally confront Sebastian and end the years of fear.

She clicked the radio on in the car and watched the sunlight outside painting the trees red and gold.

'Carole Dean's off today,' the CEO of the hospital, Frank Black, told Jill as she waited in his office for someone to accompany her to Mercy's rooms.

They sat in awkward silence until Black's phone rang and, relieved, he dived upon it.

One of the nursing staff poked her head around the door, and smiled. Jill had met Kim once before when she'd come to visit Dr Merris. They walked together through the hospital towards Mercy's rooms.

'People here are pretty shook up about Mercy's death,' said Kim. 'Not just her patients either. The staff liked her, too. She used to be great. But she just went right off towards the end.'

Jill walked and listened. They left the plush foyer of the main part of the hospital and moved into a more sterile section of the building. The private psychiatric hospital had previously also offered medical–surgical procedures, but the cost of maintaining the equipment had rendered that part of the business unfeasible, given that psychiatric beds could pull in as much money for much less outlay.

'You see it a fair bit in the mental health field, but no-one wants to be told they're burning out,' Kim continued. 'I tried to talk to her, but she was just unreachable, you know?'

'Yeah. I do. I'm hoping that her files might tell me some more about what happened to her. There could also be some information that helps us with the charges against the men we caught at the house where she died.'

'Let me know if I can help. Sick bastards.'

Their footsteps echoed on the cold blue linoleum-tiled floors. Mercy's rooms lay underneath this disused part of the hospital. She had told the other staff she liked the silence, and if her patients were particularly distressed during sessions, they did not disturb anyone else. The lighting was kept to a minimum here, to save costs. Virtually new desks sat empty. Signs seemed brand new. They passed examination rooms where shiny, expensive-looking machines sat in shadows, unused.

They clattered down two bare sets of stairs. The lifts here had also been decommissioned. When Jill had been out here for sessions with Mercy, she'd parked in a bottom level carpark closer to the doctor's rooms, and had entered through a back entry Mercy had arranged to have opened for her. That way, most patients didn't have to make this gloomy trip.

They arrived at last, and Kim unlocked the big door in the shadowy corridor.

'Jill, just call if you want to ask any questions, or can't find something you need. All the numbers are programmed into the phones. Mercy's files are in the storeroom over there. These are the keys. This one opens her desk. Good luck with it.'

Jill thanked her and entered the outer office as Kim's footsteps receded down the empty hallway.

Dr Merris had a self-contained suite of four rooms – a comfortable waiting area, a storeroom where the files were kept, a small kitchen, and her spacious therapy room and office. Jill walked into the storeroom first. Six white, four-drawer locked cabinets held Mercy's personal patient files. When she saw in-patients, Jill knew that Mercy also used to make notations in files held in the unit upstairs, however these were often just perfunctory notes, kept devoid of many details because they could be subpoenaed for court at any time.

Jill walked back into Mercy's main office and thought about the last time she'd seen her there, so flustered and anxious. Why couldn't you have asked me for help? she thought.

The afternoon came quickly to this part of the hospital, and Jill pensively watched a couple of finches playing in the last of the light in the courtyard outside the doors.

'We did some good work in here.'

Jill cried out. The man in the doorway put his palms forward, apologetically. The rooms beyond him had fallen into darkness.

'I'm so sorry. I thought you might have heard me walk in. I'm Dr Noah Griffen. My rooms are just down the hall.' He held out his hand.

'Sorry. Jumpy lately.' Jill felt a little embarrassed. 'Sergeant Jillian Jackson.' She shook his hand. He smiled. He was very good looking.

'I was Dr Merris' clinical supervisor. I'm afraid it will take me a good while to get over all of this.'

Jill nodded. 'I'm sorry. There must be a lot of sadness at the hospital at the moment.'

'Indeed. Are you here to take her files?' He looked around the room.

She nodded. 'There could be evidence in some of them related to the ongoing investigations.'

'I see.'

Jill knew she had sounded formal, and tried to explain a little better.

'I also thought that maybe I could understand why she behaved the way that she did towards the end.' She trailed off. There was only so much she could say while the investigation was still open.

'I tried to get her to slow down, you know,' Dr Griffen walked a little further into the room. 'She just wouldn't stop. I mean, we both knew our work was very important, but one can't keep helping others when one is not caring for oneself.'

'Did you work together a lot?'

'Very closely, yes.'

'Did she mention her cases to you?'

'Why yes. In fact, that was the nature of our work together. Mercy would bring her cases to me for supervision, and we would discuss them, her progress, how she felt towards the patient.'

'Did it seem to you, Dr Griffen, that she had become fixated on any cases in particular, or that she had developed a

313

fascination with the offenders who had victimised her clients?'

The light in the office was fading more with each passing moment. They stood in the gloom, the room full of shadows. Jill suddenly wondered how she had first thought Dr Griffen handsome; in this light he seemed reptilian. She moved towards the door to hit the light switch.

'Have you ever thought, Sergeant Jackson, that it might be preferable to not bring some of your suspects in? To just ensure they had an accident of some description, saving everybody the trouble of a trial, all the expense of keeping them incarcerated, all the heartache they would cause when they re-offended?'

Jill wrinkled an eyebrow in annoyance. Not just because his question was a little close to the bone, given recent happenings, but because he'd shifted slightly to the right, blocking the light switch.

'It's getting a little dark in here,' she said.

'Mercy and I had worked together for many years, Sergeant Jackson, before she came to share the same level of hatred I have for paedophilia.'

Jill noticed his body also blocked the door.

'Did you discuss the offenders at any length?' she asked.

'Oh, indeed. Many of our discussions took place in here. In fact, I'd prefer that you didn't take Mercy's files today, for that reason. There are many patients we shared, and revealing all our secrets could be detrimental for everyone. Do you see?'

A snare drum started in Jill's brain. This man stood too close.

'Yes, I understand, Dr Griffen. I hadn't thought of it from that angle. If there are some of your patients involved, we shouldn't compromise confidentiality.' She moved to indicate to him that she was leaving.

'The problem, Sergeant Jackson,' he said, moving still closer, 'is that you *have* thought of it from every angle. When you were speaking to me just then, your eyes moved to the left – you were creating your response. You should never try to kid a kidder. Isn't that what they say?'

'I'm not sure exactly what you're talking about, Dr Griffen, but it's pretty bloody dark in here, and I would like to leave. Are my eyes looking in the right direction when I say that?' Jill spoke in her cop voice, no sign of the trembling she felt inside. She suddenly felt very aware that she could not see both of his hands.

'But I'd like you to stay,' his voice was low and menacing now. 'Won't you have a seat?'

Jill stayed standing, eyes on the door over his shoulder. Could she make it around him?

As though he sensed her thoughts, Griffen moved his hand from behind his back. He had a claw hammer. He held it casually, but it was balanced. He seemed well-practised, confident.

'What is this?' Jill tried to sound irritated, to keep the fear from her voice.

'You haven't guessed yet? I'm surprised at you. Aren't you a detective, Sergeant Jackson?'

'Yeah, okay,' Jill wanted to stall for time, and now she also wanted to know. 'I'm guessing that Mercy brought the names of these offenders to you, told you she'd decided to follow them, try to catch them in a crime, report them. Basically, it sounds like she wanted to do my job.'

'Go on.' He seemed amused.

'But you couldn't let it go at that. Who knows why – maybe you're trying to deny or repress your own sexual deviancies? There was a claw hammer used in the killing of David Manzi. Was that your work?'

'Yep. He was a cockroach, but your amateur psychiatry is beneath you, and regarding my motives you are completely wrong.' His loose-handed grip on the hammer had tightened. 'And you are only half-correct about the way those men died.'

He paused. Jill remained silent.

'Think it through, detective. Do I look big enough to you to have alone inflicted those kinds of wounds upon four men? As I said before, Mercy and I have worked very well together.'

Her mind raced. Had Mercy and this man killed these men together? If so, she must have completely broken under the pressure of all of the horror she'd worked with over the years. Jill couldn't imagine it. He must be lying, but why?

'Oh come on, why would Mercy help kill those men?' she said, taking small steps backwards. 'She sent me evidence. She called me and saved a child.'

'Indeed. She became much harder to control towards the end. But that's another reason you can't take the files. She often recorded our supervision sessions and there may be evidence of the hypnosis I used with her to help her to unleash her primal needs. She wanted those men dead. Most people in society do. She needed only a little assistance to see that society would be best served by her helping me take them out.'

As they spoke, Jill became aware that they were playing a physical game of chess. With the light behind her, he had a visual advantage, and he took slow, careful steps towards her.

She countered each step with one of her own, aware that he was trying to herd her, to corner her at the back of the room. She did not need to look at the hammer to know he held it ready. Once more she listened in the dark for movements that could save her life.

'What about Sebastian?' She had to know. 'Was he involved in the killing?'

'He was next on the list.'

'And Jamaal Mahmoud?' she asked calmly, as though they were having a normal conversation. She'd seen offenders like this before. His ego was so inflated that he wanted her to know the genius of his actions. Of course, she was not stupid enough to think that he wouldn't end all discussion as soon as he was within striking distance.

'Another scumbag. Nothing to do with us.'

Us. So Mercy really had been a killer. Griffen lunged forward suddenly, but Jill had heard him tensing and, anticipating the move, she sidestepped quickly. From her peripheral vision she knew she had little room left. Her heart skidded along madly, her body steeling itself to fight for her life again.

'So you killed Mercy too?' She did not care what he answered. She had to keep him talking while she figured out a way out of here.

'Of course not. You are being deliberately obtuse, I fear. Mercy had become much too unstable, and Sebastian saved me the trouble of putting her out of her misery. A pity she could not keep it together. We had much work to do. Work you could, and should, have been doing, Jill.'

He stopped moving. She could sense him calculating his final approach. She had to do something.

'Have you had much to do with forensic psychiatry, Dr

Griffen?' asked Jill, relieved to note his head tilting in interest. She could now see only his silhouette.

'A little, yes, Jill. And you're asking because . . .?'

'Well, while investigating this case I got to speak to a specialist in mass murder. A psychiatrist. Very interesting man.' She took silent, deep breaths between words, deliberately hyperventilating, pumping herself full of oxygen to increase her body's defensive mechanisms.

'Do you know, I think you'd count as a serial killer,' she continued, watching his body posture tense. 'And I learned that serial killings are always sexually motivated,' she lied. 'Do you think I didn't know that Manzi had his pants down when he was killed? Did you service him before or after you bashed his brains in? You have to admit, that's a fucked up way to get off.'

Rage made him rigid; she could feel it. She took another deep gulp of air, ignored the spots in front of her eyes caused by the imbalance in her blood between oxygen and carbon dioxide. She kept talking.

'Or maybe you're a closet rockspider. That's it, isn't it – you can't deal with your own feelings, so you kill the people who do what you really want to be doing. What's that called again – a defence mechanism? When you try to deal with your own unacceptable impulses by doing something you think is the opposite.'

With his bellow of fury Jill threw herself forwards and to the left. The move left her closer to a wall, but she was further from the hammer, the motion of which she felt just missing her shoulder as he lunged.

'Stupid! Stupid! You know nothing about the mind.' He breathed heavily; the hammer still raised.

Jill knew she was in trouble. Her back was now to a wall. There were two ways out of here – to the right, into the path of the hammer, and straight ahead. She'd have to throw herself into him and knock him over. There was no room to take a run-up. She sensed she would not have the weight behind her to push him backwards. She heard him breathing. He tensed to lunge. She sprang.

A voice calling her name from the front of the room over-balanced them both. Noah's head swung to the sound, causing him to stumble over a low table behind him. Jill, in mid-lunge, fell into nothing, and landed awkwardly. A hiss of breath next to her warned her to roll. The hammer struck the carpet next to her head. She moved from the roll to her feet in a single lithe motion.

'Hit the lights!' she yelled, as she threw herself to where she knew his body would be. She closed her eyes before the room flooded with light, and dropped with all her body weight onto her knee in the centre of his chest. She opened her eyes with his woof of pain and, one knee still in his gut, she scraped with her other foot down the arm that held the hammer, digging deep. His hand opened reflexively, the skin from his forearm now on the sole of her heavy, cop-issue boot. She pushed harder when she reached his hand, and felt his wrist break. She stood, stamped down hard again, and kicked the hammer away, ignoring his cries of pain.

Jill looked up at the stifled scream behind her, and saw Kim, white-faced, staring at her in horror.

'Take my phone, please, Kim,' she said steadily, reaching out with her mobile, giving the nurse something to do. 'The last number dialled is my partner. Press the send button now for me and get him on the line.'

In the moments it took for Kim to open the mobile, almost drop it, and fumble for the correct button, Jill had unplugged a computer cable from the desk nearby and rolled the moaning Dr Griffen onto his stomach, putting slight pressure on his broken arm to force him into easy compliance. Using noose knots, she tied one end of the cord around his unbroken wrist and the other to his opposing ankle, leaving him immobilised without further injuring him. She'd yet to face Internal Affairs over the death of Sebastian. She wasn't going down for excessive force on this one.

She slumped against a chair and waited for Scotty. I need a holiday, she thought.

Epilogue

CLAUS ZIEL AND BELINDA BEHM had been walking for two hours, but Claus was insistent that they not stop and rest yet. Belinda moaned and hooked her fingers into his belt, forcing him to drag her up another slight incline.

'Not long, baby, it's not far to go,' he said, looking at his map, putting on an extra spurt to help Belinda up the hill.

Claus and Belinda had travelled halfway around the world together, backpacking, and today, at a waterfall he had read about two years ago in his dorm room in Germany, Claus intended to ask Belinda to be his wife. He looked back over his shoulder at her, red-faced and trudging gamely up the hill. So beautiful. She'd fallen behind a couple of steps, and he decided they should stop for just a moment. He could hear the falls close by. They'd stop for a drink and arrive refreshed. The moment should be perfect. He'd waited two years.

As Claus and Belinda shared a water bottle on a rock, deep in the bush in the Blue Mountains of New South Wales, a fat blue-tongue lizard skittered off the path ahead to avoid the noise they made. It waddled into its favourite hiding place and looked back at the path, blinking. It flicked its cobalt-coloured tongue across one of its eyeballs and sat back to wait for the humans to walk by.

Many more years would pass before anyone discovered the lizard's hiding spot, the eye socket inside Jamaal Mahmoud's skull. Around the time Claus Zeil had been sitting on his bed in Germany two years before, planning this day, Jamaal Mahmoud's brother-in-law had thrown Jamaal's badly beaten body off the ravine fifty metres above.

The blue-tongue lizard shifted a little and went to sleep.

Dr Leah Giarratano has had a long career as a psychologist. An expert in psychological trauma, sex offences and psychopathology, she has had many years' experience working with victims and psychopaths. She has worked in psychiatric hospitals, with the Australian Defence Force, and in corrective services with offenders who suffer severe personality disorders. She has assessed and treated survivors of just about every imaginable psychological trauma, including hostages; war veterans; rape, assault, and accident victims; and has worked with police, fire and ambulance officers.

Now available

Voodoo Doll
By Leah Giarratano

Sergeant Jill Jackson has been promoted and is stronger than she's ever been. But with the promotion comes a transfer to a taskforce targeting gang-related home invasions in south-western Sydney, a new partner, a whole new team to work with, and some of the grisliest cases Jill's ever encountered.

The gang is believed to be responsible for at least five brutal home invasions over the past two months, with the most recent culminating in a vicious machete attack that has left one of the victims crippled.

When the violence escalates to murder, suddenly Jill and the team find themselves hunting a psychopath, and delving into the pasts of victims and witnesses in a race against time to uncover what links them to the killer.

The thrilling follow-up to Giarratano's bestselling debut, *Voodoo Doll* will have you double-checking the locks on your doors.

> 'If your bookshelf contains any of the following names: Cornwell, Deaver, Patterson or Reichs, then I urge you this month to forgo foreign imports and sample a new domestic label.'
>
> *Readings Monthly*